I0667094

The
MoonCursers

The

Sherlock Holmes and
His London
Through the Eyes
of Scotland Yard

by Marcia Wilson

Edited by David Marcum

MX Publishing

ISBN Paperback 978-1-80424-647-4
ISBN AUK ePub 978-1-80424-648-1
ISBN AUK PDF 978-1-80424-649-8

Published by
MX Publishing
335 Princess Park Manor, Royal Drive,
London, N11 3GX
www.mxpublishing.co.uk

David Marcum can be reached at:
thepapersofsherlockholmes@gmail.com

Cover Design by Awan
Illustration of The Yarders by Marcia Wilson

Sherlock Holmes and the Scotland Yarders
by Marcia Wilson

Further adventures forthcoming . . . .

Author Foreword
by Marcia Wilson

Looking back, it was a strange time. High school in the late 1980's meant Tolkien, King, Christie, and Poe were always checked out of the school library, but we had multiple copies of Sherlock Holmes on the shelf. If students were going to apply for English-oriented scholarships, by gosh, we were going to read the good stuff, and that meant short stories with murder and mayhem. In emulation of the masters, our choices were usually ACD or . . . Hemingway. It wasn't much of a contest. Hemingway didn't have a demon glowing Death Hound on the moors.

High school segued into college, but we had *Mystery!* re-runs on PBS, even if we had to visit people to watch it, and besides Jeremy Brett, we had Christopher Plummer's compassionate Holmes against Jack the Ripper, a role that shattered the domination of Rathbone and Bruce. Our classmates swore it was necessary for our sincerity as fans of Sir Arthur to see it.

If that sounds like pithy stuff for high schoolers, my generation had a flexible relationship with media – or even power grids. Even if they existed, they weren't exactly as reliable as the sun coming up every morning. The further into the West Virginia panhandle you got, the bigger the library room in the house. Even the poorest of houses, be they on blocks or wheels, had at least one shelf of sanity to rely on when the power was out, or the brownouts made hash of anything but AM radio. When a flood took out the local libraries, it was devastation.

There was media, but there wasn't enough – there's never enough – but as far as the books printed in the wake of Sir Arthur . . . it really was never enough. You were lucky to find something in a thrift store or library sale, and your odds were no worse than combing the bookstores in the mall. Oh, for the days when there was more than one bookstore in a mall. If something was found, readers had to buy it on faith that it wasn't a waste of their time.

Look, our standards weren't low, they were desperate. We made a lot of poor book-buying choices, which were hastily returned to the ecosystem of flea market sales for some other poor shmuck to buy up. One girl, bless her, would donate the books after carefully penciling in every sin the authors made against Canon, history, plot contrivance, and attempts to pair Holmes up with a romantic partner. I like to think she cackled as she returned the much-improved dreck to the public. She always cited her sources . . . .

It shouldn't be a surprise when we wound up obsessing, ever so slightly, with what little we could find that wasn't terrible, and (*Hooray!*) didn't go against The Canon. I wonder if anyone has ever tried to list all the knockoffs and illicit print runs out there. Probably not – I'd like to think nobody could be that crazy.

Fan fiction was the outlet for a crying need that had hit breaking point. Paper fanzines of decent quality were even harder to find than a decent paperback on the shelf – you have never bought a pig in a poke until you've combed through a hand-printed zine catalog, squinted at the type, and decided to spend your allowance on what sounded the most promising – and too bad the cover art was rarely as good on the inside.

Fanzine editors lived in the twilight, trying to put out their passion projects between the obligations of home, family, and keeping a roof over their head, as well as hanging on to entire drawers of receipts to make sure a rival 'ziner didn't get spiteful and report them to the IRS. (That actually happened.) Zines were non-profit only, which is partly why the zines we could afford were always shipped Media Mail on whatever paper was on sale. If you were very lucky, you got your order in three weeks.

Maybe we shouldn't talk about the pastichery in animation . . . .

The Internet found its feet and bloomed with forums and places to hide and talk about the lack of stories, and that led to posting paper zines online, and people began writing fresh stuff, online, and showing it for reading and/or critiquing. Almost overnight there were clubs, groups, and social organizations that could get their fix on the stories between the boom-and-bust world of conventions and newsletters.

There were friendships made that I miss to this very day. The sheer power of a small number of people who were intelligent, thoughtful, and mindful of Canon encouraged so many of us. They helped with research, knew how to spell, and learned different languages in this world. They reviewed books, scrounged supplies, and let us know if someone was copying our plots just a little too much for comfort. Plagiarism and how to address it was a real eye-opener when it came to intellectual property that wasn't yours to begin with, but you could claim the OC's (Original Characters) were yours, and debatably, your unique perspective on the people, places, and things created under the pen of Sir Arthur.

I was a fan of these fans. They were amazing and – honestly – damn good writers. *Damn* good. They were role models. They read the whole Canon, and they kept track of everything, and they led us to places like *fanfiction.net*, where we could post with a minimum of fussing.

I could write about anyone I wanted, but it was partially out of respect for these writers that I began to veer away from making just one more story about Sherlock Holmes and Dr. Watson. I loved the stories, but part of their appeal was their world. And there was a lot to that world that was relevant today. Methods may alter crime, but motives rarely do.

At the time, there was a pretty well-represented group that was pro-Watson, and they wrote some of those "damn good stories" with Watson as the protagonist – or at least, a powerful, equal voice. The Granada series was a huge influence, as well as the Russian series, and throw in some of "the radio show" for good measure.

These fan writers may have loved the tight scripts and drama of the Rathbone and Bruce approach, but as they grew up, they said, collectively, "Man, that was bad for Watson!" There were other words, much less polite. Burke and Hardwicke were a positive force for the shift in the thinking that pointed out Watson was *not* an idiot and we couldn't do a decent job showing how smart Holmes was by surrounding him by idiots. This had already been tried, during Classic Dr Who, and nobody had been left happy about it. Nobody blamed the actors for doing their job too well.

Fine, I thought, *there are a lot of really good writers writing for Watson. I can do that.* But I also caught on that if Watson illuminated Holmes by writing of the man from his point-of-view, *maybe I could write about Watson through other people's eyes.* The question was: *Who?*

Enter a re-visit to the Granada Series, and "The Norwood Builder".

I make no secret of the fact that I am heavily synesthetic. Face blindness comes with its own challenge, and I have to train myself to recognize people. With an irony that approaches opera-grade comedy, I literally could not tell Holmes from Lestrade in Granada's "The Norwood Builder". Also, Lestrade made me angry when I was a hero-worshipping teenager watching the show with other hero-worshipping teenagers. *How dare Lestrade challenge Holmes? Couldn't anyone see Holmes was the smartest man in the room?*

Older adult me revisited that part of my life and went *Oops!* because there were some of those Fanfiction Demigods that rather liked Lestrade and had plenty of backup reasons. I wish I could remember the name of the one who mused, *"Colin Jeavons is the only actor who could be bulldog-like and also ferrety."* I was doing a lot of research at my job, and that included the Victorian era and law enforcement. Somehow it all started clicking together, piece by piece.

A writer whom I regret losing (her entire message board went the way of LiveJournal – only, it vanished for good. Poof. No trace) challenged me on whether or not Lestrade was stupid. He knew more than he let on, she said, and I . . . kind of said, *"Oh? Prove it."*

Ouch. She did, lining out events in "The Boscombe Valley Mystery" and "The Second Stain" and a few other bits and pieces, and I ate crow. A lot of it. I was wrong. Still, I could at least write with this new perspective. Bad as it was to be wrong, it would be worse to stay with it.

Add to this a sleep disorder that can politely be called *insomnia*, and a marriage turning into a nightmare of violence, and no health insurance – but writing was the cheapest therapy out there . . . Lestrade slowly woke up and came to life. I'll blame Colin Jeavons for knowing what the writers wanted out of the scripts. It's on him.

"Trust your characters," my old English teacher would say, sternly, so I did. I wrote short stories that could connect with others to make a fuller piece. A necklace is made one bead at a time. I wrote at night. I had to. I needed to stay awake, listening to any sounds that might be my ex-husband's return to stalk us – tampering with my car, crawling under the house, draining the well his own children needed to drink from, and taunts to the police that tried their best, but could only work within the limits of the system. They failed, but it was the system that failed. They cared, and they shared my rage that when the ex was finally brought to justice, it was too late for one of his victims.

There is only so much a policeman can do against so much collective injustice out there. If Sherlock Holmes had existed on that force, they would have begged for his help against my ex-husband. They knew he could go where they couldn't, and they would know when not to ask the awkward questions about how information was collected. They would have sniffed and said, "Well, that's a pity," and shrugged and did things according to the law – *their* law – but not expecting civilians to follow the same oaths they swore.

I empathized with Gregson's ability to buck the rules, and I empathized for Lestrade's inability to do so. The Yarders took on their own lives and, without knowing it, the job had changed. I was now sitting back and watching the stories unfold, writing them as fast as they told them. They had a lot to say. They still do, but the stories are whispering now. We are safer, there is no need to listen for danger. I am learning how to sleep.

More years ago than I'd like to recollect, I received an email so startling I forwarded it to my sister before a family dinner at the pizza parlour. It wasn't a fantastic day. Before long I would be needing their help to flee across the country in the middle of a winter snowstorm. The mood was glum. We were subdued.

My sister looked at me over the table and said with uncharacteristic bluntness, "You impressed that man."

That man was David Marcum.

Marcia Wilson
February 2025

Scotland Yard's Story
Editor Foreword
by David Marcum

Back in 2008, it was still a different Sherlockian world from today.

In those days, the quest for more excellent Holmes adventures beyond the pitifully few sixty Canonical adventures was still quite difficult. Each year, only a few slipped through the needle's-eye clutch of the moribund major publisher model. (In fact, if one is still publishing by that route, then this fact remains true.) But there were many Holmes adventures waiting to be revealed, and they just needed an outlet. Is it any wonder that the Internet was that path?

Holmes pastiches have been around since William Gillette's 1899 play, *Sherlock Holmes*, showing that Our Heroes' adventures did *not* have to pass across the first Literary Agent's desk. Some amazing and accurate adventures appeared on the radio in the 1930's, courtesy of visionary Edith Meiser. And the door kept getting wider, with more radio shows, films, and the occasional book giving us more traditional, authentic, and Canonical Holmes.

But it was not enough.

In 1998, *fanfiction.net* was created, allowing another outlet for sharing Holmes's adventures, wherein those who had discovered them could get them directly to starving readers immediately, without facing the impossible discouragement of the faceless soul-dead major publishing model. I was fortunate to discover the site a few years after that, and began to visit regularly to read and print and archive stories about the True Holmes. There are thousands of Holmes stories located there, but many are parodies, or anachronistic, or related to modernized and offensive simulacrums, or with incorrect ghost-busting leanings. Others were clearly written by individuals who have no clue about Sherlock Holmes, or have hijacked him for their own agendas. These stories may be ignored, even if they have to be waded through – for buried in the muck of this backyard goose lot, for those who take time to look, are some true and rare jewels.

And in April 2008, the beginning of a couple of stories were posted, "An Ordinary Meeting" on the tenth, and "Truth is the Critic" the next day, both as written by an author going under the curious sobriquet of *aragonite*.

"An Ordinary Meeting" gives details of Lestrade's first consultation with Sherlock Holmes, and "Truth is the Critic" is written from the perspective of the Scotland Yard inspectors as they read *A Study in Scarlet* – and providing their reactions when see how Watson has described them. These were well written and interesting, and this approach really hadn't been attempted before.

(To be accurate, there had been some stories about the Yarders, but they were inconsistent. For instance, M.J. Trow's long Lestrade series veers wildly from legitimate mysteries to unreadable parodies, with particularly bogus attacks on Sherlock Holmes, and Trow inexplicably gives Inspector G. Lestrade the first name of "Sholto".

In "Truth is the Critic", *aragonite* was already painting the Yarders – Inspectors Lestrade, Gregson, Bradstreet, and Hopkins in particular – in well-rounded and respectful ways that hadn't been seen before. They had their own life stories beyond The Canon, and weren't just the inspector *du jour* appearing in this-or-that Canonical tale. Who knew then that this new author, slipping quietly onto the scene, had such an overall vision for these individuals, with fully realized details about their personal lives, their backgrounds and histories . . . and a plan for a massive overarching adventure that would span decades in their lives?

Over the next few months, more stories quickly followed – "A Cookout in Cornwall", "Route to Madness", and "Just Inspector Will Do" (my all-time favorite of these works, relating the events on the Paddington platform when Mary Watson awaits her husband's return from the Continent in mid-May 1891. I re-read it every year on Reichenbach Day.) But on April 17th, 2008, *aragonite* raised the stakes, publishing the first chapter of a novel, *A Sword for Defense*, the first of a massive story arc relating what Watson and Lestrade and the other Yarders faced in the months after Holmes's supposed death at the Reichenbach Falls.

While keeping one story going would overwhelm many authors, *aragonite* – whomever he or she was – had even greater ambitions. New stories and chapters began to be posted at a feverish pace. A week after *Sword* started, another serialized novel began, *You Buy Bones*, telling how Watson, in early 1882 and fresh from his first year living with Holmes in Baker Street, comes across a monstrous crime that directly and personally affects the Scotland Yard inspectors. And a few months after that, *aragonite* started another novel that served as a prequel leading to *Sword* called *The MoonCursers*, telling of Lestrade's own terrifying adventures in late April and early May 1891, occurring at the same time Holmes and Watson were playing cat-and-mouse with Moriarty, on their way to a fateful encounter in Meiringen.

Over the course of that summer, nearly every day brought some new chapter: Sometimes another episode in *A Sword for Defense* or *You Buy Bones* or *The MoonCursers*, and at other times a seemingly stand-alone story that that filled in some crucial and interesting aspect about the Scotland Yarders that only made the overall painting richer and deeper.

Imagine if Charles Dickens were writing and publishing three serialized novels at once, and adding in short stories too. And they were going straight from being written to being posted for public consumption as soon as they were complete. And clearly the overall storyline wasn't being generated along the way – there was a *plan*, for little threads mentioned here and there about Lestrade's boyhood or Bradstreet's family had massive importance much later.

Over many months during this time, *aragonite* was also constructing another massive work, *Test of the Professionals*, which related the events after *You Buy Bones* and served as a set-up for *A Sword for Defense*, telling us much more about Lestrade's past, his unfortunate and dangerous life-long connection with Professor Moriarty's agent, the truly evil Jethro Quimper, and the escalating and terrifying events surrounding his courtship with Clea Cheatham.

In August 2008, with all of this going on, *aragonite* started another brilliant novella, *A Secondary Stain*, the *other* events of "The Second Stain", in which Lestrade was not as clueless as he appears in Watson's manuscript, actually working behind the scenes to assist Holmes's investigation. It was the brilliance of this story that finally prompted me to write a fan letter.

Using the fan fiction website's messenger feature, I emailed an extensive message to *aragonite* in October 2008, and soon received a wonderful and informative reply.

First, I learned that *aragonite* was really Marcia Wilson. In subsequent communications, I learned that *aragonite* – which curiously I'd never looked up before then – is calcium carbonate used by marine organisms to build their shells and skeletons. Since aragonite can be found in cave formations, and since Marcy is a caver – the evidence of which can be found in some of her stories brilliantly dealing with caverns and London's Lost Rivers – I suspect that's why she chose the unusual pen-name.

Over many emails over many years, Marcy has explained to me that she wrote so prolifically in those early years because she had insomnia, and that was a very productive time to write. She also could *see* all of these scenes, and almost couldn't write fast enough to convey them. In her very first reply to me in October 2008, she explained, how she approached telling the Yarders' story, and why she named Inspector G. Lestrade *Geoffrey:*

> *I've never liked the playing down of characters. It's a lazy way to pump up the character in your mind. I have to be very careful not to wander into the Fangirlyverse. Usually I deal with it by giving a character a name I dislike, and for some reason, I dislike Geoffrey so naturally I stuck it on the poor guy.*

She also explained that:

> *I was so bleeding tired of writing against another person's notions on Holmes and Watson that I just went to another character that I rather liked. (When I was younger, I hated Lestrade. He should have been kowtowing to Holmes' genius like all of us!) Later on, I realized that it took a pretty remarkable man to refuse to see Holmes in a reverent light. [The] clues about Lestrade were subtle and interesting. There had to be a reason for someone who was supposed to be such a good cop to stay a police inspector after his initial promotion. I made him a Celtic Breton out of a half-thought. I was seeing Colin Jeavons in my head, and he's so Welsh he's probably half-Neanderthal! Being a Breton or a Channel Islander would have made [Lestrade] an English citizen, but he would not have been accepted as an equal in race or status by many people.*

Our communications continued, as did her writing. By early 2009, *A Sword for Defense* was complete, and the next book in the ongoing saga, *The Narrow Path* had commenced. Those were great days to be a Sherlockian and to be reading *fanfiction.net*, as there were other great authors there as well – *Westron Wynde* and *KCS* among them, all with powerful and correct understandings of the *True Holmes*. These authors were writing for the fans, and also for each other, and I was privileged to be in contact with many of them. In a few years, Marcy and *Westron*

Wynde – who turned out to be amazing pasticheur Sarah Bennett, whose works are slowly being made available from Belanger Books – began to take down their online works and publish them in real books. (It was at this time that I let Marcy and Sarah read my first Sherlock Holmes pastiches, written in 2008 and at that point seen by no one but my wife, and with their encouragement I started publicly publishing my stories too.)

Marcy initially published *You Buy Bones*, along with some related short stories, in 2010 (from Lulu Publishing. That version is now out of print.) Next came *Test of the Professionals: Leap Year* (2013, also from Lulu and out of print), also collecting the original online novel and working in some supplementary material.

In 2015, I came up with the idea of *The MX Book of New Sherlock Holmes Stories*, and of course Marcy was in the initial list of invitees. Since then, much of her writing has been turned to contributing stories to these anthologies, having submitted nearly two-dozen. Through these books, she became associated with MX Publishing, who issued a new edition of *You Buy Bones* in 2015, as well as splitting *Test of the Professionals: Leap Year* into three planned smaller volumes. The first two, *The Adventure of the Flying Blue Pidgeon* and *The Peaceful Night Poisonings*, were published by MX in 2016 and 2017, respectively. Unfortunately, due to a combination of events, the third part of *Test* – the much larger piece called *Leap Year* that relates the exciting conclusion to that narrative – was not published.

So for the wider public, those who were never able to read Marcy's massive *ouvré* on *fanfiction.net*, her available works consisted of these three novels, and her well-respected stories in the MX anthologies. (Unfortunately, Marcy, Sarah Bennett, and several others were forced to pull their Sherlockian content from *fanfiction.net* several years ago after some of their works were stolen – copied-and-pasted and then republished under other author names by way of Amazon's self-publishing program.)

In late 2024, I was in the process of working toward assembling and editing the final volumes, Parts 49, 50, 51, and 52 of the MX anthologies, a process which would continue into early 2025. While looking around in my computer files, I found something I'd forgotten: Years earlier, I had saved and formatted the files for five of Marcy's novels – those relating to Watson and Lestrade's adventures during The Great Hiatus. Since the late 1990's, I've printed and archived every traditional Canonical Holmes adventure that I've found online –

thousands of them – and I have over 175 binders of pure Holmes adventures – including all of Marcy's now-withdrawn stories. But luckily I had these novels as Word files. And I had an idea . . . .

I contacted Marcy, who hadn't had time in several years to think about publishing more of her works, and asked if I could shepherd these five novels to publication – *pro-bono*, just because I was passionate about other people reading these incredible stories. Marcy was willing, and so I started editing with great enthusiasm – even as I was supposed to be editing the final MX volumes, stories for which were rolling in every day.

It soon became apparent to me that to publish these five novels without readers knowing the events of the missing *Leap Year* would be a confusing mess. Too much happened in these books that continued from what happened in *Leap Year*. Clearly, that missing volume would need to be edited and published too. And while I was at it, why not re-edit the previously published three books – *You Buy Bones*, *The Adventure of the Flying Blue Pidgeon*, and *The Peaceful Night Poisonings* – into an overall cohesive narrative?

MX Publisher Extraordinaire Steve Emecz, THE Sherlockian publisher and the Sherlockian Gutenberg – the man who made Sherlockian publishing accessible to real people instead of guarding a narrow doorway, or deciding that Sherlockian publishing should only be available for a very narrow cadre of self-described elites – was enthusiastic, and ready to proceed immediately. But I needed to actually finish editing the nine books first. It was a joy, and a labor of love to do so.

I had read all of these books serially as published, hopping from story to story as new chapters appeared, back in 2008-2011. But to read the story now, in one place, in order and available in its entirety, made it even more amazing – and exciting for the thought of new readers able to discover this magnificent world: *Sherlock Holmes's London, as seen through the eyes of the Scotland Yarders.*

Even as I dug deeper into Marcy's Scotland Yard adventures, I was remembering the other stories – the previously mentioned *A Secondary Stain*. Her Yarder's Christmas novels, *Gunnysack Goose for Christmas* and *A Mouth of Ivy*. Short-story collections like *Devilry* and *It's All in a Name*. Other novels and novellas like *The Muse of History*, *Ghosts in the Making*, *Courage Rises*, *The Kings and Queens of London*, and the World War I narrative, *The Days of Our Years*. I had amazing fun editing the first nine books that are being published in

2025, and with any luck, I hope to be able to edit the rest of these, along with a collection of Marcy's MX anthology contributions, over the next year or so, in order to fill in Marcy's *Great Scotland Yard Tapestry.*

There are certain authors who "own" other Canonical characters by taking hold of them and defining them. The late Carole Nelson Douglas was Irene Adler's chronicler. Michael Kurland gives us the best portrait of Professor Moriarty. Will Thomas has absolutely defined Barker, Holmes's hated rival on the Surrey Side. The late Gerard Williams claimed Dr. Mortimer (even if only for two books), and Susan Knight is easily becoming the definitive voice of Mrs. Hudson.

But Marcia Wilson tells the True Story of the Scotland Yarders – and presents an amazing viewpoint of Holmes and Watson along the way.

I've said it many times before, and can't say it any better now:

Marcia Wilson has found Scotland Yard's Tin Dispatch Box.

David Marcum
January 2025

SPIRIT LEVEL©2015

The MoonCursers

Chapter I – MoonCurser's Night

"You crossed my path on the fourth of January. On the twenty-third you incommoded me. By the middle of February I was seriously inconvenienced by you. At the end of March, I was absolutely hampered in my plans, and now, at the close of April, I find myself placed in such a position through your continual persecution that I am in positive danger of losing my liberty. The situation is becoming an impossible one."

– Professor Moriarty to Sherlock Holmes
"The Final Problem"
April 24th, 1891

April 21st, 1891:

The tiny pellets of ice, flinging against the worbled glass of the bedroom window, stirred the boy out of his fitful sleep.

His first reaction was to feel cheated of the warm comfort of the thick quilts his mother had stitched together with Aunt Elizabeth. Nicholas slept on, as warm as a hot water bottle in their shared bed. His older brother envied him. Nicholas was a year younger, but somehow, he never seemed to worry. He was already Martin's size and getting bigger. He was even losing his baby-teeth faster than Martin was.

Martin rested where he was, the bed pleasant enough in the cold February night. Ice clicked and spat like cats against the window.

There was a time when patience meant nothing. Martin finally slipped out of the covers and donned his dressing-gown over his night-robe. The slippers that were his aunts' Christmas gift fit warmly about his feet. He belted everything tight and pushed the bedroom door open. His was six years old. Sometimes he was still mistook for a precocious four year old. His soft round face only helped that along.

The hallway was deathly quiet to his roaring ears. He slid into the narrow walkway as easily as he'd slid out of the covers, and made his way to the small sitting room. The sight of the fire burning low in the grate always soothed him. His parents had grown used to that habit, but he for one did not understand it.

"Well, Martin?"

Martin blinked. His father was sitting up on the battered sofa, a blanket about his shoulders. He stared, and his father smiled. The firelight caught on the creases deep in his face.

Martin had seen the chromolithographs of his mother and father at their wedding, seven years ago. His mother to his mind still looked the same. But his father looked almost as worn as his grandfather in the firelight.

"I couldn't sleep," Martin confessed. "I'm sorry."

"Come over here, then. We can sit up together." His father held out a part of the blanket, and Martin was glad to snuggle up. "And you needn't be sorry for not being able to sleep at night. I'm afraid you get that honest. I never could sleep some nights myself."

"*But I'm sleepy*. Why can't I sleep?" Martin wondered. He rubbed at his eyes.

His father only shook his head, at a loss. "I took it from my mother," he said. "She always said it was the tides that caused us to be that way."

"How do the tides make us not sleep?"

His father laughed without a sound. "I don't know. But the moon, if you could see it, is growing full, and the tides are pulling. If it weren't for the ice, we'd have a perfect night for mooncursing."

Martin stared up at the man, a strange thrill in his chest. *Mooncursing*. It sounded strange and marvelous at the same time. "Mooncursing," he repeated to himself.

"That's one of the names of the smugglers who would be sailing right now."

"How do you know so much?"

"I hardly know *much*, Martin. But your grandmother's people were known for their smuggling." His father's large hands reached up and gently stroked the soft, dark hair at his ear. "They survived on the art for generations. I've chosen a legal form of livelihood . . . but I suppose blood will out." He leaned his head back on the divan. "There's something of a smuggler left in me, perhaps. And in you."

"Why would they break the law?"

"There are always men who want the quick dollar as opposed to the slow shilling . . . and there are people who know nothing else but what their own fathers taught them. I know people – I work with people – who only know the thrill of what they do. That's why I'm glad to be just a Yarder. I have enough on my plate without being a policeman for the entire world!"

Martin thought about it in comfortable silence. "Sometimes Mama is angry at you when you get home. Because you're a policeman."

"Martin . . . you know what it is I do."

"Yes, sir."

"You know what I do isn't safe."

Martin hadn't thought much about it. "You get hurt once in a while," he said slowly. "And Mum gets angry."

"She's not truly angry, Martin. She's frightened when I come home hurt. And I can't blame her for the way that makes her feel. I do whatever I can to make sure she doesn't feel that frightened. That's what it comes down to. She's angry because she's frightened, and when I get hurt, she's frightened." He patted his son on the back gently. "And she has a right to be." He shook his head, making the cloth of his dressing-gown rustle softly. "I'd rather spend my nights here with you lot."

"Even if you had to walk the floor when we're not feeling well?"

"Even if."

Martin realized with a sense of surprise, he was still small enough to snuggle up against his father's ribcage and there was plenty of room left over. "You used to tell us stories, when we were little."

"You have a good memory." His father said wryly. "Ever since you were born, we'd be up walking the floor-boards with you in our arms when the moon was full."

"When did you stop telling stories?" Martin buried his face in his father's side.

"You started sleeping the night through."

"I miss them." Martin's responses were difficult to combat. He kept his sentence structure too short for one to find loopholes in them. *Has to be the Cheatham in him.*

"What – do you remember them?"

"Mm-hmm. You said that where Grandmother lived, there were castles scattered all over the land, and many of them had crumbled to ruin . . . ." Martin paused to yawn. "You said that there were nights called, 'werey-wolf nights' where people locked up their doors and windows, because men who had sold their souls to the devil were donning wolf-skins and riding on Devil's nights in search of prey." For all the alarming content of his recollection, he was rather undisturbed by it.

"You remember *all that, then*?" His father whispered, soft as a feather. But Martin was already sliding from wakefulness with the touch of his father's warm hand rubbing his back.

The little boy's breathing lulled in sleep. His recounting of fairy tales had stumbled and blurred with his voice as, without knowing it, his father's gentle touch had sent him into the slumber he had wanted. Geoffrey stopped stroking by degrees. He rested his hand on his son's shoulder but he failed to wake. *Poor boy,* he thought. *Night is hard enough without having to bring nightmares into it.* He stared into the flames of the battered fireplace in silence, as he'd done before his son's sleepy shamble into the room.

19

A puff of cooler air drifted across the floor. Geoffrey pulled himself out of his own hypnotic state to see his wife leaning against the jamb, a loose throw around her shoulders and her hair spilling down her back and shoulders like a waterfall of black silk.

"And what are you smiling at, Inspector?" She asked softly, the smile in her voice.

"You," he answered. "I couldn't sleep." He glanced down, ruefully, at the sleeping bundle wrapped against his chest. "Nor could Martin, at first."

"However did you get him to succumb?" Clea Marie Cheatham Lestrade stepped lightly in her slippers across the floor, missing that one squeaking plank on instinct. She knelt and rested a small hand on her son's back, against her husband's.

"I just started stroking his back." They spoke softly in the firelight. Clea was smiling as she reached up to touch her husband's face.

"It works for cats," she agreed. "Let's see if we can get you into bed, Geoffrey."

"How, without waking him back up?"

"Oh, ye, of little faith . . . ." Clea smiled, and began stroking Martin's small shoulders. "Slide out," she whispered.

It took something that resembled a balancing-act and a lot of breath-holding, but very gradually, Geoffrey slipped upward and over the back of the couch. Martin mumbled once, softly, but remained buried in the cozy warmth of the blanket still heated by his father's body.

"Very good." Geoffrey smiled and bowed from behind the couch to his wife.

Clea rose by degrees from her son. She smiled. "Now what's got that look in your eyes, Geoffrey Lestrade?"

"I'm thinking," he said in the same voice, "that you haven't changed a bit. You're as gorgeous as ever."

"And I'd say you were as sleep-addled as ever," she retorted. The blanket tucked snugly around their oldest son. "Come to bed," his wife said softly. "You're better than a warming-pan and it's chilly in there."

"Yes, dear." A shadow darkened his face as he reached up to touch her cheek.

"You're thinking of the case?" Clea guessed.

"I wasn't good enough at the meeting." Bitter salt coated his voice as he spoke. His wife slid inside his arms and rested her head against his collar bone. "Clea, I couldn't . . . I couldn't convince them that . . . we should be working with the Tinkers."

"You think the Tinkers can truly help us?"

"Padriac's tribe can. They spend part of the year in France. They're in France *right now*. We've established that they're an easy source of information between ourselves and the crime rings we're against." Clea felt his head bow. His lips pressed against the top of her head. "*It doesn't matter*," he said faintly. "I'm just the regular inspector. If I were Patterson or Gregson, I'd *know* how to speak."

It was an old wound. Clea understood that, due to stature and colouring, her husband had been selected for subterfuge among many different races. It had given him an arsenal of bizarre experiences, and a degree of sympathy for those who did not normally have a friend in the eyes of the law. He believed in the people he was usually spying against – people few of the others really knew them other than in the context of "outsiders from the law."

"I mourn for the world that doesn't value simple speaking over a clever tongue." Clea circled her arms about his neck and kissed him lightly on the lips. "At any rate, come to bed. You have one more night with us before you go off, and I'm already missing you."

"But I haven't left yet." He smiled, wanting to be convinced.

"I know." She kissed him again.

They gently closed the door after their sleeping son. There was no sound on the other side of the door. Clea pulled her husband close and drew him to the bedroom. He bent her head and kissed her hair again, and was surprised when she pulled him into her arms.

"Clea?" he whispered as thin as a July breeze.

"What is it?" she whispered.

"Martin." He wrapped his wife in his arms until their dressing-gowns wrinkled against each other. "He was remembering stories I'd told him back when he was a year old – maybe as old as two." She felt his frown in the darkness. "He *remembered all of that*. If I had known . . . ! I wouldn't have told him a thing."

"Were they so terrible, Geoffrey?"

"No, perhaps not, but they were . . . vivid." He didn't know how to explain it. "There were . . . *hunts*, that the gentry activated. I suppose it was part boredom and part need to establish control . . . The priests called it meetings with the Devil, but they were careful not to say that too loudly." He took a deep breath. "The hunters would wear wolf-skins, and they would hunt down something . . . It was a cult. I suppose you'd call it a version of the Ku Klux Klan. It wasn't always a wild animal that was being hunted."

"Oh." Clea said softly. Her arms never changed their grip about him.

"Quimper's father was quite involved with it. That meant, his son was too." *Sons*. Old, painful memories flashed in the deep. "One day, at the summer estate in Portsmouth, he and my brothers decided that they would play at having a Wild Hunt." Clea watched as her husband's features dissolved into the past. "I was small, I had a twisted foot. I can't run very fast."

"*Oh, my God, Geoffrey.*"

"They couldn't use the horses. The men were already out on their version of the hunt. But some of the dogs were left behind, and they knew to obey Quimper." He swallowed dryly. "They obeyed Armoricus, too. Paul . . . I suppose Paul really *did* think it was all just a game. He was too trusting that way. But he could see at night like an owl, and it was because of him I couldn't shake them off."

"And you don't care about dogs to this day," Clea supplied in an unsteady voice.

"No. I finally got to the barn, where the dogs weren't allowed to go. The horses didn't like them, and I was hoping my father was still there. But he'd gone home. Perhaps he was even part of Ivo Quimper's hunt. I don't know. But I climbed to the hayloft. Quimper hated – *hates* – heights, so Armoricus went after me."

"Is that how you broke your leg?" Clea could feel his heart drumming against her breast. Her own was rapid.

"Yes." He shivered a little, wanting to leave the memory. "I was tired, Clea. I was telling Martin *all kinds of stories* that night because the sound of my voice seemed to soothe him . . . I don't think I told him any of that, but I must have told him something about the Wild Hunt. I shouldn't have said a thing."

"You aren't the only one who told him inappropriate stories, love." Clea pointed out. Inwardly, her heart hammered. "I think I was reading parts of the suffragettes' newspaper when it was my turn to sit up."

He snorted, and gave her a rueful look. "Really."

"Well, I needed something that would keep *me* awake," she pointed out. "Some of those women are utterly ridiculous. Thinking women are too good to fight – really." She obviously still carried a disgruntled recollection.

He looked like he wanted to laugh, but cobwebs of guilt remained in his eyes. "I'm just going to be very very careful about what I say around that boy from now on."

"Martin doesn't seem to be upset, Geoffrey." She squeezed him a little tighter. "That's the important thing."

"Clea, I do love you," was all he said to that, and he was returning the kiss she placed on him with enthusiasm.

"What happened after your leg was broken?" Clea asked. "You've started the story. It couldn't end there."

"I was sent to live with my grandfather for the rest of the summer," he admitted. "It was really the only time I spent much time across the Channel. My father did *not* approve, but that was the only time I think my mother ever defied him." He shook his head in wonder still. "Honestly, I don't think she even consulted him . . . she just . . . sent me across to Brest and I stayed there until they ran out of excuses."

"You sound like you liked it," Clea offered.

"It was . . . restful," he said succinctly.

"I can imagine. You must have been angry for a long time."

"I was at first . . . but my grandfather was a bit of a patriot – strange, but a lot of smugglers are. He'd point out that the small ermine will fight a fox."

"Hmm . . . Quimper does remind me of a fox." Clea answered softly. "Clever like a fox, too clever by half, until his cleverness chokes him."

"He can't live forever." Her husband knew her own feelings for the man.

"Come to bed," she repeated softly. In moments they were back under the covers, but as Clea listened to the sound of her own breath against her husband's neck, she knew his mind was very much elsewhere from sleep. His thoughts were on the world outside the sleet-driven window outside their bedroom.

She knew he hadn't spoken of the entire case they were on. Clea was an Inspector's Wife, and as ignorant as any other's on what their husbands were doing until after the fact. But he was worried. She felt it in the depth of his embrace, and the way he held her without moving, like she was something that would get up and leave forever.

Which had almost happened. They had spent so much time facing the possibility of his death, they weren't fully prepared for the idea of losing her. Nicholas' birth had been a hard one, with complications that had nearly been the end of mother and child. For all the trauma of his arrival, Nicholas had faced existence with unconcerned aplomb. Clea was back to her full strength, but she had learned a lesson about mortality in herself, and Geoffrey would carry an ice-chip of fear in his heart for the rest of their lives together.

Clea wished for a daughter, but Geoffrey was unconvinced that she should put herself at risk for motherhood again.

"How long do you think you'll be gone?" she asked. His mind was on the job anyway.

"Hopefully, no more than a day once we get there," he admitted. "I'm just not . . . looking forward to it. At least the weather will have warmed up . . . ." He paused to stretch suddenly. "But . . . after that, we'll be waiting on the word from Those Above on how we're to go after this gang."

23

"Something to be grateful for." Clea reached up to stroke his hair. "We'll miss you." She leaned up to kiss him on the lips.

"I'll be back as soon as I can." He kissed her back. She began combing his hair and neck with her fingers. He made a contented sound and managed to melt deeper into her arms. She smiled against his neck, and kept going. What worked for Martin could work for his father. She was still smiling when he slipped off to sleep without knowing it.

Chapter II – A Raid Gone Wrong

"N'eus den nà tra heb e si, hag alïes en-deus daou pe tri"
Translation: *"There is no man nor thing without his defect,
and often they have two or three of them."*

April 27th, 1891:

The tiny coastal village known as Corentin-avel was little more than a twenty-house, two-tavern depot against the sea and protected from the ocean itself by the height of the land. Only one single winding trail, skirting old upthrust rock and freshet-tracks, permitted access for the people and the small cove that plummeted twenty-five yards below. That cove was *just* big enough to support the port in seafood and trade, and that only when the weather agreed. One single "main street" with two rival shops for outsider goods, the chapel, and the *ti-ker* [1] comprised the municipality. Because the weather was calm between spring storms, one could now see the resting boards, docks, and single pier of the port itself.

The little old man, hard and spare as grapevine, paused at the top of the hill and searched over the end of the land with his dark eyes. Only a few stone houses sprinkled over the grassy slopes, and some of them were round in shape – a stubborn holdout against those newfangled Romans. Small vegetable plots, a few fruit trees, and one herd each of goats and small cattle comprised the agriculture. The *ti-ker* rested at the highest point that permitted the perfect view of the port. Like many small places, the *ti-ker* fulfilled many functions: Legal offices, town hall, and in the cool stone basement, the holding cells, and morgue.

The old man was not large. Age had shrunk him further, as if he had been formed of the native clay of the peninsula only to be baked down into something smaller and harder than his first form. But his spine was straight as a rod, and his dark eyes were clear underneath the thick grey of hair and beard. The *poliser* standing with their tobacco on the front steps paused as they took in the little man. Eyes widened with dawning awareness. They stepped aside and gave him a respectful nod as he walked inside the cool depths of the medical examiner's office.

Gouelanig, they murmured. *The Seagull. The* smuggler of his generation. Triaged Potier was no stranger to the *ti-ker*. He had walked the halls to bail out his less fortunate friends, hired lawyers to keep himself from such fates. He had delivered food and news and had worked side by side with these *poliser*'s predecessors, aiding them when the storms would

25

have crushed them all like matchwood. Like the seagull aloft on its wings, he had been untouched by his foes, be they legal opponents or smuggling rivals. He had lost count of the number of times he had walked its halls. Mr. Death worked abroad, but he parked his cart here in Brittany.

"Ah . . . *demat*, Monsieur Potier," the youth was every *polise*: Excruciatingly polite, but awkward in his youth. He carried the traces of the Romantic *Oil* speech from the eastern side of the peninsula – his mother, perhaps. He did not use the "*auotrou*" of Breton's address of respect. "You *are* Triaged Potier, sir?"

"I am he." *I am withered and old now, but I see you remember my name.*

"It is my honour, sir." The boy's head dipped. "I am sorry to have called you at such an early hour."

"Time and tide wait for no man, officer. Nor do they wait for the sun." Potier permitted a bit of sharpness to his voice. "If I am to identify my flesh and blood, sir, I would prefer to do so now."

"Of course, *Monsieur*." The two fell in step, side by side in the long confines of the cool stone walls. Potier was either too buried in his thoughts or too dignified to notice how people ducked away from them in the stone hallway. Someone opened the thick wooden door that led downstairs to the too-familiar cold room in the basement.

"*Setu*," he was told – (There it is.) – but it was the only body on the long table. He caught a shiver from his guest. "*Yen*?" He held up the stray blanket kept for the purpose. (Cold?)

"*Yen-yen*," Potier agreed, (Very cold.) but refused the blanket.

Potier waited a few breaths for the usual bustle and clatter of thought to die down before he spoke again. "How did it happen?"

"We aren't sure." The *poliser* surprised him with his frankness. "The English police, *Scot-lund Yaard*, they had three of their men on a smuggler's boat. The boat was heading into the heart of the Sea and a storm came up. The story is, one of the men died en route and they threw his body overboard."

Potier made a low humming noise in his throat. "*Skrapers*?" He asked.

The boy jumped slightly. "I don't think they were really kidnappers," he said hastily.

Didn't think . . . Potier knew what that meant. The boy had already been told what to believe. He held his peace. Already the stench of corruption was in his nose.

"I would like to be left alone, if you please."

The boy was only too glad to comply. He looked like he would thank him, but stood in the doorway instead.

26

Potier stood before the canvas-shrouded form on the slate table. It was not a large man underneath. Potier had prepared himself from old practice, but still . . . that he would be placing eyes on the remains of his youngest grandson?

He must. Even if it was a nightmare come to life, something wrong was happening. An undertow of corruption sang in his ears as soft as the roar of the sea inside a cave. He stepped forward with the cold detachment of experience. When his brothers drowned in the storm of '56, he had identified all three, though the reefs had torn Pierrick's face to shreds. When his only nephew drowned off Brest, he had been the one to claim the body. This was a duty higher than that of any squeamishness he could carry. He could not afford to be selfish enough to weep yet. His strong brown hand tugged on the heavy cloth and pulled it away.

The body was in terrible shape. It had been immersed in the sea for too long. The eyes were gone. The lips too. Potier had never understood why the fish preferred those. But the hair . . . he remembered dark brown hair . . . .

It was the body of a small man, his own stature. Potier forced his mind into cold lines. He reached into his pocket and produced thin gloves. "If I may satisfy my curiosity," he said in French. The boy nodded from the doorway and hastily turned his back.

"Is . . . there anything I might help you with?" he asked.

Potier hesitated while donning the gloves, touched by the boy's courtesy. "I may," he said slowly. "But I will not hold you to an imposition. For now . . . please . . . a moment alone."

The old man closed his eyes for a moment, collecting all the memories of his youngest grandson. Jeanne's last boy, the only one who favoured him. Triaged never took favourites, but in the eyes of his smallest, beleaguered grandson he recognized a force of will that reminded him of his ownself standing fast against a world made of thorns. Let the world think that Geoffrey was his father's son. He carried the legacy of will of his *tad-kohz*.

He avoided the eyes, which were ruined, and the water-bloated flesh. There was one thing that he knew would mark his grandson. He began kneading the remains where foot met leg.

His wife had been the first to hold the *bugel* upon his entrance to the world. Worn out from birth the baby she had ignored the fuss, but Triaged's arms had been satisfied at the feel of the small weight.

"His foot." Margit-Jeanne leaned her head on his upper arm and they looked at the infant. Soon enough Thomas would come home with the other sons. "His left foot is twisted. Not much – just a bit."

27

"A small thing." Triaged had answered lightly. Women took such things deeply. They believed all babes were perfect.

And it *had* been a small thing. Between mother and grandparents, the boy's foot had been well on its way to correcting the twist, until Armoricus had, for reasons unexplained, thrown Geoffrey out of the top of the barn. "An accident," he had protested, but Triaged had not been convinced.

Such a strange world. Margit-Jeanne had thought the defect a large thing. He had thought it small. Now fate was proving it to be the most important moment in Potier's life.

The old man ignored the muffled choke from the policeman as he worked his fingers deeply into the soggy flesh. It was leached of blood and lymph from seawater, easier to mark. Flesh wore away more quickly than the hard calcium of bone, or even the tough material of the tendons and ligaments.

If it was his grandson, the marks would rest in those sinewy bands under the skin and in the fault-lines of bone.

The policeman was trying not to pay too close attention to what was happening. Finally the horrible wet sounds stopped. He refocused reluctantly to the old *floder*. [2] He was standing like a statute, not even breathing.

"Sir?"

"Yes." Triaged Potier turned to face him. Choked-in emotions crept through his voice. "I have found what I was looking for." He straightened, ramrod straight as a soldier and the boy's intestines lurched inside the cool morgue. "Tell the authorities that it is my humble opinion that these are the mortal remains of my grandson, Geoffrey L'estrade." He worked his mouth for a moment. "May I have the body, please?"

"I . . . Forgive me, sir." The boy whispered. "But the authorities wish to return the body to Scotland Yard. His wife and her people would like to see to arrangements."

Wife. Triaged blinked a moment, thinking. "My apologies, young man. I had . . . quite forgotten myself."

The boy gulped and pulled out his notebook. "I may state for the record that . . . You are convinced that this is the body of your grandson?"

"Please record that I have been convinced." Potier said heavily. "And if you will excuse me, I must go." He threw the spoiled gloves in the waste-can, caught the open, child-faced worry in the other man, and forced himself to smile kindly. "Not to worry, *Mab.*" He reached out and patted the big arm inside the sleeve. "I must see to my own grief." He cleared his throat and again became the epitome of dignity. *"An trubuilh ne varw den ebed gantañ"* Sorrow. Nobody dies from it.

Bretons died of many things, but they had no time to run to the Ankou's cart. Slow as it was, the ghost would come for them speedily enough.

LeCorre watched the old man step very carefully back up the steps. He swallowed hard. All his life he had heard the stories of what it had been like to patrol the law with men like that.

They were called *floders* – screech-owls. Corsairs and smugglers, but the truest name was the *MoonCursers*, and their ships were the *Moonfleet*. It was their kind that had protected Brittany from the crushing weight of the French Government. They fought for the English as much as the French, but they had never been defeated. LeCorre could glimpse why.

Even faced with his grandson's death, Potier was as solid as the rocks against the coast.

April 25th, 1891:

The *Athene* was large enough to move quickly over the choppy North Sea, but once it set its will against the Channels, events grew rough both outside and inside. On the other side of the small glass portal, waves lashed from the bottom while rain washed the salt from the top.

It made his head hurt even worse than before, but there was no time to wait it out. As long as the storm was causing havoc among the smugglers, the captain would have all available hands at work. That meant no supervision.

Just a few minutes, that was all he needed.

A slight toss, like riding a sleigh over a knoll. The small man lying on his shirt-front in the bottom of the hold turned colour for the worse and quickly slapped his palm over his makeshift pen and paper. Nothing escaped. Heart pounding, he waited a moment and turned his hand up. He breathed outward, silently, and risked a glance upward. The crude stitches pulled at his temple, threatening to open up again. He held his breath and returned to writing.

> *. . . Wiltson confessed. Captain of Hyssop. Faked Quimper's death in '84 . . . Q's valet on board with cargo . . . dissent in ranks . . .*

A lemon fished out of a tea-glass. A splinter prized off the floor-board. Two devices not known separately for their trickery, but when put together . . . a child's toy and a last chance.

It took more concentration than he liked to squeeze the slice out for the drops of ink. The splinter was suited for nothing more than shorthand.

He'd written plenty of notes on his cuff, but never on his collar. There wasn't much time. They would be back soon. They never stayed away for long.

In truth, Lestrade couldn't blame them. They were desperate men.

The small ship pitched slightly with the waves. He winced slightly, schooled himself to concentrate on the task at hand. Just a little more time . . . just time enough to get the message out . . . He swallowed as the *Athene* faced forward into a roll. Beside him his fellow prisoners continued to sleep. No wonder – they were exhausted. The detective paused to look at them, worried in the lamp-light. Cooper and Forbes were good men, but they should have never been caught up in this.

Patterson had much to answer for. Lestrade fully intended on having him do so if they survived. Especially for Cooper's sake. What fool had assigned the boy to this job? The inspector had watched a member of this very gang, his own brother, put a bullet in the man's father seventeen years ago. Did they think grief would make him a better fighter? Fools. He breathed out quietly, rested the detached collar flat on the floor and kept going.

These idiot boys will stay behind for my sake even though it means their own death. Have to lie. Won't be responsible for any more killing . . . .

> *. . . sorry . . . head won't stay clear. Sawbones isn't much. Thinking comes and goes. They're bringing ship to port. Name changed to* Galliou, *think it Quimper. Gregson right. Crime ring. Big. Got them under thumb. If they disobey, families forfeit. Ask mercy in court. Upholding law doesn't mean another father dancing hempen jig. Ship heading to Brittany's west coast Clea hold boys, be there if could –*

Footsteps. The hold-hatch screeched open. Someone upstairs scolded a sailor for not oiling everything that was metal on the ship. He moved with speedy economy and yanked the collar back on, hiding the unbuttoned end by his still-present scarf. They might take that from him soon. These smugglers weren't the brightest, but eventually they'd start thinking of his wardrobe in terms of weapons . . . He rose up despite the ache in his head and began playing the part.

They pushed open the door, spilling open dripping daylight into the dimly lit cabin. The detective was sitting upright, tin cup in his hands as he drank.

April 28th, 1891:

"Constables," Inspector Bradstreet spoke as gently as possible. Forbes and Cooper were sitting with stiff propriety, but they reminded him of his own sons when things were bad. They were all but huddling together in their shared misery. "Please remember that we are not gathered here to condemn, or to criticize you. With CI Miller in the hospital, we're trying to merely expedite matters in his absence. We are simply here to learn the truth of what happened aboard the *Athene*."

The PC's nodded in unison. Bradstreet wondered if he had *ever* looked that fragile when he wore the wool uniform. Forbes was sweating like a racehorse. He looked breakable with his wounded arm pulled inside its bulky sling. He saw Bradstreet's slow nod or permission and he loosened his thick collar awkwardly.

"Yes, sir." Cooper took a deep breath. Despite the collection of injuries they carried, not to mention the wind burn on their faces from the salty ocean, they were ready.

Bradstreet sighed as he took up the pencil. Lestrade was always better at shorthand than he was. He tapped the pencil on the desk. Against the wall of the conference room, Sergeant Hopkins, Inspectors Gregson and Lanner waited in their chairs, hands resting on the conference table. There was nothing in the way of blame in their eyes, and to the already-self-loathing constables, the patience made it worse.

Bradstreet had a thought – an unpleasing one. "Where's Patterson?" He demanded.

"Where do you think?" Gregson snipped, but low-voiced and deadly calm. "Off on his own affairs."

"I'd dearly love to see him here." Bradstreet said under his breath. Aloud: "We'll do this in alphabetical order. That makes it no more fair or unfair than any other system. Cooper, just tell your side of the story and we'll stop you once in a while if we have a question."

"We were . . . taken by surprise." Cooper took a deep breath. He suddenly looked sick.

Hopkins stood, his walking stick tapping against the floor as he leaned on it for support. His wounded leg thrust out stiffly, removing his usual grace and economy of movement. Cooper looked at him with an almost-frightened face until he saw the soft package of cigarettes offered in his hand. He took one with unsteady hands.

"You're not on trial, lad." For Hopkins to call the much larger and probably older constable "lad" was almost diverting . . . but it was what

31

Cooper needed to hear. He calmed by degrees and struck a match to the tip. One puff – he seemed to calm just a bit further.

"We . . . we were following Inspector Patterson's orders to get to the aft of the ship," he began. "Almost as soon as we went up the gangplank, I lost any sight of the rest of the raid. The inspector had 'is bull pup out and we had the guns we'd requisitioned out of the office." [3] Forbes nodded at his side in agreement.

"Forbes here, he was on my left. It was hard to see. The moon was behind the clouds, but there were a lot of barrels piled up like . . . like a child's set of blocks. Forgive me sir. They didn't seem to have any more order than that." Bradstreet motioned to continue. "This big cove with a bright yellow fogle [4] around his neck jumped on us with a bloomin' life-preserver in his hands – stuck out like a sore thumb in 'is dark dunnage [5] . . . He was going to split open Forbes' skull, right down the middle, but the inspector, 'e put 'is fist inside his middle and twisted him over the edge and into the water."

"That'd be Kerjean." Hopkins said to Gregson, who nodded without taking his eyes off the tableau. "I fished that one out of the water myself."

"He'd been blocking the hatch, so with him gone, I kicked the wood down and we went inside."

"As you were ordered." Gregson pointed out. By now, it would be an exceptionally stupid man who didn't see the guilt rolling off the constables in the room.

"Yes, sir." Cooper was slowly crushing the cigarette in his fingers. "There were a few shots. I never got to fire any off." Apology.

"Can you describe the hold?" Gregson asked.

Copper bubbled into an unhealthy-sounding laugh. "Sir. Yes, sir, I believe I could." He smashed the cigarette to his lips and struggled to breathe smoke in. "Yes, sir, I believe I could describe it to you."

"Forbes?" Bradstreet had the sense to drop Cooper for now. "Do you have anything to add to Cooper's account?"

"Well, we did as Inspector Patterson ordered, sir. And after the inspector tossed that thug in the Thames, we got into the hold as ordered, and it was a right *dewskitch* [6] after that. I got off three shots of the Webley, but I don't think I wounded more than one. The inspector, I know he hit two of 'em, but I don't know what happened, I jus saw the bodies fall down. They were desperate men, sir. They weren't going to be taken if they had any say."

"That fits what we know." Lanner cleared his throat. "I have a question," he rested his hands on the table. "Do you have any idea how long the fight took?"

Forbes looked bewildered. "I . . . no, sir . . . It couldn't have taken any more than ten minutes. It happened so fast . . . but I don't know how long exactly."

"That's quite all right, Constable. Carry on . . . ."

"Yessir. Right sir." Forbes was not a smoker. He drank from his teacup instead. "We hit the bottom of the ladder and a man with a scarf wrapped around his face had a small bottle in his hands. About the size of a claret bottle. He threw it down and jumped back. It broke right at our feet, and the chloroform came out of it, and put us all out. That's all I remember of that part . . . ."

Bradstreet was as close to nausea as he could get in public without disgracing himself. He rested his head in his hands for a moment, elbows throbbing against the desktop as the constables filed out. He waited for someone to say something. *Anything,* he thought. *Say anything. I don't care what it is.*

Hopkins cleared his throat, very very softly. "Do you think he might have made it?"

"Hard to say." Bradstreet astonished himself for the cold even voice he owned. "If it was at all possible . . . he would have."

"I'm afraid to aim in that direction." Gregson rose to his feet. A moment later the stench of his vile fags tickled Bradstreet's nose. "He'd survive if it was his first priority . . . but stopping the *Athene* . . . that would be something on his mind."

"We'll know soon enough." Bradstreet said. They both studied in silence the battered rectangle of blood-stained cloth in his big hand. Lestrade's collar, a message smuggled out at the literal last minute, stared up at him with the delicate brown streaks of lemon juice exposed to heat. *So much effort, and only one name to show for it . . . one name.* Galliou.

NOTES

1. Town hall
2. Smuggler
3. Contrary to popular belief, bobbies were permitted firearms, but under special circumstances, such as walking the beat in dangerous parts of London at night.
4. Silk handkerchief
5. Clothing
6. Beating

Chapter III – Over Authority

April 29th, 1891:

Scotland Yard was an organized mess. The new building was all but finished, but there were still the piled stacks upon stacks of files, papers, reports, and informants' accounts. In this world, a secretary who remembered everything could wield true power.

Somehow, word had gotten out. Constables who should have been in bed were huddled around the front of the main office, passing around endless cups of tea bought from the street-vendor on the corner as they murmured in low voices. No one could keep their eyes off the silent street that rested at the bottom of the steps.

Sergeant-Detective Hopkins felt as though someone had injected hot sand underneath his eyelids. The harsh lights of the building made it even worse. Tired to the point of physical illness, he put his head down and shut his eyes. When had he last eaten? It seemed as though he should have . . . at the normal supper-time, but for the life of him, he couldn't remember what his meal had been.

His wounded leg throbbed. Soft burning strands of glowing colours twisted slowly behind his eyelids, pulling him into a state of half-hypnosis.

He must have fallen asleep. It wasn't something he had sought. PC Harry Murcher was standing there, shaking him awake, his street-battered face open and sympathetic. 'Sir," he cleared his throat, "sir . . . they're here."

"Thank you, Constable." Hopkins stood on his own flimsy power, and made his way to the front of the building where the ambulance was pulling to a stop.

Inspector Bradstreet jumped down from the back doors and wobbled on the cobblestones. Two orderlies carefully stepped out, bearing a shrouded body on a gurney between them. Behind Hopkins, Gregson was just coming out. His big hand pushed Hopkins aside impatiently.

"Roger?" Athelney Jones was in the process of straightening his collar. It was so late at night everyone was slacking, even he.

"*I can't tell.*" Bradstreet choked. His face was a dangerous colour. Abruptly he swayed on his feet. "I can't . . . tell . . . ." Hopkins leaped down the whitewashed steps and grabbed him. The big man whirled to the gutter and vomited.

"That bad?" Hopkins asked. His face was so pale his lips were blue.

"We can't let his wife see." Bradstreet was clinging on to Hopkins with everything he had. Cold sweat ran ribbons down his face. "Oh, Good *God*," he stammered. "Oh, God."

Hopkins remembered belatedly that Bradstreet and Lestrade had served together as bluecoats over twenty years ago. There were a few years between them, but their history had been friendly. He didn't know what to do in the face of such a loss.

Gregson's lips thinned. "Get him downstairs," he snapped to the silent orderlies. "*Now*. Get Roanoke," he added. "And I mean, *Right Now*." He swept the air with his arm. "He's not dead unless we get the proof!" His cold eyes sank into Bradstreet. "*Athelney Jones*! See to Bradstreet! Where's Roanoke?"

Roanoke was a naturally pale man, his complexion hastened by his long hours in subterranean morgue rooms kept in chill temperatures. By then the word had spread throughout the Yard. "You wanted to see me, Inspector?" He asked roughly.

"I want *proof* that's Inspector Lestrade." Gregson pointed at the sheeted body underneath his hand. "Either confirm or deny it, but I want proof."

"The identification on his body . . . ."

"Could have come from anywhere." Gregson snarled. "*Anyone* can claim to be his grandfather. I want *proof*, Doctor."

"In order to do that, I'd have to have his medical records." Roanoke winced but kept his voice calm and professional. "The condition of the deceased . . . ."

"I've got his records." Gregson cut him off. He stamped to his folded overcoat and pulled a file out from underneath. "Start examining. I'm *not* telling his wife and children a god-damn thing until I know the facts to *be* facts."

April 22nd, 1891:

Two shots shattered the darkness. Lestrade heard them impact behind him. Forbes grunted, a bull-like sound and he crashed to the floor. Lestrade and Cooper both flung themselves down with him. A man with his face hidden in a mummy-like wrap of scarf emerged from the shadows. Lestrade's gun-arm was pinned under Cooper's body. He saw a small glass bottle gleam for a moment, and then it burst on the planks before them. He was unconscious before he knew it.

The raid had not gone as planned.

Patterson's habit of keeping details close and private was never so bitterly regretted among his cohorts. The ship had too many people on it.

The crew consisted of too many hard-bitten smugglers north of Essex ready for a fight or paranoid of failure.

Gregson stared, pale with sickening dread as Sergeant Hopkins moaned in pain, clutching a leg that dripped blood through the weave of his trousers. He rolled on the dirty planks of the decaying short-pier, trying not to faint and scream at the same time.

"Easy, Sergeant . . . ." Bradstreet was already bending over the younger man, his avuncular instincts soothing the poor man faster than any opiate. Gregson wiped the sweat off that face-had any of them looked that young? listening to the cloth rip. Below the *Athene* and blocking the ship by an embargo of floating police, the Thames Division had lined up a dangerous barricade.

The smugglers had not been completely surprised.

After the initial startled skirmish, the gangplank had been drawn up and the ship tugged away from the dock. She floated now, too far away from a land-boarding, and her gun-men sat invisible in the night, ready to pick off any copper who floated too close.

Stalemate.

"Well, at least we can see where they are," Gregson tried not to sound too insubordinate while Patterson was standing at the lip of the water in his inscrutable prig expression . . . .

Gregson decided to hell with it. He was wet, exhausted, sweating like a pig in his pea-jacket, and sore from too many blows from too many frightened criminals. Hopkins was lucky not to be shot *through* the leg-bone. That would have meant a slow, agonizing death through bone infection if he hadn't chosen an amputation. As it was, the bullet-graze was sending him through all kinds of Hell. "Isn't this what the Pinkerton Yanks call, 'Ketchable but not Fetchable'?"

Patterson shot him an icy look, his face hot. In that moment, Gregson made an enemy.

"Oh, my God." Bradstreet staggered up, wringing Hopkins' blood from his handkin, his face chalk-white. *"Where's Geoff?"*

Youghal blanched. "He was with Cooper and Forbes!"

"Cooper and Forbes are missing too!" Bradstreet barked. "Patterson, you sent them aboard that damned ship!"

Patterson didn't hesitate. He whirled and barked orders – or began to. *"Halloa!"*

A dark lantern gleamed, tracking a slender line on the oily water as it chopped against ship and dock alike.

Gregson stared in disbelief as a white handkerchief – How could anything be white on *that* ship? – flapped in the air tied to a stick. *"Halloa the shore!"*

"*Halloa the ship!*" Patterson snarled back. "What say you, Captain? Do you surrender?"

"Excuse me, sirs," The Captain held up his hands in a signal of truce. Slowly, the policemen paused in their attack. "Excuse me, Officers . . . Thank you." The captain's accent was strange – tints of Norway mixed with round vowels. "Which of you is in charge of this operation?"

Patterson stepped forward, his eyes narrowed. No one would ever criticize his courage. "I'll have you know that if you're asking merely to find a target, there are plenty of my rank present to take my place."

"That *wasn't* the reason why I was asking, Officer," the captain answered back reproachfully. "We simply wish to . . . open negotiations with you for a moment . . . ."

"Your ship is loaded with contraband!" Patterson shot back. "We have proof that you're a supplier for Moriarty's gang, Wiltson! – A long-term supplier."

The captain blinked in the lamplight. No doubt he had thought his true name sacrosanct. "Very good," he bowed slightly. "But nevertheless, we wish free passage out of the estuary."

"I don't see how we could possibly go against our morals and give it to you." Patterson shot back with heat. Behind him the other policemen, with their deeper experience of working in teams and groups were beginning to grow uneasy with a dawning suspicion.

"It seems we've taken on a few unexpected passengers, Inspector." Captain Wiltson spoke coolly, but his eyes burned with a mad delight in thrusting his power onto Patterson. "Now that they're aboard, I really do hate to go through the trouble of going back to shore . . . ."

Patterson went white as a ghost in the starlight. "I don't believe you!" He barked back.

Bradstreet lifted a big hand and clamped it down on the other man's shoulder. "Hold on, now," he grunted. "Captain!" He roared. "Prove your statements, sir!"

Wiltson grinned like a skull. "You heard him, boys." In the black shadows where no one could aim a bullet, two seamen scuffled up with a blood-stained Constable Cooper between them. The big man was missing his helmet and leather collar. A bruise was gaining on his left cheek like a cancer. He looked completely disgraced and ready to die of humiliation.

"Inspector," Cooper gritted his teeth. He looked past Patterson to Bradstreet. "Inspector Bradstreet sir."

"How is it, Constable?" Bradstreet asked gently.

"Sir. They were ready for us in the hold. Forbes' been shot, but it's not a bad'un. He should pull through." Cooper sounded like he was trying to convince himself.

"Is that it, Constable?" Bradstreet held his breath.

"The inspector, sir." Cooper said heavily. "He . . . he's not too well, sir." The young man swallowed hard. "Got a head wound." He swallowed again.

Bradstreet's face slowly turned the colour of Burgundy. "Captain Wiltson," he said sharply, "State your terms."

"You can't be serious!" Patterson shouted. "I am in charge!"

Bradstreet didn't even look at the man. He simply moved his fist backwards and it collided with Patterson's face. The other man went down like a bag of sand. Even the smugglers were impressed. Wiltson's eyebrows went up in a sudden show of respect.

"I said *state* your terms, Captain. I didn't say *name* your terms." Bradstreet's face was hot. His voice cold.

Wiltson ducked his head in a sudden grin. "Fair enough. You want your men back, and be assured, if I do not fulfill my business transaction, I'll have no more reason for using up any more of God's marvelous oxygen." A thread of seriousness wove through his voice. "You'll have your men back to you in one week, sir. I promise you no harm will – that is, no *further* harm – will come to them – " He put his hands on his hips and sniffed expectantly. " – provided they don't get themselves into any more mischief. There is rank among you. The inspector will be the first to face the consequences of his men's actions."

Bradstreet was breathing through his beard in long, shallow gasps. "I'll need more information than that, sir."

Wiltson tapped his fingers on the rail. "We'll contact you with the location where you can pick up your men," he stated. "I have no intention of dancing the hemp, Inspector, and I am quite aware that killing a policeman in the lines of his duty is a straight ticket to the event."

"Ye'd best be thinking of this, then, while you're conductin' your unlawful business, Captain." Bradstreet's voice was rarely so used. It was a black glacial cave. "All three of the men you have – they have wives and children at home. If we have to answer to them on their fate, no place in the sea will keep you from answering to us."

Wiltson pursed his lips, giving him a briefly spinsterish look. "A fair enough warning, Inspector, but you keep to your side and leave us to do our business." For one last time, he grinned. "This sort of thing happens quite a bit among our little business wars, sir. You'll forgive us for treating you as if you're a rival organisation for the night . . . ."

PC Forbes tried to take a deep breath. It was stuffy and humid in the confines of the ship's hold. The only light shining through was due to the placement of a few glass pyramids set in the wood and a dark lantern suspended far above their heads. The men had been leg-shackled to the wall by heavy iron rings, and Forbes tried very hard not to think of those implications.

"Looks like we're not the first hostages to ride first-class, eh, Forbes?" Cooper tried to smile, but he was still in a great deal of pain. Every breath dragged the scrape of his coat against his bruised ribs. "Now what?" Cooper asked.

"*Hsshhtt!*" Forbes answered just as softly. Even talking hurt the bullet hole in his arm. His eyes strained to make out Lestrade. The small man was lying in the same position in which the smugglers had left him. Blood on his face made a black gleam in the murky lantern-light. "Inspector," Forbes asked softly. "Are you all right, sir?"

It took a long time, but the inspector finally responded. His eyes opened by degrees and blinked against the curtain of drying blood.

"Inspector," Forbes tried again, pitching his voice as softly as possible. "Sir . . . we're riding with them as a guarantee the police won't follow. The captain promised to drop us off somewhere where we can be picked up in a week. I don't know where that might be."

Lestrade gave the barest nod in response. His eyes slipped shut again.

"Damn." Forbes licked his lips. "He's none too good." As if he could claim any different.

"They'll check on us in bit," Cooper pointed out. "As rough as these boys play, they got ter have a fake Crow on board with 'em." It wasn't much, but it was something to hope for.

Bradstreet's first thoughts of what he would say to Clea – not to mention the Mrs. Forbes and Cooper – were halted by the sight of Chief Inspector Miller rampaging around a stack of files and document-crammed boxes. "Bradstreet! What's this about you laying hands on another inspector in violence?"

"He wouldn't shut up during the hostage negotiations," Bradstreet spoke with the same cold voice he had on the waterfront. "He was willing to put their lives at risk, sir."

Miller vibrated with fury. "That was our last link to Moriarty's partners!" he hissed. "*The very last.* You let our proof go sailing to God knows where, and you have no idea if they'll keep their word on our men or not!"

"I had no choice." Bradstreet said heavily. "Patterson was about to instigate a firefight, and that would have been a *guarantee* of killing Cooper on the spot! We wouldn't have found Forbes or Lestrade in time!"

"You went above the authority of the man I placed in charge of the case." Miller's shaking hands locked at his sides and he stood, taut as rawhide. "You are suspended from all duties, without pay, until further notice."

Bradstreet felt himself turn into a statue at the words. He simply stared at his superior over the Atlantic roar in his ears.

"Take your personal effects out of your office now." Miller finished. "You will be notified when you may return – *if* you may return."

"You might be in need of this." Gregson proffered one of his terrible smokes.

Bradstreet wearily agreed. In the cold light of dawn, the alley was a terrible place for contemplation. Bradstreet realized he had been using it for self-pity.

"I feel like I've just dipped myself in filth," he choked. "How am I supposed to tell Clea her husband's off the map, in the hands of smugglers?"

"As I recall, he's the one what had to tell Hazel *you* didn't stand a good chance of pulling through that bullet in the chest back in . . . '79?" Gregson said evenly. "And that was a bullet meant for him when you stupidly got in the way . . . Now what's this about you being suspended?"

"Didn't you hear every blasted word floating through the air?" Bradstreet's hands shook as he lit a match. The match went out. He cursed. Gregson wordlessly pulled out his own box, and his hands were the usual extension of his cold and calm self as he lit the tobacco for Bradstreet. "I should think the little men on the moon would have heard."

"All I heard was Miller's side of things." Gregson said icily. "And *that* was from the perspective of Patterson – who, I'll allow, is a brilliant man, but he doesn't play well with us, man. That's the whole reason why he's allowed to work solo for the CID. He'll sacrifice three of us to get *one* of the enemy, because he seems to think we lost our rights to be protected as soon as we agreed to take the crowned badge." He blew out a stinking cloud that was like tobacco mixed with sawdust and a trace of mud.

"You can't know that," Bradstreet protested, shocked.

Gregson only nodded. "I keep my eyes out on people like that," he said succinctly. "Any time you run into a man who can't work with a partner, there's a problem."

Bradstreet felt his nausea deepen.

"I may be the smartest of this lot, but I can't make bricks without clay, Bradstreet. Give me something to work with."

Bradstreet swallowed something even more bitter than Gregson's smoke.

"I need your help," Bradstreet said bluntly.

"I know you do." Gregson answered. "And you'll get it."

"I'm not about to see you get suspended too."

Gregson smirked. "Give me some credit, man. Give me some credit."

Chapter IV – A Change
in the Wind

April 23rd, 1891:

"**J**ust to take a look, would you?"

PC Cooper opened sleep-heavy eyes to see one of the smugglers nodding at Forbes as he set down a wooden trencher of sausage rolls and a jug of what looked like *very* dark beer. He blinked his lids as Forbes lifted a roll up for a fish-eyed inspection. "S'going on?" He asked softly.

"Got them to see about us," Forbes broke the bread open, clumsily and one-handed, and sniffed at the contents. "Pig-liver sausage . . . Could be worse," he decided. "Go easy on that beer, will you? Smells like the good stuff."

"First-class accommodations *indeed.*" Cooper managed to slosh some of the jug into a wooden cup without spilling it. He took a taste. "*Whew*! That's the Sabbath special, that is! Well, I suppose it's cheaper than drugging us."

"Aye, clever. I need to make a private note o'that for my personal files. Might come in handy when interrogatin' a recalcitrant prisoner . . . ." The constables shared a quick, nervous grin between them. Forbes sighed, his throbbing arm a deterrent to any ease. "Ruddy mess."

"*Mess* ain't a word big enough for this, Matty." Cooper leaned back and nursed his aching body. *God.* "How're you feeling?" A shrug was his answer. Cooper gave one back.

"Can you reach the inspector?" Forbes murmured.

"Probably. Be easier if he wasn't all the way against the wall." Cooper took the offered drink, quaffed it, and handed the cup back. "Here goes . . . ." His wound throbbed and burned as though there was a bullet deep in the muscle. Or a jagged splinter. "Damn," he muttered. "This just plain *hurts*." His fingers caught on the cloth of Lestrade's sleeve. "Go' 'im," he panted. He pulled more of the sleeve into his grip and reeled in the inspector's wrist. "Hang on . . . ." Lestrade was dead weight. Cooper held his breath against his own pain and tried to pull. "Damn," he breathed. "Bloody damn . . . ."

"Here they come." Forbes hissed. "Drop him and act pathetic."

"No difficulties with that." Cooper shot back. The footfalls clopped their way to the makeshift prison. A bright storm-lantern was hung on a hook by the wall and the panels taken down from the dark lantern above their heads.

"So much for me beauty sleep," Cooper grumbled.

"Ease off, bluebottle." The man performing the role of physician was *not* the kind who inspired confidence . . . unless he was meant as an example as to why one should stay healthy as long as possible. Only his hands were clean. Forbes decided they were lucky to even have that. "Get your coat off and let's see the damage." He clucked his tongue impatiently at the slowness of Cooper's movements. Like lightning the two grinning smugglers lifted him up and divested him of garments.

"Gettin' fresh, now, and not so much as a bouquet?" Cooper taunted. He was given a friendly tap on the head for his troubles.

"Hold still if you don't want this to get infected," the greasy man scolded impartially. At least he was quick. He no doubt had a great deal of practice with spot-jobs. "Sit down," he ordered as the last of the bandage-lint was tied off above the muscle. Cooper did as he was told. "What's wrong with the other one – Oh, lovely. Head wound." The proclamation was critical. "Who had that brilliant notion?"

"I don't truly think he took it on to spite you," Forbes said gently. He wondered if the man was a little mad.

"Hush, I'm working." The Crow flipped Lestrade on his back with a toe of his boot and pulled out a fresh bottle of carbolic-water. Most of the inspector's face was masked in caked-over blood. Cooper felt his weakened guts clench as a large sponge turned it into a red rivulet onto the planks. "Going to need stitches, I'll vow." Again, he sounded as though Lestrade's medical condition had been an act of deliberate spite against his schedule. He snorted under his breath. "Marvelous. Just marvelous."

Forbes swallowed down a croak. "Will he be all right?"

"How should *I* know?" the Crow snapped. He finished getting the worst of the dried blood off the wound. "Don't bother me while I'm working." That said, he sat back on his heels and muttered to himself in a mixture of basic English and not-so-flattering idle obscenities. A spool of thick black waxed thread was unrolled half a yard and knotted to a curved needle with a slightly hooked tip. Almost in afterthought, the whole thing was dipped in a bottle that reeked of rum and *then* he went to work. Forbes was beginning to feel a very genuine sense of alarm. No one wanted to deal with a Crow who hated work.

The larger man that had held Cooper suddenly shifted his weight and went to the other side of the ring. His pale eyes gleamed brightly as he stared at the unresponsive inspector.

"What the devil is it now, Craddock?"

"That's Inspector Lestrade," Craddock said slowly.

"Never met him," the Crow retorted.

"I got ta tell the captain."

"You will when I'm done here." The Crow snapped.

Forbes and Cooper looked at each other. The situation had abruptly changed, and they knew it wasn't for the better.

Craddock twitched. He waited with an eagerness the constables found worrisome. The moment the filthy man finished stitching up the inspector, Craddock stepped in and riffled his pockets. "No badge," he muttered. "Where's his badge?"

The constables shrugged. Forbes was glad Cooper was keeping his mouth shut – it had to be an effort on his part. The Crow sniffed again and stood with his stained canvas bag in his hands.

"Harker, go get the captain." Craddock was trembling. "I'm not letting my eyes off these bobbies." Ignoring the situation, the fake doctor had already left.

Cooper tried to pass on a message to Forbes with his eyes: *What's going on?*

Forbes sent one back: *I haven't the slightest idea.*

They both looked at Lestrade, who hadn't so much as moved while getting stitched up by a man who apparently thought a rope and a harpoon made for decent medical sewing.

Captain Wiltson tromped down with a strange expression on his face. "What's all this, Craddock?"

"It's Inspector Lestrade." Craddock nudged the senseless inspector with his boot. "The boss would like to ask him some questions."

Wiltson was dead silent for a quarter-minute, regarding the man who was not, after all, an ordinary seaman-turned-smuggler. "I made a promise that I would keep to my end of the bargain, Craddock," he said at last. "So far the authorities have not molested us."

Craddock adopted a stubborn expression. "The boss would pay for the privilege, Captain. He's said so in my hearing before."

Wiltson wavered, his strange-sea-coloured eyes moving over Lestrade. "I did not know his identity, Craddock. I struck my bargain. If our employer wishes to question him, he must make his own arrangements."

"Then holdover once we get to port," Craddock persisted. "Do that, and give him time to respond to my wire."

The captain sighed through his nose – a strange, defeatist sound. "I *may* go *that* far," he admitted. "But bear in mind I have no control over the spring squalls. We're riding ahead of a large one as it is!" He turned his back and stomped back to the surface. Craddock paid them all a dark look and followed. The constables were left, sweating in the close, dank air of the hold.

"What's . . . going on?" Lestrade whispered.

"Hold on, sir. Can you get your strength up?" Forbes was stiff from inactivity. He passed the beer and rolls over to Cooper, who did his level best to help the inspector to an upright position. Prospects were not favourable. Lestrade went gray as soon as he lifted his head, and it was a good quarter-hour before he could stabilize himself to the point that he could drink some of the bitter brew. *Then* it was a matter of waiting to see if he could keep it all down.

"Sir," Cooper took the initiative from Forbes. His mate was ready to drop from lack of sleep as it was. "We're being held hostage to ensure the authorities do nothing while they sail this ship to their destination. The captain – Wiltson – says he's going to deliver us to some place where our mates can pick us up in a week."

"A week?" Lestrade whispered. He would have frowned his concentration, but it simply hurt too much.

"That was the *first* plan," Forbes corrected, his voice was thick with fatigue. "But things just took a change, and it's a-seeming to be for the worse."

"What's . . . that?" Lestrade asked softly.

"There's a big demander by the name of Craddock who says their boss wants to speak with you." Forbes was so weary his tongue slurred on the syllables.

"Craddock . . . ." Lestrade's dark brown eyes briefly opened all the way. "Tell me everything, gentlemen."

Between Cooper and Forbes, Lestrade got the whole story. Well, that was their hope. He reacted very seldom to what they were saying.

"Sir," Cooper finally took the jump. "Are you at all well? You took a nasty knock on the head."

"Just a . . . scalp-scratch. Always . . . bleed well." Lestrade suddenly swallowed hard. "S'the . . . Chlor . . . form . . . ," he clarified faintly. "doesn't . . . suit . . . Well . . . ." He blinked in the poor light.

"Aye, I understand," Forbes was worried. Once in a while you ran into someone who was plain wiped by the drug. It made them fair useless for days, and their wits were addled as sharp as if they'd been dropping on their head. It looked like Lestrade was in that category. "Good to know about your head, though. They didn't really take a close look at you."

"Spring . . . storm . . . ." The little man worked his mouth, trying to bring some moisture out with which to speak. They passed him a cup of the bitter beer and he gulped it down without a blink. "Did they . . . say any more . . . to that?"

"No. Just that they were riding ahead of a spring storm."

They watched while the inspector slipped back into a still level of consciousness. He never moved and barely breathed. Forbes and Cooper must have napped then, because when he spoke next it startled them. "Brittany." His voice slurred. "Not headed . . . to . . . North Sea . . . after all . . . Sea of . . . Brittany . . . spring storm, heading 'cross from peninsula . . . in newspapers." His dark eyes closed for a long time, and they were forced to watch, unable to help him. "Brest," he forced out. "They're heading to . . . the sea-caves . . . smuggler's ports . . . Brest . . . only . . . sensible place . . . ." Lestrade's dark eyes closed again, as surely as someone turning the gas down from a light. "Cooper . . . ."

"I'm here, sir." Cooper whispered.

"You . . . in . . . charge." Lestrade stopped to swallow. "I'm going to . . . cause . . . some distraction. You need to get yourself and Forbes . . . out of here."

"We're not leaving you, sir!" Cooper blurted – he barely remembered not to shout in the confines of the hold.

"Listen." Lestrade lifted a head that looked as heavy as a concrete block. "Senior . . . rank . . . ." He smiled thinly. "They'll be taking us to Brest . . . or one of the outlying islands . . . Either of you . . . swim?"

"We both do, sir. You know that."

"Men . . . faked reports before." Lestrade was by now speaking with his eyes closed. "Be . . . patient . . . need to time this . . . with storm . . . be . . . ready."

"What do you want us to do, sir?" Forbes asked softly.

"You . . . take care of each other . . . and . . . wait . . . ." Lestrade's groggy eyes opened one last time. "Next time they come down . . . convince them I need extra . . . attention."

"I don't think we'll have much trouble of that," Forbes whispered. He stared at Cooper, sharing the same worry in the other man.

"Hoi, you!" Cooper lifted his voice. The seaman removing their wooden bowl paused. "The boss needs medical attention, like." Cooper used the slang of his childhood – the type that his grandparents always whipped him for using.

The smuggler paid Lestrade the courtesy of a long-eyed look. "I ain't promising nothing," he warned. "You comprehend that, Copper?"

"I'll comprehend anything that means you won't call me a pig," Cooper made a rather pig-like exhalation of contempt.

The smuggler grinned, showing he was missing at least half his teeth. "Got me there, so help me. You just sit tight. I'll tell the man upstairs on deck what's going on." He departed with the bowl.

Half- an-hour later – it felt like eternity – the Crow came down with the captain. The latter waited while the former poked and prodded and muttered, then gave his decision. "Needs better light," was the grudging verdict. "Hard to work on him down here."

Wilston nodded. "Get him out," he snapped at the waiting servants.

In the cleaner, more active circulation of fresh sea-air flowing in from the deck, Lestrade's mind opened by degrees. For the first time in what felt like ages, he could think in coherent structures. Dawn was breaking over the grey waters and the crisp wind did much to take the groggy feeling out of his head. God, but he *hated* chloroform. In its own way, it was as bad for him as morphine. Lestrade had never encountered anything that resembled sea-sickness before, and he absolutely did *not like* it.

"Settle you down," Wiltson directed evenly, and they helped him lean up against a large oilcloth-covered mound of rope against the cabin wall. The breeze shifted, clean and cool. It felt marvelous. "Leif, wash your damn hands." The captain said in disgust.

Lestrade wondered if the man was any good at all, besides his ability to hold a gash together with what the constables *swore* was a canvas needle and waxed thread. The blood still tracked from his left temple down the cheek-bone and stiffened his collar like starch. *Clea will kill me*, he thought ridiculously. She *hated* bloodstains.

Things were made worse by the cold-eyed glare of Craddock. Consciousness asserted himself to the big man's glassy gaze. Lestrade's first impression was that he would find a quick death over the side of the ship at the first opportunity. That was dispelled at the presence of the captain, who seemed concerned in his welfare in a shallow, materialistic way.

"I'm to see that you survive this jaunt, Inspector." Captain Wiltson seemed uneasy at his "guest's" potential fate. Lestrade was willing to give him a bit of credit for that. The "caught-in-pincers" expression on the outwardly confident face reminded him too much of people who worked for "families" of crime. "Anything I can do for you within reason?"

Lestrade lifted his hand to his aching head. "Something for this," he rasped. "Cup of something with lemon to keep things down?"

Wiltson grimaced with sympathy. "Aye, a good cup of black tea with lemon and ginger ought to do the trick." The captain crossed his arms over his chest – a more belligerent move than merely folding them. "Dare I ask what it is you've done to get on the bad lights of M. Gaillou?"

"It doesn't take that much, as I'm certain you're aware." Lestrade was guessing there. His reward was the firefly flicker of guilt in the salt-beaten brown face. "You were the captain of the *Hyssop*, weren't you?"

47

Wiltson's lips tighted. "Aye, back when my name really *was* Wiltson."

"Good job you did there . . . back in '84, wrecking that new ship so he could get away." Lestrade smiled, using his polite-rascal demeanor. Quimper had to be Gaillou . . . "I've always wondered . . . Did he request a first-class lifeboat?"

Wiltson laughed, palm slapping his thigh. "That he did." The First Mate grinned as well. Both ignored Craddock – *everyone* was ignoring Craddock, hard as that was to imagine, which clued Lestrade that the big man was not well-liked, and probably forced into a position of respect.

His presence only confirmed there was something big on board. Not the elusive Professor Moriarty of Patterson's dreams, but *something*.

"So . . . ." Lestrade let his head lean back against the boards. "What next?"

"Mostly, keep you from dying." Wiltson admitted. "You and your men'll be dropped off at a safe spot . . . We'll send word on where you can get picked up but we'll do it after we set sail." The captain was carved on hard lines and sun-browned even under his neck. "Probably one of the little islands on the Channels . . . Haven't made up my mind yet. Of course, if we fail to keep ahead of this little squall, you may be a guest longer than you care to."

"Mmm." Lestrade already didn't much care about it. "They never tell us much about what's going on. I don't even know who we were looking for."

Wiltson snorted. "Sounds like your ruggers and mine aren't too different," he commented. "All I know is, I'm fair on my end, and that's fine with me." He paused to glare his distaste at the returning Haus. "Well?"

Haus' water-clammed hands made Lestrade shudder, and damned if he'd be ashamed of a simple ordinary reaction. The quack perused his head slowly, squinting in the pale ocean dawn. "I suppose he'll live." And that was that for the pronouncement.

"Buy a bloody Ouija board next time I need a doctor," Wiltson muttered under his breath. Lestrade was forced to feel sympathy. "A few minutes up in the air should set you right. We'll see to that tea. I suggest you get your constables to eat their rations. It will make my mind rest the easier if they're well cared for."

And keeping them half-sauced will do it. Lestrade leaned his aching head in one hand, propped on his knee as he peered wearily up to the man. "I don't think I'll have much trouble getting two Aldgate constables to drink your ruddy tar-water."

Wiltson snorted. "I won't drug 'em if they behave," he cautioned.

48

"I'll be sure they understand their responsibility, Captain," Lestrade said blandly. Wiltson nodded – then looked suspiciously. The little detective only looked tired out and slightly green. "Harmless" was the word for *how* he looked, and by default, Wiltson decided to go with that impression. He wasn't keen on this job anyway. The sooner it was finished, the happier they'd all be.

The constables were relieved to see Lestrade looking more human as he was returned to the hold. He wryly ignored the return of the shackles and was stirring a good half of a lemon in a cup of what looked like some sort of limpid brownish liquid when they were left alone again.

"What is that, sir?" Forbes was within his rights to ask.

"Tea." Lestrade said succinctly. "That's what they said it was."

"I'm not one to argue with my host, sir." Cooper snorted. Despite his extreme discomfort, he was managing a smile. "How long have we been down here, do you know?"

"It's dawn." Lestrade set the lemon aside and passed over the cup with a grunt. "Hold that for me . . . ." He sucked in his breath carefully and stretched out on the floor, running his fingers along the cracks and crevices of the planks. "It would just figure," he said under his breath. "The *Hyssop* was a junk ship that looked good on the outside . . . This old scow is ugly as sin but solid on the in – *Ha!*" He managed to work a long, thin splinter up.

"Both of you," he blinked. "Keep your ears open. First sign of a visitor you clap your boot-heel on the floor or something." He tucked the lemon in his pocket and sat back on his heels, blinking as a sudden wave of exhaustion hit.

"Sir?" Forbes asked softly.

"I'll be fine . . . ." Lestrade sighed. "Still . . . still feel sick as a dog." He swallowed and tilted his head back, began to work on his collar.

They watched him work. The ship began to move with more aggression and less grace as the sea grew feisty. Once Craddock came down to guard them. Cooper gave the signal in time, so all the big man saw was Lestrade sitting Indian-style and nursing the tin teacup in his hands, but the squall worsened. Craddock was sent up to help with the crew, giving them the time they needed. It was still hard going. Lestrade had to lie down to keep himself stable as he made a message with lemon juice and a splinter.

Chapter V – Because of Trust

April 29th, 1891:

"It isn't Lestrade." Dr. Roanoke said it calmly, matter-of-factly, as if it wasn't the most important thing in the world to a family and to Scotland Yard. As the four expressions of relief collapsed faces all over the conference room, he ignored the fuss and reached for his tiny Irish pipe. Tobacco, dust-fine, glowed in the bowl and he puffed softly, letting the emotions settle down.

"It almost fooled me, though," the graying man added as soon as there was a lull in the room.

Gregson breathed out. He leaned back in his chair as Sergeant Hopkins shakily poured himself a cup of coffee. The young man and the poor PC's were grinning from ear to ear, but Gregson couldn't fall into the temptation of joining him.

"Can you give us some details, Doctor?" Gregson asked quietly. It was the tone of his voice that made the others straighten up.

Roanoke puffed a moment. "Everyone knows that Lestrade has a twisted left foot. A few more know his foot was broken in childhood. Whoever identified the body as Lestrade's . . . He *may* very well have been his grandfather. When I went searching for that proof, I couldn't find very much. The tendons that would have shown the inturn were mashed and pulped by someone's fingers." He seemed unaware of the reaction to his words. "Complete mess. It was hard to look at the bone for the old fracture line too. The surmise is that someone wanted to convince us it was your cohort, and the blurred the evidence that would have proven otherwise."

"Sir?" Cooper cleared his throat. "What convinced you, then?"

"I recalled one of you – Hopkins? Yes, Hopkins. – said that he'd been injured in the fight, so I took it upon myself to find the PC's who attended him." For the first time that month, Roanoke smiled, and that was at the young men in uniform. "They independently described in rather colourful detail a scalp wound that 'bled like sin', whatever that was supposed to mean. The body wasn't in very good condition, but it was quite clear there was no such scalp wound on the skull." Roanoke shrugged. "*Ergo* – not Lestrade. Someone else who matched his basic requirement for height and build. I suspect the body had been in the water a bit longer than the half-week claimed."

"Mmm." Hopkins had Lestrade's blood-stained collar in his hands. He turned it around as his spoke, absently taking in the faint message. "What do we do now? Do we tell the wife?"

"We should, but we've got to be *exquisitely* careful." Gregson tapped his fingers on the table. "I'll have Bradstreet speak to her . . . It will look like we're in an appropriate state of mourning. Bradstreet and his wife are close to the Lestrades."

"You're saying we should keep this under wraps?" Hopkins was pale at the thought. "What will the Chief Inspector think?"

"I'll have to explain it," Gregson did not confess he hadn't come to that part yet. "But I'll think of something. We need to convince the remnants of that gang we've swallowed that story." He rubbed his jaw. "We'll tell the truth to Mrs. Lestrade, but we'll also encourage her to . . . move out of London for a few days. That'll lower the chance of word accidentally getting out . . . ." He rose to his feet. "This goes no further than the room, gentleman."

Hopkins nodded, face drawn thin. The PC's could have been standing attention at a funeral. Roanoke merely shrugged. Reports were his work, not the actual verbalization.

April 25ᵗʰ, 1891 – What Happened Aboard the Athene*:*

It took slow leverage, but Forbes had finally prized up the tiny nail from its hiding-place deep in the crack of the floor-boards.

"Forbes . . . if I recall . . . you were rather good at the lock-picking contest on Hallows Eve two years back." Lestrade smiled wearily at the sight of their freedom in the man's narrow hands.

Forbes managed to blush. "You heard about that?" He muttered awkwardly. But he set to work with a will.

"What, you don't think we were never in those contests back when we wore the blue coats? Get us loose." Lestrade winced suddenly and put his hand to his temples. "We don't have much time. The storm will lull soon, and we need to work within its parameters. The two of you will hit the life-boats, and . . . I'll hold off their attention as long as I can." The short speech had openly drained him of the little strength he'd collected in the fresh air of the above-deck.

"We can't leave you here, sir." Cooper protested. "That Craddock doesn't want the captain to keep to his end of the bargain. We don't know what will happen to you. He looks like he'd kill you before letting you go."

"Doesn't . . . matter." Lestrade set his teeth. "They want to change the rules – Well, so can we." He leaned into the wooden post for support.

Forbes' shackle fell open with a clatter. He set to Cooper with a fever. "Get into the lifeboat. The current will take you to the archipelago. Don't waste time. Once you get there, wire back home. Tell them everything."

"We can't leave you, sir!" Forbes persisted. "It's not right."

"You can and you will." Lestrade closed his eyes against another wave of surrealism. Back in the close confines of the hold where the chloroform had been dropped, his weak nausea was returning. "I'm not going to make a trip in this, nor are you going to get away without help. It's risky, but there's the chance we have to take." He reached up and slowly undid his collar. "Forbes, switch collars with me. I wrote a message on it in in case things get bad." The inspector's eyes briefly went hard. "Don't pass her the message unless things are very bad," he warned. "I mean it. The Yard can read what I put on it, but there's one message to her."

Forbes nodded and complied without a word. "What shall we do, sir?"

"First, we get loose. Then we spend *exactly* five minutes looking through this peculiar cargo that they want to protect so badly. Then . . . the lifeboats . . . ."

Forbes would have never dreamed that his choice of career as a police constable would have led to actions considered sabotage by rules of the sea.

A chill sheet of rain in a night black as bog-oak struck their faces. Forbes, bringing up the rear, hurriedly closed the small hatch after them and they ducked into the relative safety of a space between two columns of strangely shaped objects lashed down under oilcloth. A sharp odour like oil and metals assailed their faces. Lestrade blanched.

About their heads the wind had picked up. It carried with it the smell of wet earth over the salt spray, and something like flowers – but surely it was too cold yet for even Brittany. Lestrade paused, lifting his head and inhaling deeply, his eyes closed. He reminded the constables of a compass trying to settle on north.

"Cooper, go ahead."

"Sir." Cooper lisped softly. He slunk sideways like a great turtle against a jungle of barrels and ropes. Forbes had seen his vanishing act before, and it still managed to surprise him. Lestrade leaned himself into the shadows, keeping his head down so the sudden moonlight escaping the clouds would not reflect off his pale face.

Cooper was a marvelous man to have in any situation that called for cleverness, muscle, or both.

"I remember that smell," the little man said distantly. Above their heads and against the splash of salt, crewmen were yelling orders out to each other and constant updates. "We're in the Sleeve."

"Sir?"

"That's what they call it . . . the sleeve that connects the North Sea to the Atlantic . . . ." Lestrade's faraway expression was growing ever deeper, pulling out what bits and pieces of memory the past would surrender. "*Mor Breizh*," He said softly. "The water's warming up. That's what makes it smell like flowers this time of year . . . warmer water and the smell of the earth . . . ." His eyes suddenly snapped alert. "This is going to happen *quickly*," he warned. "Be ready."

"*Must* I remind you that I am the captain of this ship?"

Few people heard that tone of voice from Wiltson. Craddock was not impressed by it – only his employer had that power. But he did respect the sudden way everyone within earshot just . . . paused in their work and idly drifted their working hands to the nearest knife or gun.

Careful. Craddock possessed little in the way of native genius, but he hadn't been Quimper's valet for so many years and not learned something. He scowled and took one step backwards, which greatly reduced the sudden tension on the ship.

"Very well." Wiltson's lips were pressed tight and drear. "If I don't stick to the bargain, the police will make me their concern. Nor will it do my reputation much good if I'm to exist as an oath-breaker. You will have to find your opportunity, Mr. Craddock, off my ship. I leave it to you to do so."

Craddock glowered, but his deepset eyes held no quarrel in the face of such opposition. Not trusting himself to speak, he spun on his heel and went back to the other side of the ship.

Cooper had created a risk by grabbing not one sailor, but two. He felt there was little choice – they were the only ones breaking away from the group and he decided their mates would think they were simply off nipping the brew. To his relief, Lestrade merely lifted his eyebrows and accepted the matter as Forbes helped him strip the unconscious men for anything useful.

"Now let's take a look," Lestrade whispered, holding the dark lantern close. The axe felt heavy as a timber, but the weight was a comfort. As quickly as silence would allow, they slipped to the nearest tarp-wrapped mound lashed in the center of the ship. A lid creaked open with a single, short scrape.

Lestrade would have sworn – had he the breath to spare. Cooper gasped softly, his face white and suddenly terrified.

Forbes said it: "Counterfeiting." He held up one of the minting-stamps in question, eyes round and frightened. The barrel was full of them. "For coins from all over the bloody world . . . *My God, sir*. No wonder they risked a hanging by using us as safe passage."

"That's what tipped me off." Lestrade admitted in a pale whisper. "It *had* to be high stakes. Help me. We can't throw the barrels out, but we can throw the contents!" He glared at their shock. "We can't risk it getting in their hands! You just *think* of the damage this could do to the economy of *just England and France alone* – We're looking at the start of a war here!"

"You stand watch, sir." Cooper said sternly. At Lestrade's surprise, the constable looked even sterner. "You said I was in charge. We need someone to stand watch, and Forbes'n'I'll start dumping."

Lestrade managed to grin at the logic of it. "Yes, sir, PC." And because he would probably never get another chance, he slipped in one last Parthian shot: "Just like your father, Cooper."

"I ought to hope so." Cooper kept his control, but a quick grin escaped his lips. "Everyone else takes after my *mother*."

"Hurry!" he hissed. There on the wall – finally – a lighter-weight axe. Lestrade hefted it up and nodded. "Inside," he rasped. "Now." The constables scrambled to obey, their eyes white in the dark. "Start cutting."

Cooper sawed frantically. The stolen knife had been kept sharp, which helped. A thin core of metal was inside the cordage for strength. It gave suddenly, like a strand of hair, and the boat was free.

There were three in all – When they came to the last one, the PC's tumbled in first. Lestrade hefted the axe

Letting them go was the hardest moment of Lestrade's life. He waited with his heart threatening to burst and his head splitting as with the quick *chop* of the axe-bit, the lifeboat cut loose into the ocean. The current would take them where they could reach the authorities. Without any other lifeboats, the crew had no hope of following in the storm.

The boat slipped away into the night almost instantly, and with it, his ties with home.

The feel of Martin's small body was still fresh in his arms. Nicholas always grinned when he saw his father walk into the room, the smile reaching his mother-given Prussian eyes. Clea's own smile was enough to make him wish he could kill everyone who placed their authority over his. Above his head, people were screaming in alarm, but it was too late to turn against the wind. Time to delay the inevitable. Every second helped the constables . . . No one was going to die while he could prevent it – especially another Cooper. Lestrade pushed himself back to the last place they would be looking for an escapee.

54

The darkness in the hold was a physical thing. Lestrade fought against it, knowing his consciousness could collapse like tissue-paper without warning, and crept to the smallest, dingiest space in the hold sheltered by two misaligned crates. His head fell to the floor when he was done, and in seconds, he had passed out.

April 29th, 1891:

Back in London, another sort of tension was being exercised.

Gregson had quite coolly dismissed himself and traced his steps to Bradstreet's blocky tenant-building. One knock at the door and his tight-lipped wife – who always made Gregson a slight bit nervous – nodded in the direction he should go. Gregson thanked her and traveled down the narrow hallway, noting that the seashell artwork on the walls and table were a bit on the startling side.

"Still no word."

Within the privacy of his little office inside his own home, Bradstreet took the bad news stoically. Sleeplessness and guilt burned his eyes. He offered a smoke to Gregson, who seemed askance at the higher-grade leaf, but took it politely. The tow-headed man sank down in the empty guest chair, appreciating the fact that here he didn't have to worry about sitting in something small or fragile.

They smoked for a few minutes in silence.

"The North Sea's a hard place to look for anything that doesn't want to be found," Bradstreet said at last.

Gregson snorted. "That's assuming they actually went to the North Sea. You'll recall, Lestrade got his head bit off for suggesting they *might* be headed south."

Bradstreet shook his head. "Patterson was awfully sure of himself."

"Always was." Gregson slipped an uneasy confidence to the darker man. "Even Holmes seems not to care for him, if that tells you anything."

"When did Holmes ever care about any of us?" Bradstreet wondered with his old bitterness. "We're just fools to him."

"I can't think of anyone who isn't a fool compared to that one – save Watson, and I don't think he *can* be figured out. The point is, have you ever heard Holmes call us corrupt, or greedy, or in a case for selfish reasons?" He nodded as Bradstreet froze, astonishment widening his eyes as the epiphany struck. "Ayeh." Gregson drawled. "He's never called us any of those things. But you just think of this. Has he ever *demonstrated* any lack of trust in us other than that charming habit of not telling us what he's on about?"

Bradstreet shuddered. "It's bad enough."

"Aside from that . . . you just think about this." Gregson licked his lips. They were suddenly dry. "Patterson's missing vital information from Sherlock Holmes. The last bit o' paperwork that would prove all the connections with the gangs. Holmes up and left the city and left this to Patterson. What do you think that means, as far as confidence in Patterson is concerned?"

Bradstreet tried to think. "Strategically, Holmes probably shouldn't have trusted any one person with that much information."

"Oh, I quite agreed. It'd mean Patterson's life easily. But . . . perhaps – just perhaps – Patterson was arrogant enough to convince Mr. Holmes that he had everything well under control?"

"*Ha!*"

April 25th, 1891:

Lestrade had forgotten just how silent – and strong – Craddock could be. He remembered everything all at once as the man latched his arms around him. His startled gasp only galvanized the big man to move faster. Arms like a tree trunk wrapped around her head and neck. The detective could only believe that he was trying to snap his neck. He grabbed up, twisting out of his smothering grip from desperation and kicked backwards. Craddock grunted and slacked his grip.

Lestrade staggered forward, falling against a hogshead as he tried to breathe around the stabbing pain between his eyes, but Craddock was already scrabbling to grab him again. His head pounding, he tried another kick, but his luck stopped as the boat shifted to the side. Instead of trying to grab him again, Craddock pushed hard with the slant of the ship. Lestrade hit the stab'bard and sank to his knees. Craddock cuffed him on the head almost absently and wrenched his hands behind his back. The derbies snicked around his wrists. *Damn!* Lestrade swore in his mind. The cut had reopened. He felt the trickle over his skin.

Then Craddock did something that made no sense.

They were panting for air in the stillness of the hold. Craddock's pox-pitted face was badly lit by the wall lamps, slick with sweat as something made his head jerk upwards. Lestrade looked up too, scraping his face against the rough floor-boards, but heard only the tromping of heavy seamen on the deck, and muffled commands in different languages. Panic widened the thug's eyes – such an emotion Lestrade had never seen on him, and he threw Lestrade down to the boards, pinning him with his knee until it was all the detective could do to breathe. Clumsy with frightened haste, Craddock yanked out a large fogle and forged a large knot in the centre. He stuffed the knot in his ersatz prisoner's mouth and tied it in the back. Lestrade had no idea why Craddock was doing this, but he knew it was against Wiltson's orders, involved Quimper, and thus was no good for *him*. And he wasn't in any shape to give his own opinion about it.

Craddock grunted as he stood and slung the detective over his shoulders. He was close to being genuinely frightened. He hated the feeling, but Wiltson didn't understand. Wiltson might have made a deal with the Bluebottles, *but he wasn't the boss. Quimper was.* Lestrade couldn't be let loose. Better dead than loose. But if Wiltson caught him directly disobeying orders, he could easily toss him over the side of the *Athene* with a hole in his skull.

The only recourse was not to get caught.

Craddock climbed to his feet as quietly as he knew how. Above his head, the sea-men were continuing their search, but the man over his shoulder had grown unresponsive and limp. Probably fainted. His head was bleeding again. Just as well. Craddock couldn't afford his waking up right now. He needed to work fast . . . .

"No sign, Captain." Craddock's large hands clenched at his sides. "All three must've gotten away."

"Damn." Wiltson swore under his breath. Moist sea-air battered his face and he reached up with a handkerchief to wipe it off. "Damn," he said again. "We'll have to move fast. It won't take that boat long to get to shore, and we've got to get to the rendezvous on time."

Craddock nodded. "I'm going to see what else they ruined," he announced.

"You do that," the captain said listlessly. Craddock busy was a Craddock out of trouble. He watched the big man lumber off, and knew he would be completely relieved once the lubber was out of his hair. "I'd sooner take on a cargo of sea-gulls and starfish than one of you, ever again," he said under his breath.

Several minutes and a strong pipe later, Wiltson was considerably calmer. Craddock threatened that fragile mood. He poked his head back in with a glum expression. "They dumped all the equipment we really needed," he said slowly. "All the hydraulics parts, the stamps and the types."

Wiltson was a moment collecting his voice. "Not unexpected," he said at last. "But a deal is a deal. I daresay Mr. Quimper can cut his losses." He puffed his pipe again. "After all, we were just a decoy for your Professor, were we not?" He smiled mirthlessly at the flick of horror on Craddock's face. "Come, now. The Yard would adore the prestige of grabbing a counterfeit press on its way to another country, but I think the mastermind of the scheme would prefer to sacrifice it if it meant his own skin was saved. We're not stupid over here." He puffed one last time. "Write up your report. I'll write up mine."

"Wasn't a total loss," Craddock grunted. His eyes were thrown down, and Wiltson wondered what he was really thinking. "We got the hogshead of sealed paper and two barrels of water-marking stamps. That's the hardest thing to nick. Worse than types and gears."

"Well, should help his mood, one would hope," Wiltson murmured. "Go ahead and batten it all down, because I want it off the ship three seconds after we dock."

"My boys will be ready," Craddock promised.

"Bob's your uncle, then." Wiltson smiled to see Craddock turn his back and leave. The smile froze at the dark, wet shine staining the big man's wool jacket.

Wiltson gulped hard, his throat suddenly swollen.

You will have to find your opportunity, Mr. Craddock . . . I leave it to you to do so.

My God, he thought. Betrayal swarmed in his mind, cold fury and horror and a nauseating sense of falling off a precipice. *He killed him. He killed him, and we'll all hang for it.*

The only hope was that it couldn't be proven.

Chapter VI – Deeper

April 29th, 1891 – Little Venice:

"Still no word."

Lancashiremen were no strangers to emergencies or family unity. The two went hand in hand. Still, things had been relatively quiet for the Cheatham sept since moving to the homogeny of London – a few forays outside the straight and the narrow, but overall upstanding citizens who never – quite – forgot their noble family was deeply rooted in the art of combat.

Nine years had not dulled their instincts. An eavesdropper through the dining room window of the Cheatham House might have guessed with some accuracy a Council of War going on: Seven large men cut from the same large stamp and a tiny woman were collecting around a teapot with grim, stubborn faces.

Myron Cheatham moved slightly off to the side to make room for his youngest brother. Bartram grunted, his only way of showing Myron's silent courtesy. Bartram was not unwilling to discourse – he was just incapable. "I don't completely understand this mess, Clea," he confessed to his sister. Next to him, Andrew was fussily adjusting the lamp-light on the table. In its shine, their sister's eyes were wet, but her control was as firm as ever. "They *want* us to act like he's dead?"

"Mr. Bradstreet explained it to me," Clea swallowed and picked up the teacup her father passed to her. Charles Cheatham was stone-blind with cataracts, but navigated with more skill than most people with perfect vision. "There is a war going on between Scotland Yard and the people who . . . you might call them the true employers of Mr. Quimper."

Just that hated name was enough to send a ripple of anger throughout her father and six brothers. Bartram's fight-blunted face turned dull red. He had his own history with the man, and blamed himself for the terrible time when Jethro Quimper had pursued Clea's hand in marriage.

"They must keep it as quiet as possible," Clea took a deep breath, "because there are lives at stake. A body was found in the Channels by the French gendarme. They claim it was positively identified as Geoffrey by his nearest relative . . . they found his grandfather from somewhere on the peninsula. He . . . he said he was convinced it was his grandson, and they accepted it, even though it's been . . . decades since they last saw each other." She swallowed hard and took another drink of tea. "Mr. Bradstreet and Mr. Gregson believe that . . . Geoffrey has slipped their grasp and they're buying him time by pretending to go along with it." Clea's throat hitched. "For all anyone knows, he truly is dead, but if keeping up the pretence means they can put an end to this . . . ." She lowered her gaze and fell silent.

Charles Cheatham broke the silence at last. "How are we certain the dead man isn't he?"

Despite the severity of the situation, a faint smile quirked Clea's lips as she picked up her cup. "We have Bartram to thank for that," Her smile bloomed at his blink of surprise. "When you broke his hand in that so-called charity wrestling event, Big Brother, Geoffrey and the others kept it quiet. The only people who knew he had a broken hand were his physician and the two officers who took him to Dr. Watson. Mr. Gregson must have nicked the file to give to the coroner. When he couldn't find proof in his ankle, which was a flaw most people knew about, and he couldn't find signs of the scalp-wound the constables reported, he found a third confirmation in the lack of a broken hand."

"Huh," was Bartram's verdict. "So what do we do now? Keep you and the boys under wraps?"

"I suppose we could say I'm in shock and deep mourning," Clea said thoughtfully.

Andrew made a rude sound from the other side of the flower bouquet. "Let's just hope it doesn't turn into the real thing, Sister." His brother Cutler promptly struck him in the ribs. "Just stay here. We'll do the rest." He was the best-looking of the Cheathams, for all that he used it like a weapon to get what he wanted. He was smiling now, his crafty brain already moving ahead and pondering possibilities. "People believe what they want to believe. It won't be difficult for the rest of London to think you've been sequestered from shock while your poor children are kept ignorant as to the true state of their father's sad fate."

Clea tensed inwardly, but Andrew was just . . . Andrew. "That we can," she said softly.

On the night before April 22nd, 1891:

"*Nicholas Bartram,*" Lestrade didn't bother to look up from his desk. Sharpening quill-pens by hand might be horrendously old-fashioned, but at least it was a skill he *knew*. Paying for metal nibs meant trading money for convenience.

(And being married to a cook who took pride in roasted goose and turkey, it wasn't as though he would run out of feather-quills before the next century . . . .)

He held the tip of the goose-quill up to the lamp-light, looking for minute flaws. The giggling down the hallway diminished. "If you've *really* got that stomach-ache, you wouldn't be trying to spin tops on the floor."

Abashed silence. "Sorry, *Taddiz*," Nicholas normally called him "Papa" or "*Tad*". *Taddiz* was for when he was trying to compensate for a tactical error.

Long practice kept the smile out of his voice. "You need your eight hours if you're going to meet your mother at the station tomorrow. You and your brother both."

Pause. "Good night, Tad."

"Good night." Lestrade looked down at his paper. Nicholas had been a welcome distraction from this ugly business. He exhaled through his nose and picked up his ink-pen again. Ink for deep thoughts. The frequent pauses to refill the quill gave him time to consider the words as they slowly emerged.

He read what was already on the paper:

Clea-bihan,

> *With any hope, you'll never read this. Yet, you aren't like most people, and the not knowing would go harder than the truth. You're out now, getting into mischief with Hazel no doubt at her new* soiree, *and that's how I like to think of you when I'm away.*
>
> *Martin suspects* something. *He won't talk about it, but you know how his eyes go right through you. Nicholas, who prefers to let Martin take the lead, has caught up on his brother's unease. They've clung to me all evening. I took them out for those wretched meat-pies they so like . . . (I* still *think the vendor is making use of the stray cats.) At any rate, they finally had their fill and dropped off to sleep after the bath.*

Leave it to Nicholas to wake up a half-hour later . . . .

> *Today did not go well at the Yard. I'm still acclimating myself to the ways of Inspector Patterson, who is as much of a lone wolf as a human being can possibly get. He's got us all wrapped up in this case, and a large, fairly dangerous one it is too. Not dangerous for us Yarders so much as for the consequences of our failure. We cannot fail in this.*

. . . and perhaps the fear of failure is the reason for Patterson's hard head and sharp tongue. Lestrade couldn't begin to imagine the emotional stakes of over ten years of criminal research, about to avalanche down in one fell swoop . . . .

> *To begin with, Patterson is one of those sorts who place absolute and unswerving faith in his few hand-picked men. Everyone else must earn his trust, and thus his confidence. I'm not in the former category, and I doubt a recommendation from the Home Secretary Himself would change his perspective. A rigid outlook is his particular strength. To be honest, we've been rushed in this. There is no time for our adjustments with each other. Patterson even clashed with Gregson, and you've seen for yourself the mark of the man's intelligence.*

Lestrade's problem was not intelligence, but the quality of the company he kept.

> *Patterson's clean and narrow outlook, which is a severe contrast to the criminal pig-swill he works in on a daily basis . . . is as different from my own work as can possibly be. He cannot afford to trust my informants.*

In Patterson's experience, Tinkers and Gipsies were unreliable, self-absorbed, filthy, and incapable of constancy. Lestrade's surname implied a life on the road, and because of that, Patterson had conjectured that Lestrade was part Gipsy himself. It was a clever conjecture, but wholly flawed.

> *Gregson even stuck up for me (which just shows to you we may be approaching the end-times.*

"Patterson," Gregson drawled, "Leave off with the *battre l'estrade*." Lestrade gave Gregson an unfriendly glare. As puns went that was fairly atrocious if awfully clever . . . but Patterson never caught on . . . . [1]

> *In the proverbial nutshell, Patterson believes his quarry is headed in one direction where there are two possible routes. The overlooked route has my informants already stationed. It would be a simple matter to alert them . . . .*

"We know Moriarty's contacts are just across the Channel. It would be the work of a few hours to contact the Tribe and ask them to keep their eyes open – "

"We are not paying dirty Gipsies to do our work!"

Lestrade stared down at the remaining clean paper. Would it do any good if he pointed out those so-called Irish Tinkers were actually English in origin? He sighed and finally re-dipped his ink-pen.

> *I'll be doing what I can to make sure we see an end to this. Please believe me that I'm doing my best. I may have to step on a few toes and go behind a few backs . . . but we can't afford to fail. If we don't crush this gang, we'll leave the entire city open to criminal anarchy. No matter what happens, remember that I did my best.*
>
> *Yours always,*
> *Gffry*

He swallowed hard, uncomfortable as always with giving Clea a hard truth. Still, the difficulty had strengthened his resolve. He blew the paper dry and set it inside the small safe. Clea knew where the key was kept. She would find the letter on her own if he didn't return – as well as the (God forbid) other documents, letters and things he'd left. He shouldered into his coat and reached for his everyday hat . . . He just as swiftly discounted that and went to his closet. A few minutes' work and Lestrade was gone: Galvin the Tinker was back, sun-browned, battered, his coat patched up at the elbows with a sky blue *diklos* about his throat.

Lestrade devoutly hoped no one recognized him at the telegraph office, but sod it. He could afford to pay Padriac out of his own pocket for a few hours' watchfulness.

Five times in his life, he'd had to walk to the house of a cohort and tell the women to their face that their husband . . . or father . . . or son . . . would never come home. He would not shirk his responsibility, but damned if he'd let someone put that expression on Clea's face.

There was something Patterson would never understand. Gipsies didn't look sharp because they were waiting for an easy mark. They were trying to avoid the predators around them. They were the first line of intelligence when it came to anything going on in the country . . . so long as you understood how they thought and acted, which was completely different from what other people could be like.

If all went well, this gang was watching the chief players – Patterson and Gregson. They wouldn't be liable to skulk out his quarters. Who would bother to confide in Lestrade?

He slipped out the back door. The grape-and-hops-vine crawling up the back wall masked the pegs driven deep into the brick years ago. A moment's work and he was over the side.

Fifteen minutes later, a slight, ruddy-faced Tinker, bare-headed against the elements, entered the Whitehall telegraph office and garrulously requested a wire to his *"Gan'faer"* in France in between sips of something that reeked suspiciously of potato vodka. The clerk was a decent sort and tried to be universal in his courtesy, but still, he held the filthy coins in his hand no longer than necessary, and dutifully copied out the message the illiterate man had asked him to pass on *"waird fa' waird, sair . . . sae th'ganmaer c'n rest aisy."*

It was none of his business if the recipient in question could even read, and the clear couldn't make out the message anyway: *"Solk us awae from the Taddy"* was sheer gibberish to his schooling. But business was business, and the Tinker was willing to tip him for his troubles. Sheer ignorance incarnate when it came to literature, those Gipsies. But they knew *money*.

Present Day London:

"No new developments, but Clea is safe with the children at her father's. I would almost welcome the notion of someone trying to get through that family."

"You wouldn't be the only one." Gregson admitted. It really was an attractive image. Gregson indulged in that a moment. Would the Cheathams punch out all of the gang-members' teeth first before they dumped them into the Venice Cut, or would they break their knee-caps first and neatly take them out of the world of Organized Crime on the technicality of medical disability? "Patterson's not exactly eating crow right now, but he has admitted that his men aren't doing much good in the North Sea . . . They're being moved south."

"Moriarty's gang had ties in either direction. I wonder if Patterson will ever make allowances for the human factor next time." Bradstreet sighed. "If only we'd known what sort of cargo they were carrying!"

"Mmm, that *would* have made things easier . . . ." Gregson tapped ash restlessly. A slow grin emerged on his face. As Bradstreet watched, he began to chuckle.

"Private joke, Tobias?"

"Just imagining the *look* on the gang's face when they realized Lestrade sent all that expensive, irreplaceable counterfeiting equipment straight to the bottom!" His chuckle grew louder.

Bradstreet was still ill with worry for his best friend, but it was impossible not to laugh too. "Can you imagine *Patterson's* reaction?" He wondered. "Destruction of evidence?"

Gregson exploded. He put his pipe down before he dropped it. "The problem with that lot," he said when his breath returned, "is they can't figure out Lestrade. Man can be a royal fool, but they think because he's not as smart as they are, he should be easy to figure out." The big man rolled his eyes, supplicating the ceiling for patience. "Everybody makes that silly mistake."

"Except for *you*." Bradstreet pointed out wryly.

"Of course." Gregson agreed with his usual calm arrogance. After years of the man, Bradstreet no longer had the urge to slap him. "Hell, even Sherlock Holmes makes that mistake. But the more a man displays his brain, the more *predictable* he gets – You can't tell me that's not a lot of the reason why Holmes didn't want Watson to publish his stories. It's like a magician who gives his tricks away at the end of the show." Gregson puffed in silence, pondering. "Looking at the whole schematic, I'd say Quimper makes it a point of pride *not* to study Lestrade too closely. That would be admitting his own mental powers aren't up to the snuff."

"It's true that Lestrade seems to be the root cause of all of his . . . interesting failures," Bradstreet admitted. "But Quimper went through *effort* to fake his death."

"Quimper is a flawless genius, and I'll allow." Gregson pointed a finger thick as a chisel at the hapless Bradstreet. "But you force him to think on his feet and he makes mistakes from the start. His impulses are not of the sort that should be allowed. As long as he has time to pull back and think coldly . . . Well, he's perfect. But when there's no time to pull back and he's thinking on his feet? He makes mistakes." Gregson leaned back and re-packed his pipe. "Which means up to that point, Lestrade was still alive." Gregson said it with a confidence that Bradstreet really wanted to shake off. "Alive, and, I'm betting you, he's escaped from him. Quimper's covering his mistakes to his superiors."

"You *can't* know that." Bradstreet protested. "Much as I want to believe you . . . ."

"Nothing else makes sense, Roger. If he was dead, he'd have sent the body back with a horrible little sympathy card addressed to his wife!" Gregson ignored Bradstreet's flinch. "No, they turned their back on him, and he got away. Take that train of thought further, and it just proves that they didn't plan on keeping him originally. If they had, it would have been

Quimper's idea, and Quimper makes plans long-distance. This Craddock character, he's the reason why everything fell to pieces, because he knew Lestrade was wanted for questioning." Gregson stubbed out the cigarette to ash. "He escaped, and Quimper had to think of something fast. He's brilliant at long-term plans, but when it comes to improvisation . . . Ha! That's a good part of why he keeps losing when Lestrade's concerned. Lestrade's a better man when it comes to adjusting to a snag."

"I wonder why Quimper's like that?" Bradstreet mused. "When you put it like that, it makes me wonder who the smarter man really is."

"People like to compare Quimper to a fox, don't they? Remember that Aesop fable about the fox who had a hundred tricks and the cat only one? The dogs came and the cat used the one trick it had, climbing up the tree. While the fox was still trying to decide what to do, the dogs tore it to pieces." Gregson smiled.

Somewhere in Brittany:

Oh, damn.

Lestrade's mental compass had been completely scrambled in the chaos of being pounded, half-smothered, and then stuffed into a crate full of small, hard metal objects that reeked of machine-oil. Losing consciousness several times during the pounding of a hasty wagon-ride had been a damned relief in comparison to the experience. Now . . . the compass had aligned itself in the light of day. He was in a place that was *much* worse than his last quarters.

Seawater lapped ankle-high in the floor of the cylindrical room, which was about the size of a half-starved hermit's prayer-cell. It might even have been used for that reason, back when the foundation had been above the tidewater. Lestrade *never* understood why religious aesthetics would embrace all other forms of discomfort in the name of their faith, but refuse *water*. This place would be miserable enough for the most arrogant martyr. Even without the heavy manacles around his wrists. He shook his head at the brusque workmanship. They must be antiques or a consequence of a poorly funded crime ring. They could have been used in the Bastille during the Revolution.

Well, perhaps someone was nostalgic about crude iron rings . . . Lord knew, the French carried all sorts of hereditary insanity . . . .

One of Sherlock Holmes's *more* annoying habits was his insistence on breaking into some poignant or pointed quote about a situation in French in Lestrade's presence. The little detective still didn't know if he was just showing off – most people in his experience couldn't resist the temptation – or if he was making some little underhanded jab about an idiot policeman who failed to keep in touch with his own history. Lestrade honestly could not care less. He knew peasant French and some of the *Gallo*, but study the finer Romantic language? *Ha.* He rattled the chain in sheer annoyance, wondering what Stone Age fortress these things had been found in. *The French are lunatics.* This was just further proof.

The detective frowned at the iron ring welded *around* the smaller links that connected the wrist-bands together. Recent work, carefully done. The links slid back and forth freely, but they couldn't pull out of the ring, which in turn was connected to a large, dense iron chain that was more suited for deep-well drilling. The width of that metal rope was thicker than a young sapling. Eyes sliding upward, he tried to see where it led to. The sun blurred and burned his eyes, but it seemed as though it ended at a point well above the surface.

And I'm at least twenty feet below said surface. He studied the tight stonework around him. A silo. Limestone blocks, hand-dressed dimension-stone, generations of seawater causing a slow weep of calcite crystals to collect like tears through the flaws of the rock. Illuminated by the indirect light, they glowed strangely. Lestrade blinked upwards in the epiphany. The sunlight burnt like needles into the wet darkness. *One of the old pits dug out for grain storage*, and some enterpriser – probably a dimwit Roman engineer under the payroll of some deluded satrap – had lined the earth structure with stone. On reflection, it might not have been for food storage. Armorika had been a *tense* place for Caesar's folk. It would have made an ideal cache for weapons or – *Heaven forbid* . . . contraband.

Coastal architecture faced the shifting nature of the sea with resignation and a shrug. There was no choice. The Romans had been the most hard-headed about it, which had led to some interesting creations. Such as this prison.

Layers of salt-lines suggested the level of water was fairly regular. It no doubt flooded during severe storms. The highest water-level was – he swallowed dryly – halfway up the shaft.

Lestrade found himself wondering what Clea's opinion of all this would be. No doubt she would have something scathing to say. *Something scathing, and true.*

The sky was overcast, but after being below ground for hours, it burned his eyes like fire. Lestrade's first thought was confusion: The stone courtyard was hardly done up any better than his prison. Decaying nobility? The large castle-like structure had no basis in his memory, which meant he was in some part of the peninsula the family had never taken him to. That in itself was both good and bad – good in that he was probably in one small part of the province . . . bad in that he didn't know much about the land itself.

He recognized Craddock again, but not the short, stocky man who stood at his side. Going by the expense of his clothing, he was the *pro tem* leader for the lot. Ink-black hair and matching eyes gleamed in a face that was too pale to be normal or healthy for any species on earth. Instead of the ubiquitous walking stick, he had a cane of spiraled applewood. When he took a step forward, it was clear he needed that cane to walk with.

"Allow me to introduce myself," the man spoke coolly and quietly. "My name is Jean Groix . . . in the colloquial of the land, they call me '*Aotrou-Illiz*' – Mr. Church – perhaps because I have been witness to so many confessions." Groix smiled slightly. "Last-minute confessions," he clarified.

"I see," Lestrade said grimly.

"This, you might call my chapel." Groix aimed his cane at the black pit that had so-recently disgorged him. "My penitents never seem to spend a long time in it . . . ." He smiled again, and it was still a false thing. Lestrade felt that if the man's smile was ever genuine, it would be too private for another person to see it. "They want to 'see the light'. When the tide rises, it can be a most uncomfortable thing for the inhabitants. You may dislike the shackles, *igounier*, but they keep you from drowning in the pool."

"Not a Druid in a past incarnation?" Lestrade rasped. "This obsession your gang has with *drowning* isn't healthy by modern standards."

"I never liked the notion of reading the future in a victim's entrails. Very messy and leaves all sorts of evidence." Groix answered dryly. "But that is a good point . . . We seem to have a gift for this type of arrangement." He looked about the stone courtyard with his usual cool pride of possession. "Let's be frank, L'estrade . . . your friend *Padderzon* was operating outside the lines of information that he could have received from your lapdog, Holmes."

Lestrade had heard just about *every* word that could be applied to Sherlock Holmes – often uncomplimentary. His eyes widened at the implication of servitude. *I can't wait to tell him about this . . . He'll spit out his pipe . . . .*

"We need to know where he came across his information." The agent tapped his shoulder with his stick. "I'm not giving up until I have it in my hands, L'estrade."

Lestrade sighed. "This is beginning to sound terribly familiar."

"Remedials usually do." Groix answered quietly. There was a low, grim cut to his voice that was a sharp divergence from Quimper's cocky and smug sadism. "You have no notion just how important that information is."

"I don't even *know* the man, you *nouch*." Lestrade said wearily.

"You don't have to know him, L'estrade." Groix knocked him backwards. "I want the constables who worked with him."

Lestrade absorbed this bizarre demand in slow-building bewilderment. Who a constable worked with was a matter of public record. They would find what they needed by poking through the files when someone wasn't looking.

"Can't think of any." Lestrade answered. *I didn't even recognize some of them. Patterson brought them with him from Surry . . . If he wants to know, it's not a good thing. Patterson must have put false information in the reports to throw them off the scent –*

He hit the stone palazzo like lightning. Groix sighed and stood over him, the tip of his stick resting lightly on his throat. He could feel his heartbeat thrumming against the metal tip. *Surrey. Constables brought in from outside. Who were they, really?*

"Allow me to say this for the record," the agent said in that same quiet, collected, businesslike voice. "When my employers needed test subjects for their particular mix of morphine, M. Kemper made certain to include you in the roster. We received many detailed reports on what our subjects were raving about under its influence – Yes, I know it would be more humane to use animals, but animals can't *speak*, can they? Now, let's add to the fact that you have continued to have sporadic but disturbing recollections about your repeated baptisms in Lord Beckett's pond. This old silo isn't a very useful well. It connects to the sea-caves all the way to the harbor. It fills with salt water every day. More than enough to drown a man."

The stick moved, very slightly, to rest under his ear. "Either way you're going to die, L'estrade. Do you want to die in a way that will traumatize your lovely little wife for the rest of her life? Would you like her to receive a chromolithograph of your corpse in the post? What if we sent it to those charming little children?" Groix' lips parted over his teeth. It was not a smile. It was a yawning pit. "Terrible thing, to traumatize a young child like that . . . ."

Groix had been so wrapped up in his carefully rehearsed speech he hadn't paid complete attention to his environment. A dull pain clubbed his shin. As he reflexively looked down L'estrade's other foot was coming up and kicking him in the throat.

The agent struck the stones, choking. Around him his men were pushing in with their fists and kicks, embarrassed at the break in security.

"Enough!" Groix shouted – or tried to. His voice cracked from the strain. He lashed out at Craddock. "*Choma-sav!*" That was better. Craddock obeyed, pulling the others back. Groix rose, rubbing ruefully at his throat. Like turning one's back on something vicious. Groix had broken one of his own rules. He felt no animosity to L'estrade for doing what he himself might have done. The fault had been his for dropping his guard.

"Put him back in." Groix coughed slightly. He ran his finger across his collar. "Shorten the chain high enough that he doesn't drown tonight."

"M. Kemper is coming in at midnight," a man pointed out.

"All the better." Groix smiled. "We'll just get him ready for his arrival."

Craddock knelt to obey, but kept one eye on Groix as the man spoke quietly to one of the other men. They were planning to question Lestrade before Quimper's arrival. Craddock's ability to read lips was a secret only Quimper kept. The big man kept his bland features from showing his thoughts. Long experience had taught him to create a plan on the fly.

Lestrade had caught Griox' betrayal too. His dark eyes locked into Craddock's for a moment. Not in fear but determination. They were on opposite sides of the wall, soldiers on the chessboard. Neither man felt any particular emotion for the other. The sensation of being small players in a large game was too overpowering. They both knew they were insignificant in the grand scheme of things.

But neither would hesitate to kill the other.

Craddock wordlessly eased the detective over the side of the pit and put his hands on the crank. By degrees he lowered the chain back to the silo. Water would rise soon. High tide would have to be adjusted for. *Plans* would have to be adjusted for. Craddock knew better than to match Griox' subtle betrayal for an overt betrayal. He would have to think, and quickly.

NOTE

1. The French phrase, *battre l'estrade*, can be translated to "go and procure intelligence".

Chapter VII – The Fox and the Empire

There were times when Jethro Quimper (otherwise known as *M. Kemper* or *A. Galliou*) hated the demands of his profession.

The agent said nothing, nor did Mr. Byrd – he never tolerated the companionship of those who spoke without permission. The carriage ride was painfully slow, made worse by the sheets of rain that seemed to strike sideways as oft as straight down. Farm horses had been drafted for the work, being stronger and less capable of bolting at the sudden eruptions of thunder and lightning over the sky. The packed rock and clay of the road was so far holding fast, but he was glad they did not have far to travel.

Much as he appreciated the rewards of his unique skills, there were times when being an agent for less-than-legal bodies forced him to act swiftly and decisively. A windfall was appreciated and longed-for, but it by definition forced one to hasten and take advantage of it before someone else did.

Quimper pulled his watch out and peered at the faint glow of phosphorous numbers on the face. He would not arrive precisely at midnight, but it would be close enough. He snapped his watch shut, his expression slightly pensive as he stared out the window. Occasional bursts of light illuminated the rocky earth and distant mountains, scraps of forest and uneven farmlands.

He felt no more tied to this land than he did any place else on the earth, but the ancestral bonds were *convenient*. It just reminded him on occasion (such as now) that with those ties came the inconvenience of protocol and courtesy he really felt little patience for.

Griox was an excellent business partner. He was even colder and more meticulous than Quimper, and their work had benefited from the collaboration. But Griox was . . . irritating, like a grain of sand trapped in the shoe. He had the intolerable confidence rooted in the fact that he never suffered defeats or setbacks that couldn't be regained.

Only hours ago, he had the poleaxed sensation of the coded message he still held in his hand:

> *We are pleased to announce the sale of Rennie's Estate on Peninsula. Have liquidated majority of estate accordingly. Inspector will be present to confirm proceedings. L'estrade village antiques and tools are part of estate. Spring weather*

is uncertain, please dress accordingly. House will be sold on the 14th at closed auction.

Taking the first letter of each sentence, the true message was hard as bedrock: *We have Inspector Lestrade Spring House.*

Griox was crowing about his trump over Quimper. Quimper felt it in his bones. He also knew that Griox was interrogating L'estrade hurridly, trying to glean what information he could before his arrival. Cold as he was, Griox wanted very warmly to be the superior in the partnership.

When Moriarty's heirs took over the Empire, there would be a massive reshuffling of the ranks. Quimper knew from experience with his father's political downfall that it could easily turn him into a true exile. He was too important to be killed at this point, but he could be ordered into a flat, static retirement.

Death would be preferable, he thought angrily.

He snorted to himself. Let Griox think he could wrest information out of the little detective. He had *no idea* what kind of grief he was putting upon himself. The Intransigent Inspector L'estrade would be *more* than a match for his colourless intentions. Of course, Craddock was there. He would be certain to keep things from getting too out of hand . . . .

Cheatham House:

Martin's small face was glum as he stabbed the tines of his fork into his roast. The six-year old had fallen into a dull pall since Geoffrey failed to return. He spoke little, and made deep scores into his food. Next to him, Nicholas was eating well enough, but then, he always did. He would outstrip his older brother in size if things kept to their present course.

Regarding them over the dinner table, Clea took in Martin's dark eyes and wondered how her father had faced seeing her every day since her mother had died. Martin was enough like his father in appearance and demeanor that the reminder was sharp and painful.

"Martin, dear," she said softly. "Please do eat."

Martin reflected upon his mother in silence. He never reacted to the slight lull in conversation as uncles, cousins and aunts halted to pay attention.

"Yes, Mum." He bowed his head and obeyed mechanically. Nicholas stared at his older brother, who was eating with no enthusiasm, and stopped eating himself.

"Nicholas, you too." Clea spoke around a tight throat.

"When is Ta' coming home?" Nicholas dropped the shell flat into the centre of the table. No one pretended to talk after that.

Martin looked at him. "He might not come back home, Nicholas." Martin continued to eat. It was what his mother wanted.

"Why not?" Nicholas protested.

"He got caught by some criminals." Martin summarized a complicated tragedy in six words. "He might not be able to get away."

"Martin," Clea gulped hard. "You know he'll come back." She had to believe that, for her sake as well as Nicholas, but her first born was looking at her with a too-sober look in his dark eyes.

"I don't think he expected to, Mum," Martin said softly.

Clea put her shaking hands down on the tablecloth. "Martin, what do you mean?"

"The night before." Martin continued to dutifully eat, but his manners kept him from eating and talking at the same time. "He told me he was getting ready to do something dangerous, and he might not come back."

"Why?" Nicholas persisted. "If it was dangerous, why'd he go?"

"'Cos he had to." Martin said sensibly. "And he said there were too many *childer* in London who didn't *have* parents because of the people they were fighting." Martin's dark eyes were thoughtful on Nicholas. "He'll come back if he can, Nick. You know he will."

"But what if he can't?"

"He'll try," Martin insisted with a cool maturity beyond his years.

And Clea wondered if Martin actually believed it . . . or if he was trying to put up a good front for his younger brother.

Quimper scowled, trying to see through the unstoppable grey curtain of rain. He smashed his hat down tightly and pulled out his umbrella almost as soon as he stepped out into the spring storm. He and Mr. Byrd rushed across the stone courtyard into the open shelter of the portico.

"Welcome back, sir." The butler was one of the servants from the old days. "I regret to inform you that the storm has thrown the horses into a panic. Several have broken free and took off across the countryside." He managed to divest them both of their sopping outerwear. "Mr. Craddock has left to pursue."

"Oh, that well-meaning fool." Quimper swore fondly under his breath. Craddock couldn't bear to think of any of his property being damaged in his absence. "*Which* horses?"

"The ones in the west side, sir. The storm blew out the door, and the Alsace stallion kicked the rest of it to the ground. He and four of the Alsace herd, and two of the yearling ponies, ran right through the gate."

"Well, they have the cleverness to survive if they don't run themselves off a cliff." Quimper had been through this sort of thing before.

He was gulping a hot cup of *chouchen* just as Griox was coming down the main staircase.

His business partner was frowning like one of the thunderclouds over the sky, and rattling *Gallo* French to his personal valet, LeBras. His lips set tightly upon the sight of Quimper, an unpleasant conversation about to be opened.

"Welcome back, Jethro," he began, his limp pronounced in the weather. "Did Houat inform you of the bad news?"

Quimper hastily put his cup back on its saucer and took the towel the butler offered. "We've had horse-escapes before, I'm afraid." He smiled and tried to be philosophical about it. "My Alsace line is bad for that. In all other respects they're most admirable. I suppose I should try to breed more Arabian back into the stock."

Griox nodded. He knew little of horses. "Mr. Craddock went in pursuit. I trust he knows his way through the countryside."

"He knows it quite well, but I frankly hoped he had better sense," Quimper said directly. He watched as Griox' face tightened. "Anything else to report?"

"No. Craddock was in the courtyard when it happened, so he was directly in the path of the horses. I suppose he couldn't have missed the opportunity to pursue them."

"I'm afraid that sounds just like him." Quimper admitted. "When did this happen?"

"Right at dusk. I had hopes he might have been trapped by the weather at one of the depots, and you would have met him there."

Quimper pondered that. They were jealous of the power they carried, but he and Griox operated under their own rules. Griox *wouldn't* kill Craddock, or set him up for harm. If Quimper even *suspected* that sort of betrayal, the collaboration would end in a blood-bath. Quimper's hold over Griox was only by a few degrees, but that small hold was powerful.

"So he was at the silo until that point?" Quimper handed the wet towel back and headed upstairs. The news was urgent, but *nothing* was so urgent right now as clean, dry clothing.

"He wanted to guard our guest." Griox joined his side. "He stayed there in open view for several hours, but went under the court-yard shelter as the rain grew harsh."

Quimper held his hands over the fire in his room for a moment. "L'estrade's in the Roman silo?"

"It's safe enough of a place," Griox defended himself. "I think Mr. Craddock was being overly worried, myself."

"I'm not being critical. It has proven its worth in the past," Quimper said patiently. He *wasn't* worried. The issue of Craddock was already dismissed – the man who got the better of *Craddock* was not a man Quimper wanted to meet. None of Griox' men were capable. He strode behind the screen and began his change of clothes. Griox paced before the fire, silent and controlled, but rubbing on his red-gold watch nervously. It was the strongest emotion he was capable of displaying. Griox loathed the unknown more than a priest loathed the idea of Satan in his own church.

"So." Quimper decided to get on with it. He studied the little wall mirror, checking Griox' reflection for clues. "Anything of interest to report?"

Griox was a moment collecting his voice. "He's hard-headed." That was said with the greatest reluctance.

Quimper sputtered through a snort of amusement. "Do you feel I didn't prepare you enough for the reality?"

"Well, you've spoken of his father," Griox pointed out. "Your *calliou* is intractable enough."

"Not such as you'd think." Quimper suggested. "Thomas L'estrade isn't intractable so much as *withered*. He's simply incapable of giving in to a situation if it means he has to experience an unwanted emotion." Quimper worked around a four-handed knot on his tie and adjusted his collar with relief.

"I'm surprised he works for you then."

"Old patterns, my friend. His family has worked for mine for generations. It goes against his very nature to leave a path if it isn't dissolving about his feet. Besides, my father was good to his father. Some debts can never be paid."

Griox thought about that. "*Sklav?*" [3] He asked.

Quimper grinned. "Now, Jean. That's illegal. He masters the horses at my father's old estate, and I require *nothing more* from him."

Griox made a soft sound. "Well. To return to the subject at hand, Craddock was watching the silo when the storm broke."

Quimper looked out the window. "It seems to be burning itself out," he noted. "In another hour or two it will be down to a drizzle. Ah – when you put him in there, did you make sure – ?"

"He's on a short chain," Griox joked dryly. "Considering the high level of the water tonight, as well as my own impression, I put him up a good two feet higher."

"Best to make certain." Quimper held the door open for Griox and the two made their way down the hall. "Mr. Byrd," Quimper nodded at his valet, "have someone take a check on our guest in the silo." He rubbed warmth into his chilled hands. "I am quite ready for something to eat," he announced. "We'll see to the questioning after."

Houat had laid out a hot meal. Griox joined him out of courtesy. "Is there any news from the mainland?" he asked.

Quimper frowned pensively over his *crostini* before replying. "Not in so many words," he said. "The telegrams are suitably vague to keep our rivals from learning too much. I did learn that a 'mysterious fire' struck the apartment of 221b Baker Street." He grinned as his companion's cool reserve shattered in a thousand pieces. Brandy sloshed in his glass.

"That is interesting." Griox wiped his face behind his napkin. "But why a fire and not a bullet?"

"I would venture that our employer's trackers lost their quarry. And there is the possibility that the evidence Holmes has is in the apartment itself."

Griox absorbed that in wonder. "Still," he said, very softly.

"Still." Quimper agreed. "It seems more vindictive and hasty. A gamble of luck. Which," the agent sighed as he lit a cigarette, "taken in accordance with L'estrade's accursed demolition of the printing-press aboard the *Athene*, has lifted the bar on our schedules. I shan't be surprised if the *Kelenner* [1] has declared out-and-out warfare on his favorite thorn."

Griox was carefully non-committal. He had no concept of hating an opponent enough to go past the mark to strike a blow. It made as much business sense as betting on a horse because you liked its face. "They had their chance to ask for our aid when Holmes was in France," Griox grumbled. "He was in Narbonne and Nimes long enough we could have dealt with everything – and the French *poliser* none the wiser." [2]

"I can only surmise the work Holmes was doing for the government was delicate enough that *any* of the *Kelenner*'s work would have been seen as politically hostile." Quimper mused. "The small men are spoiling for war again." He sighed. "As small men with high titles do."

Mr. Byrd appeared at the doorway and nodded. "Sir," he said quietly. "All appears to be well. I shone a lamp down and I could see movement."

"Good." Quimper examined his cigarette, gauging how long it would take to finish. "Has the rain stopped?"

"It is stopping, sir, ya."

"Well. Shall we begin?" Quimper rose to his feet. "The sooner we learn something from L'estrade, the sooner we can retire."

Griox wasn't convinced *bed* was the motive on Quimper's mind. His partner was a clever man, but he enjoyed his interrogations rather more than was considered professional. As he understood it, the man in the well had won the only suit Quimper had ever made of a woman, which was reason enough for bitter enmity . . . Still, it was little of *his* business.

Houat helped them with their coats. Quimper chose his heavier walking stick for going outside, and three men prone to silence. The door opened to the last of the rain, sweet and heavy. Puddles splashed under their feet until they reached the shelter stretched over the silo.

Mr. Byrd knelt and lifted the iron grate off. It fell on its hinge against the stones with a clatter. Used to procedure, the servants hung the lanterns on the hooks at the shelter. Quimper leaned over for a look. He could barely make out a man hanging from the bottom of the chain, waist-deep in water.

"Resting, L'estrade?" Quimper called down. His voice echoed oddly from the water and the cylindrical shape of the silo. "Fish him up, gentlemen." He pulled out another smoke and lit it, watching while the chain slowly cranked upwards.

The lantern light threw back the gleam of a furious white face. Soaking wet and gagged with his own tie, Craddock thrashed on the end of the chain.

"He climbed the chain." Groix' expression was such that Quimper dearly wished he could capture it on canvas, forever. "He . . . *climbed* the *chain*."

Quimper could have said many things, and all of them would be true. He chose not to. In an unfortunate way, it was worth it to see his oh-so-calm and controlled, arrogant business partner completely flabbergasted. He reached into his pocket and offered his cigarette case to the other. Groix took it purely on reflex. Quimper helped himself to one of the better cigarettes in the collection and found a light.

Groix was still staring at the empty pit with a blank look. Craddock was being bundled into dry blankets and judging by the amount of wine being poured in him, would soon revive enough to talk.

Quimper couldn't help it. A low chuckle escaped. "I'm afraid you fell victim to miscalculation, my friend."

Anger flushed Groix face. "He had to have had help! He *couldn't* have climbed up the chain in those shackles!"

Quimper blew a perfect smoke ring as around them, the staff scurried to lock down every square inch of the grounds, but it was too late. A case of shutting the barn after the horse fled – figuratively *and* literally.

"Did I ever tell you about the L'estrades who worked for my father, Jean?"

Groix stared at him, nonplussed. "Not besides Thomas," he said. "It was before my time."

"Ah. Very true." Quimper tapped ash on the stone. "They were performers originally. Stage actors, orators. Few people carry the anonymity of crime as well as a troupe of performers, and they had the respectability of taking the cloth the Glenan family wove and selling it where they went. Several hundred years ago, my family realized they would be useful in conveying goods other than cloth . . . a bit of an extra income on the side, strengthening of ties here and there . . . Then a rather devastating famine that ruined everything they ever owned. My family was there to pick up the pieces." He took another sip of smoke, held it in before exhaling it through his nose. "When they weren't weavers they were actors, troubadours . . . musicians . . . ." Groix was slowly changing colour for the worse. " . . . jugglers . . . tumblers . . . trick shots . . . horse-lords . . . *acrobats*." He shrugged with his eyebrows. "I confess I have little idea on how much his family trained him . . . For a while it looked as though my Thomas would raise him as a jockey, but he had no joy with the beasts. More's pity. He was skilled if indifferent." Quimper sighed. "But there's something I should have warned you about, had I thought . . . Geoffrey L'estrade is the most *intractable* man on the face of the planet."

"I don't see *how* he could have gotten out of there." Groix whispered. He was thoroughly lost. As angry as Quimper felt for the escape, it was *almost* a treat to see his confidence so shaken.

"I'm just creating a supposition, my friend, but I believe all he really had to do was climb up to the point where he could brace his feet around the bottom of the chain." Quimper held up the large iron links. "Once he was braced, he rested a bit, and then pulled his shackled wrists over his head as far as he could go . . . and wrapped the connecting links of the shackles around the larger links of the descending-chain. That held them steady as a rock and took the strain off his shoulders while he raised his feet higher up." Quimper puffed reflectively. "Then he repeated the process. When he finally got to the top, he no doubt used the cover of the storm to take Mr. Craddock by surprise. Once Craddock took his place in the well, he entered the stables and rigged that panic. A man riding underbelly at night is hard to see. Especially a small man." Quimper puffed. "I'm just betting you there's a missing girth or harness. Something he could use to brace himself. Pardon me, while I take back everything I said about his lack of interest in horses."

Groix was reluctantly forced to concede to the explanation. "I wouldn't have thought he was in any shape for such a thing."

Quimper sighed, this time in sympathy. "I *told* you, Jean . . . L'estrade *is stubborn*. He is hard-headed *beyond* the bounds of intelligence. He never stops to *ask* himself if he's capable of doing something or not. He just *does* it." Quimper shook his head. "Very well. Send out a telegram to the depots. All the *maers* [4] and city-managers, our informants. He can't go far without help. The very shape of the land is against him."

"He can't get to the mainland even if he had an armoured elephant," Griox pointed out. "More of our men are there than on the Eastern Coast!"

"We'll overlook the eastern border and the mainland for the moment." Quimper smoked furiously. Griox thought he looked like a hunter spoiling with his dogs for a full pursuit. "He doesn't know the channels at all. He's spent most of his life on the other side of the Sea. Most of what he knows I'll warrant he learned by listening to other people talking. And he certainly doesn't know *a thing* about the piracy lines."

"*But his grandfather is The Seagull!*" Griox protested. Such a notion was alien to his concepts.

Quimper grinned mirthlessly. "I'm afraid Potier-*kohz* did not get along with his son-in-law from the very beginning." Either *son-in-law* . . . . "L'estrade did not encourage visits. And since Geoffrey was disowned, Potier has sworn to have no contact at all with *any* of his kin on that side. He even included his daughter in that."

Griox sniffed. "Would he try to go to his grandfather?"

Quimper was silent for so long Griox grew impatient.

"That," the agent said at last, "is a *very* good question. He has not initiated contact with anyone in his family since Armoricus was hanged and Paul put in the asylum for the weak-minded. He knows to do so would be to put them all in jeopardy, nor is he capable of standing up to his father. He never was." Quimper smoked further. "That is the problem. L'estrade lacks imagination to a sad extent. He is *deficient* in that quality. Does he have the ability to do the unexpected when his life depends on it?"

"I suppose that would depend on his motivation." Griox said carefully.

It was only a reasonable observation, but his partner's blue-diamond eyes widened from behind the cherry-red glow of his cigarette.

"*Doue*, you're right," he breathed. "Motivation. He's got the strongest motivation anyone could have." The tall man spun on his heel. "Mr. Byrd! Get me three of your clever men! Mr. Batz – I want the list of all the *poliser* on this side of the peninsula! And find out where The Seagull lives now!"

Griox didn't understand, but at least Quimper looked decided. He watched as the agent swept to the stables, barking orders.

NOTES

1. Breton word for "Professor"
2. As Holmes briefly commented to Watson
3. *Sklav*: Slave
4. *Maer* meant "mayor". *Maer-koz* implied the Big Boss
   .

Chapter VIII – A Running Game of Chess

What happened in Brittany:

Time. I must have more time. Quimper sat by the gaping hole that had once been a Roman silo and now a worthless prison, thinking hard for nearly half an hour. No one bothered him when he was in such a mood as they scurried to obey his orders. *They knew better.*

"Mr. Quimper." Craddock came up with a large leather folio in his hands. "We believe we've found the Seagull's current address." He opened the large book to a finger-marked page. "He was paid fifteen *sous* three months ago at the ti-ker of Corentin-avel to witness the end of a minor feud of two rival dairymen."

"'Hurricane-wind' . . . ." Quimper mused. "Catches weather from all three sides. That has to be the most *neglected* port in all of Europe! He *would* retire in such a place – it barely keeps the citizens alive as it is." The agent rubbed his jawline, thinking. "Worthless even to a smuggler. I suppose he *was* sincere when he vowed to retire . . . ." He closed his eyes, mapping the land in his mind. "It isn't so far from us . . . three days by ox-cart . . . less if the roads remain clear . . . ." His eyes flipped open. "Craddock," he said softly, "I need you to find me a body."

Craddock was uncharacteristically surprised. "Who, sir?"

"Not *who*," Quimper said slowly. "Get to the Brest morgue and find me a body." He pulled his personal notebook out of his inner-pocket and wrote quickly. "Go to M. Marat. He knows me and he knows not to ask questions. This is what I'm looking for." He tore the page off with a flourish and Craddock dutifully read the paper before neatly folding it inside his waterproof jacket. "Wire me back as soon as you succeed." A great weight dispelled from the agent's shoulders as his own cleverness came to him. Salvage was more than possible. It was already happening. He stretched and stood his full length. "Now . . . if you'll excuse me, I need to see to my other business."

The plump little *maer* wiped sweat off his face. Quimper eyed him with impatient ice. The man's ancestors had originally been mainlanders and had no understanding of what things truly were like. He also had the Mainland attitude of sealing up his office from the cool sea-air. Quimper wanted desperately to hurry up with this work and move outside to the freshening breezes.

"Scotland Yard is demanding their inspector, M. Gaillou – dead or alive." He produced the folded and sweated-on telegram nervously. Quimper impatiently took the paper and glanced at its contents. "They imply they do not believe what I told them."

They'd be fools to. The *maer* was *such* a waste of space. Good to command, but not to be trusted when he had to think for himself. Quimper likened the usefulness of the man in his obedience, but the drawback was in having to hold the man's hand for *everything* that went on. He even *believed* the story that Lestrade had died en route on the ship.

That belief would make him credible enough when the Yard came to question.

"Don't worry yourself, sir." Quimper leaned forward in his chair, hands on his stick. His blue-diamond eyes soothed as he spoke. "We'll have everything sorted out."

"But . . . I can't lie!" The plump man whimpered. "I don't know where the body is!"

Good God . . . if only there was some equitable replacement for this *nouch*. Quimper frequently thought of clubbing the man to death with his shoe-heel. He was *that* infuriating, but couldn't consign himself to getting closer to the sweating man than he had to. A long-range rifle aimed at the back of the head would have to do. *Someday* . . . He briefly divulged in fantasy, even though it wouldn't happen. There was no one gullible enough to take his place.

"We don't have to *lie*, Governor." Quimper kept his voice calm and soothing. "The captain naturally had to jettison the body for the good of the ship, but he did it not a quarter-mile from port. I posted to all the sailors a substantial reward for finding the body, and sure-enough, they did find it. We know for a fact it is the missing *igounier*. His relative just identified him not six hours ago. The Yard will get the corpse in due time." He projected a pleasant, reasonable smile. "It's a fairly simple matter. If you want something done, tell the smugglers."

"They're illiterate troublemakers," the mayor protested, but weakly. He *wanted* to be convinced.

Our people were speaking the fine language fifteen-hundred years before French was standardized. You have forgotten your own past, fool. No wonder you are so weak. "You leave the dealing of the Yard to me." Quimper rose with a smile. "Everything will be taken care of." The official left, to the relief of both.

Triaged Potier walked slowly home, weighed down by a rented pull-cart full of mourning crepe and as much baked food as he could collect from the ovens on short notice. He was thoroughly shaken from his episode in the chill morgue of the *ti-ker*, and his own impromptu role within.

He took his steps with the utmost care. The heavy rains would be a long time in leaving the land. One didn't always know if one did the right thing. Sometimes impulse was the only form of instinct a man had.

Old Kerbol called out. Years had diminished his strength and the cancer had taken part of his leg, but his lungs were still powerful. Potier stopped the cart, glad for the rest as his old sailing-mate huffed up the narrow path. Urgent as his business was, he was exquisitely careful not to trod on the gooseberry bushes his daughter had planted along the trail.

"I heard," he began without preamble. "I am so sorry, old friend." The two clasped each other close, and Potier permitted himself to fall into the comfort of weeping.

"*We're being watched,*" Kerbol said into his ear – the tame folk never understood why a screech-owl would grow such abundant beards. They hid the lips. "*My sons-in-law are in the house.*"

Potier clapped his friend hard, on the back. "*I am being followed,*" he whispered back. Aloud: "Thank you, my friend."

"You were there for me when my son died," Kerbol answered sternly in the same voice. "Will you be bringing the body home?"

"No . . . They said his wife would have his body. An *English* will have my only grandson's remains." Potier allowed more tears to well up. Kerbol drew his head against his shoulder. "*It isn't he,*" he whispered. "*The body had a normal left foot.*"

"*It's the* Maer-kohz," Kerbol whispered back as he patted his best friend on the back. "*They posted a reward. He has the real* maer *under his thumb . . . He's somewhere in hiding. They'll expect him to come to you.*"

"*Or they'll expect me to find him.*"

"*We shouldn't disappoint, eh?*" Kerbol held him at arm's length. "I will bring the old crew," he announced firmly. "We shall see to things for you. A good send-off for a man who died at sea. We'll bring the food and chouchen. *You* set up a big fire. We'll do this proper."

"Yes." Potier gripped Kerbol's still-strong arm through the coat. "*We do this proper.*"

And St. Anne pity the fool who misunderstood the meaning of that phrase.

Lestrade was *more* than glad to part ways with the Alsace stallion at the lip of the forest. Horses were just like people. It was one reason why he had fairly ambivalent feelings about them – Dishonest people were grief enough without bringing in the animal kingdom. Like humans, they would lie or pretend in order to get out of what was expected of them. This one

82

was a patent hypochondriac, and like any hypochondriac, was perfectly sound despite his protests at being sent over half the country in a looping pattern.

"You think *you* have it rough," Lestrade looked the brute square in the eye and spoke through his teeth. He was standing on a pedestal of slowly softening limestone against the forest edge. The horse had complained even at that, but Lestrade wasn't about to let them find his foot-prints. "Try getting your bearings from *my* point of view." He yanked off the girth with deep relief and watched as the horse promptly enjoyed a miraculous cure to health. He shook all over and trotted to the edge of the small copse where fresh green crabapple leaves beckoned. The rest of the ersatz herd quickly surrounded him with equine admiration, paying fealty to His Nibs. "I hope you founder," Lestrade breathed. Thank God for those extra six inches. He *wouldn't* have survived life as a jockey. "*Kerzh da garc'hat!*" The long-forgotten, favourite curse of his grandfather leaped out of his mouth independent of his intention. Well, "*Get lost*" was rather fitting, considering the circumstances . . . .

Just his luck that the largest, tallest horse in the stables was also a prize-winning blooded champion. If *any* wandering horse would be searched for at the nearest opportunity, it would be he. But Lestrade hadn't much choice. He needed something big enough to absorb his weight without leaving too obvious a trail. The soft earth had made things easier. With the looping and criss-crossing and the other horses pounding their hoof-marks over his, even Quimper would have trouble tracking the difference of his weight in this mushy earth.

Not that he expected to fool Quimper forever. Since childhood the man had taken an unholy delight in the Hunt . . . .

Lestrade shut his mind on that door. It was a waste of time. He wearily hunkered down on the limestone outcrop, resting on the backs of his heels and forearms on his knees as he studied the land. He was so tired his muscles hummed. A drink of water was suddenly worth a gold watch. The vantage of the higher ground was limited. Eventually, everything led to the ocean.

The outcropping meant he was still above the cave systems . . . He twisted around, thinking through his private store of information.

Wind coming in from the south-east . . . smells of salt-water . . . He narrowed his eyes over the sweep of dark green land, dotted with grey rock and small bursts of fenceline. Someone rotated their stock in this long sweep. The horses seemed to favour it. That meant they wouldn't be likely to leave – If only they *would* get lost! – and he should put distance between them as soon as possible.

The forest behind him was girt in a loose tangle of briar and vines looping about the slow-marching vanguard of evergreens. Thickets clotted that dark canopy beyond the deep carpet of pine-needles. Boar rested in those forests. He did not like the idea of surprising one of those monsters. They were impossible to kill, even when he had his pistol. But it was a safe place to hide from the other predators.

Padriac Dooley liked forests. He *especially* liked the forests of Brittany. Lestrade recognized the looming oaks and beeches in the crown from engravings. This was the Paimpont Forest, once known as the *Broceliande* of Arthurian Romance. He was facing the beginning of the eastern border of Bretagne. Mainland France was on the other side – the side that was thoroughly friendly to Moriarty's gang.. There were dark places to hide, food for a foraging Tinker, honeycombs of caverns, and sweet springs brimming with fish. Lestrade saw no moors, so he calculated he was roughly opposite the forest from Armorika. Rennes was the nearest important city – probably thick with Quimper's people too. Some of them were no doubt his own severed relatives. He couldn't think of getting too close to those city limits.

Lestrade hoped they'd received his message of – how many days ago? It was a language he'd drafted out with the old Tinker during years of their association. In the unlikely event that someone would intercept his wire who knew the Shelta, it would indeed seem to be what the grinning Galvin claimed: A line of prayer for a sick relative. "Solk us away from the Taddy" was a line from their dialect from the Lord's Prayer.

"Deliver us from evil," had two meanings. It meant, "look out" to Padriac's people . . . and it also meant "watch it".

Padriac would be looking out for those he knew the Yard needed . . . but he would be watching from safe ground. *Again – Padriac liked forests* . . . .

Lestrade had mixed feelings about seeking shelter in there. He did not deal with the extremes of rural life well. It was a fact he couldn't run swiftly or for long. London was his element. Its nooks and crannies and bolt-holes were second nature to him, not this tangled force of nature.

Lestrade reminded himself that one didn't have to run long or hard in one of the seven black forests of Brittany – Anyone chasing him would be forced to move at the same slow pace unless they wanted to risk death by sinkhole or an angry wild pig with tusks like scimitars (but chances were Padriac was *eating* his way through the damned woods, leaving a trail of porcine bones behind him like breadcrumbs).

The horses would lead Quimper – not to mention that wretched Grioux – right to his doorstep. Lestrade set his lips and rose to his feet.

Moving as lightly as possible and keeping to the stones for their lack of foot-prints, he began threading his way through the knot of thorn and briar.

Jethro Quimper leaned against a lightning-blasted stump that had once crowned the hayfield, and made the thoughtful fixings of a cigarette. The familiar procedure soothed him. He'd been up since before dawn, searching for the watery remnants of L'estrade's trail, and was now at a contemplative crossroads.

Mr. Byrd and a very sour-faced Mr. Craddock remained on their own horses, constantly searching the land with their eyes. Craddock in particular. It was no exaggeration to say he wanted to find the detective even more than Quimper did at this moment. It made Byrd uneasy to be in his smouldering presence.

He scanned the horizon himself, but Quimper had no doubt he would see nothing of use. He checked his watch. Right on time, he spied Groix' party coming out of the small game-park and to their location.

"Any luck?" Quimper already knew the answer.

Groix' face was even more sour than Craddock – quite an achievement. "The dogs lost the scent halfway through the forest, and then we ran into a troupe of those wretched Tinkers. You can imagine the dogs went mad," he added darkly. "They were on legitimate business, so I couldn't run them off. But I did tell them to hurry up and out."

"Legitimate business?" Quimper blinked. "One doesn't hear that every day. What was the business?"

"Coffee convoy." Grioux shook his head in the wonder of it. "They're hauling an entire wagon of European-grade coffee beans to Rennes." He indicated with his fingers the size of the beans, which were larger than a child's peppermint. "Not that they're being rather swift about it . . . they had paused at a pig-roast. Blood was everywhere. You wouldn't believe the size of the brute they took down. Tusks like your forearm. And they said the larger one got away."

"All boar are elephants when they're running past you." Quimper chuckled lightly. "So that's a dead trail . . . He's somewhere in the forest, but he won't stay there for long. The man's a fish out of water in the wilderness and he knows it."

The dogs were cold-nosed, capable of finding old trails, but that also made it harder to get them to track fresh, or "hot" trails. Quimper thought very hard. Tinkers were capable of the slipperiest tricks imaginable, but it was a long stretch of the imagination to believe they had a part in Lestrade's disappearance. He blew smoke out as he thought.

"We're going back home," he said abruptly. "Summon the men."

"Which ones?" Griox was startled at the sudden drop in his partner's tone.

"All of them." Quimper was smiling. "Gentlemen, it is past time we had a Wild Hunt."

The news passed itself as he went back home along the narrow ridge of rock that divided his land with his neighbors'. News, good or ill, traveled faster than the speed of light. There were times when the old man was surprised at the adeptness of land-gossip. Somewhere in his life he'd garnered the impression that the sea was the best route for news (good or ill).

Three passers-by stopped to bid their respects as well to ask polite questions that did not quite bring out the burning question the entire province was wondering: How would the Seagull see to his grandson when there was no body?

And Potier had expected that question. The Cult of the Dead was as important to the living as it was the living itself. Unlike the English or the *Galleg*, [1] the Afterlife was not particularly different. Dead was just dead, and that was all there was to it. But to join the company of the family, there had to be a body.

He had little choice but to tell them the body was in the care of his wife and her family. That was accepted with a knowing nod. The people had lost too many menfolk to not see the sense in a woman's control of that sorrow.

A few stiff sips out of the wine bottle and Potier felt ready enough to paper the front of his cottage in mourning, gather firewood, and dig up all the sandstone blocks half-buried in the ash of his fire-pit for the night's festivities.

He was threading up a brace of hens by their feet for the next-day's meal when the creak of wooden wheels alerted him to the next wave of company. *Now, that's different.* He rose to his feet, the birds hanging limply to his knees as he stepped out of the little barn to the stonewalk leading to the limestone fence around his croft. He knew it was truly different when he took in the reaction of the nanny goats: The entire flock was facing forward, chewing on their cuds as they watched with an impolite fascination as a team of Irish Tinker horses, no taller than twelve hands at the most, tripped their way up the road to his house. Their long, feathered feet and manes blew like goose-down in the light breeze. A bowtop wagon with knotwork paint slid over the wooden sides. Several more horses and bowtops followed. The pack of dogs, which Potier was willing to swear on a Bible were real wolfhounds, were playing a game of chase underneath the cobs' large hooves and the wagons.

The lead wagon pulled to a stop, and a withered old man, who looked like those old shriveled apple-head dolls his daughters loved as children, grinned without teeth around a stone pipe. (Potier hadn't known anyone was still old-fashioned enough for stone pipes.) A bright blue cloth looped about his neck, trimmed in yellow. A young boy that could only be his scion perched on the side, his head bare against the elements but an identical scarf about his throat.

"Good even, young fellow." The Tinker lifted his beaten bowler in greeting.

Triaged Potier decided that was the *last* time he would ever hear those words addressed to himself. He recovered with admirable poise. "And to you," he nodded. "Da need sikour?"

"Ya, we could use a bit of help. A bit of advice as it were." The apple-faced man lifted his stone pipe from his mouth. "We were asked t' deliver a fine boar t'the household of a seagull driven far inland." The pipe was sucked on, thoughtfully, with a terrific sound. "If that be ya, would ya mind inspectin' the goods first?"

"I'm afraid I don't understand you," Potier confessed. "I never joined a hunt, so a portion would not be coming to me."

"For th' grandson who was lost." The old man bowed his head – he truly was ancient. Potier realized that in comparison, he probably *was* a young fellow. "Was a gift on his behalf. If you would be so kind – ?"

Triaged shrugged helplessly and opened the gate. Aware that the Tinkers were watching him carefully, he waited for the old man to hop down (which he did spry as one of the smuggler's goats) and cross to the wagon bringing up the rear. This bowtop was clearly used for storage. The stench of pig's blood was unmistakable and strong. Potier wondered if the wolfhounds had helped bring it down.

Boar were large creatures. The size of this one was of the stupendous sort, a forest lord gone to war and lost. Potier held his breath against the strong odour, and then took in the size. His eyes swelled in their sockets.

"Good God . . . *Tad-kohz tourc'h* . . . ." He swallowed dryly. "That's a grandfather boar you have there."

"Five-hundred-fifty pounds," the old Tinker noted with satisfaction. "Before dressing. He lost a hundred pounds of organs when we took care of that. He now weighs six-hundred-fifteen pounds."

"Six-hu – !" Potier stopped himself. The old Tinker's light blue eyes were twinkling like starlight. "If I may take a look at this remarkable sport . . . ."

"By all means." The old Tinker skipped straight up and into the dark depths of the wagon. It had already been gutted in the chill air. Heat still steamed faintly from its body carcass. The Tinker offered his hand. Potier hopped, sea-manlike, into the dark of the waggon.

Potier peered over the carcass cautiously. A large, smooth cut stretched frolm the boar's throat to tail. It was true there were no organs left inside. Something had taken its place.

The old smuggler swallowed hard, unashamed of his tearing eyes.

"Thank you," he choked. "I am most satisfied, sir."

There were two little-known facts about Gipsies that Lestrade was determined to take with him to his grave:

1: Coffee was one of the most successful scent-maskers in the world. Any time he saw a Tinker in the coffee business, he itched to check the bags for contraband. He'd seen trained scent-hounds walk right *past* a bag of coffee during a police raid that was later proven to hold illegally taxed Stinking Bishop cheese.

2: Gipsies had no concept of "taking a walk" for its own sake. They were always on the lookout for a way to bring in income, and that meant keeping the ears and eyes open. A half-ton boar meant nothing more than a great many steady meals for the extended clan, and possibly the added benefit of training the dogs and several years' worth of storytelling.

Addendum: Pig blood *stank*. It was awful.

Quimper's dogs had been decent enough at their task, but they had not been skilled enough to find the hiding place of a man who had been hurridly dunked in strong coffee and then smeared with pigblood and offal and buried under said offal. The dogs were a fairly gentle, timid sort that obeyed scent-trails. They had not been trained to deal with the aggressive contempt of fullblooded Irish Wolfounds (who were seven feet tall when they stood on their hind legs) and had especially not been able to endure the shock of a trio of mischief urchins perched in the tree-tops of the campground, gleefully blowing for all they were worth into "silent" whistles.

Faced with the obvious fact that the dogs' sensitive noses had been seduced by the stronger odor of pig, and unwilling to accept the Tinker Chieftan's slightly shady offer of a bag of coffee beans – "Cheap." – Mr. Grioux had hastily left the campsite, hoping the dogs would be able to find Lestrade's trail. All for naught . . . .

Inside the house with the worst of the blood sluiced off, Grandfather and Grandson regarded each other for the first time in decades.

Lestrade was shocked out of a year's growth at the sight of Potier. He'd been prepared for the sight of age. Not the cane.

"*Douaren?*" Triaged asked softly. "*Douaren-bihan?*" And then his grandson was gasping inside the pincers of a very firm embrace. *Not so aged, after all . . . .*

Old smuggling habits died hard. "Now . . . *hurry.*" The old man gripped him by the arm and began pulling him into the house. The door shut. Both men sighed in relief. He bolted it shut. "Sec'hed 'm eus. Petra 'po d'evah?" *I'm thirsty. What will you have to drink?*

"Ah . . . *Ur banne . . . dour.*" *A glass of water.*

"Dour?" Triaged sniffed. "*Kafe. Te. Chokolad!*" He set himself to throwing open a hundred little wooden doors set inside the walls. "*Chistr! Gwin! Chouchenn? Bier? Hini krenv!*"

"No, *not* the hard stuff, thank you." Lestrade found himself waving his hands wildly in the air in a fruitless attempt to get his grandfather's attention.

"Ha! *Ur voutailhad!*" Potier hoisted an enormous bulb of cloudy glass above his head.

"A full bottle *of what?*" Lestrade asked weakly.

"*N'eo ket chistr eus Normandi!*" *It's not cider from Normandy!* The bottle suddenly slammed on the table and Triaged grabbed his grandson for another embrace. "My God, it's good to see you." The old man's bones trembled. "I thought I would die before this day." Triaged was not English. He took no shame in his feelings. It reminded them both of the wasted years between. "They made me see a body. They wanted me to say it was you." Easy tears tracked into his beard. "I told them what they wanted to hear, I didn't know what else to do." Another painful squeeze.

"I'm sorry, *Tad-kohz.*" It was very inadequate.

"Drink." The old man said through the tears in his eyes. "Drink, and then we'll find a place to hide you."

"You're a *MoonCurser,*" Lestrade breathed wearily. "How hard can it be to hide a man?"

Potier grinned, a sudden display of stained teeth in his face. "Drink," he said. "Then you rest."

"There's no sign of him, sir."

Quimper made no appearance of hearing the report at first. "Keep looking," he said mechanically. "He's hiding – which is *exactly* what anyone would do if they had the brains god gave the lowly goose." He stroked his nose, tapped it as his thoughts grew deeper and deeper. "Tell the *poliser* I would like to see them," he said at last. "When in doubt, begin at the beginning."

Lestrade woke up to a sound that was as recognizable then as it had been in his earliest childhood. Triaged Potier was verbally ripping *someone* into jagged chunks of quivering flesh.

" . . . Is that what you say to an old man in his own house? While I'm in mourning for my own flesh and blood? You know what this old man says to you? He says you can talk to his wrinkled (explicative) because his balding head is busy!"

Oh, my God. He's gotten worse! The inspector's eyes shot open to a view impeded by a dark forest of dry straw. The baking-bread smells of sun-dried oatstalks mixed with the dark richness of cool, dry loam and the starchy, bitterness of potatoes. His heart pounded in his ears. He could hear his breath crackle against the thin cellulose wands. The root-cellar. He remembered. His grandfather had buried him like one of the apple barrels in a straw-lined pit and covered him back up with a solid layer of dirt on top of it.

From one storage silo to another. No one else, not even his own mother, would Geoffrey Lestrade trust with such a maneuver.

Air fed down from the clay pipe in the middle. It was the common procedure for keeping produce in Brittany where there was enough soil. The warmth of the stores created steam and masked his higher, mammalian temperatures. The pipe also brought to him the distant sounds of a quarrel.

"You call yourself the police, ya? I tell you, you don't need *my* permission to search my property! Go ahead – do it! You think I want a bullet in my brain? That's how you young pups do what you want! Go ahead!" (Lestrade could see, in his mind's eye, Triaged Potier waving his hands with the wild skill of a conductor. Only the orchestra was in events, not music) "With my blessings!"

Ah, well . . . .

Worn out, reeling from exhaustion, he'd dutifully taken his grandfather's version of tax-ignored distillate that had originated as an innocent crop of black currents during the Napoleanic Wars. By the time Potier-*kohz* had returned from his preparations outside, his grandson had been in no shape to know a green moth from an invasion of resurrected Vikings. Add to that the moonless night, and he really had no idea how deep he was under the ground – but he suspected he resided at least a foot deeper than the willingness of the local police to dig.

Potier-*kohz* would soon light his sharp eyes upon one of the unsuspecting police, recognize him as the son or grandson or nephew of one of his old sailing partners, and fall all over the Force with his effusive, romantic apologies that would only be answered by free amounts of the same shatterskull he'd poured into his grandson.

Potier-*kohz* had a nearly infallible memory. He remembered every day of his life all the way back to the cradle. It would be very, very easy to come up with a weeping account of the old glory days on the Sea of Brittany with the poor, unsuspecting policeman. Lestrade also knew from personal experience that the old man could pretend to be a perfectly besotted drunk.

Dull interest intruded into his thoughts, but vaguely. There were more important things to worry about. He knew he wasn't thinking as clearly as he should be. It could have been the strain of the past few days, or perhaps the fever that followed. A person could easily lose memory from fevers, and he truly hoped that was not the case. Clea shouldn't have to face a brain-damaged husband, nor the boys an addled father. Family was now the only loyalty he had that overrode Scotland Yard.

NOTE

1.   French.

Chapter IX – Unearthing the Past

Cheatham House, Little Venice:

*C*lick. *Click.*

> *Clatter.*
> *Click.*

It had been the only sound in the breakfast room for the past quarter-hour. Charles Cheatham could bear his own curiosity no further. "Clea, dear," he asked his daughter, "I remember a time when you were out of sorts that you would go to the kitchen and cook it out."

He heard her soft sound of amusement. "That's Elizabeth's kitchen now, *Feyther*. Besides, I don't feel so much like cooking right now."

"So you're playing with the toy blocks your nephews left behind?" Charles sipped his strong coffee with easy grace, not a drop spilling on his snow-white beard.

"Shouldn't we be glad Cutler wants his children to learn from the best alphabet that can be carved? Prime beechwood, coloured with milk-paints . . . ." Clea laughed thinly. "You'll think me silly."

"It will be the first time you've *ever* been silly, dear." Charles pointed out. "What are you doing?"

"Oh, I was thinking back to when the *childer* were beginning to learn their words. Geoffrey brought home a large *sack* full of these things from Hazel . . . Martin spent a few months learning to read on them . . . and then he independently discovered the joys of anagrams . . . 'arm tin' for Martin . . . It took him forever to find one for Nicholas, but he finally found 'cash lion' and was well pleased with himself . . . ." Charles heard himself laughing at the thought. "As long as they felt young enough for blocks, we'd play the game at night . . . looking for sentences hiding within sentences."

Click. Another toy block slid up against its brothers.

"I miss that time of their lives, you know." Clea confessed. She missed many things about their first years. Geoffrey had been home more often, the medical expenses for Nicholas' birth-complications finally paid off, and *anything* was a good year for a policeman after the horrors of 1884. Clea had never been so frightened for him since their first year of marriage with the bombings and murders of his comrades.

This was the most she'd been worried about him in . . . seven years . . . eight counting their marriage.

"Martin's clever, isn't he?" Charles mused. "When he took his first steps at nine months . . . Well, I suspected you may have a lively time with him. He's much more restless than his brother."

"Nicholas is a calming influence," Clea agreed. "He doesn't care in the least that Martin is operating on the level of a much-older boy. Martin seems to need that lack of admiration. At the same time, and absurd though it seems, Martin tries to protect his brother as much as possible. It seems amusing, I know – Nicholas outstripped him in weight two months ago . . . but the two both look out for one another."

"That's what's needed in this world, dear." A brother's love was the strongest bond a child could know. The old wrestler remained astounded that his son-in-law knew nothing of that bond. Charles had finished his coffee. As soon as the empty cup clinked down, his trained dog lifted her head, hoping that something without caffeine would drop her way. His large fingers found the tiny biscuits the maid had set aside just for the purpose, and 'accidentally' dropped one. It never hit the floor.

"Well, enough of me, Da – What have you been doing to keep yourself busy?"

"What makes you think I need to keep myself busy with this Primate Exhibit known as a house?"

"Now, Da . . . ."

"I've been modeling for Elizabeth. She's taken up painting and shoulder-muscles drive her to tears. Robert has made himself scarce as a badger in winter, so it has fallen on my shoulders, so to speak." Charles frowned lightly. "Now that wasn't at all intentional, dear. You shouldn't laugh at a pun. They're a low form of humour."

"Short people appreciate low humour, Da."

"Oh, for . . . Well, *I* wouldn't know, would I?" Charles tried not to smile at the sheer awfulness of the joke. "It's good to hear you laugh again," he said softly.

"Yes . . . Well." She scooted her chair back and leaned her head against his arm. "It's hard not to be worried. I've got to trust him to get back. Martin had the right of it."

"Am I right in feeling you partially blame yourself for what's happening now?" Charles asked quietly.

Clea was silent, which meant he was correct. "That man Quimper truly did desire my hand in marriage." She said in a low voice. "I don't . . . Da, he never had a chance, but he never realized it until late. I think it made him hate Geoffrey in a way he never had before. He'd . . . make little comments while I was staying as his guest. Called Geoffrey a . . . a *Corrigan*. I don't know what that means, and I'm a bit afraid to ask."

"*Korrigan?*" Charles repeated, his white brows drawing up together.

93

"That's a bad word, isn't it?"

"I . . . ." Charles Cheatham cleared his throat. "No . . . not at all, but it could be used very cruelly."

"I don't understand. What's a Corrigan?"

"It means, 'changeling' . . . Do you know what that is?" He felt her shake her head no against his arm. "Superstitious people believed that unclean spirits would take newborn babies and switch them with one of their own. The human parents would never know until it was too late. They'd have bonded with the false child and wouldn't be able to break the enchantment because that meant burning it with hot irons, or smothering it over coals. It's like a cuckoo's egg. And very coldly fitting to Mr. Quimper's way of thinking, for your husband fought against his brothers and saw to their ends. A cuckoo's first action is to kick the true chicks out of the nest to their deaths."

"That's . . . that's . . . He's one to talk." Clea growled in a low voice. "He poisoned the well years before Geoffrey was old enough to stand up for himself."

"Those people don't think that way, dear." Charles Cheatham said quietly. "They're landed, and they're entitled. Your husband's people were his family's servants. He committed the unforgivable when he chose not to serve them."

"You know a lot about it," Clea observed.

"Cheathams weren't always wrestlers, dear. We may have been living in Lancashire since before the Anglo-Saxon days, but we weren't always our own man. We were Celts, though we certainly don't look it now . . . . 'Homestead-Wood' is what *Cheetham* meant . . . The invaders conquered us, but we learned to fight. Do you remember the family motto?"

"'*Hold What is Yours*'," Clea whispered.

"There's a reason why we keep those words, Clea."

Brittany:

"The moon will be on our side."

Quimper nodded absently at the piece of good news. It had taken longer than he'd initially planned to summon the parties. As far as he knew, there hadn't been a Wild Hunt since his father's enforced retirement . . . .

How many years ago has it been? Quimper frowned around his tobacco and tried to think, suddenly struck at the amount of time that had passed by him unknowing.

94

The Wild Hunt was a tradition among the organized "families". It kept the peasants in a state of superstitious fear that indeed came useful. Years . . . it really has been too long.

The folk-lore of the people held that the spirits of dead men, wrapped in the skin of wolves, rode horses in frenzy, overtaking all who stood in their way. Generations ago it had been discovered to be a convenient method to both take care of one's enemies, and to keep the families in line. Once they participated in the unspeakable, there was no escape. And with the careful adjustment . . . Well, most of them grew to enjoy it.

Let the Americans commit their ridiculous conceits with white bedsheets. Walking were-wolves were far, *far* more terrifying.

Satisfied that things were moving along – if slower than he desired – Quimper leaned back in his desk chair and stared out the large glass window that overlooked the lip of the dark forest. Lestrade was probably hiding out in there. He didn't have much choice.

The agent's lips grew tight, as it usually did when faced with a peculiar difficulty.

So many problems would have been prevented, long ago, if that first Wild Hunt had succeeded. Quimper had been angry at not being allowed to attend with his father. He had been old enough. He had practiced for months with Armoricus, using Paul's sensitive night-vision to hone their skill. Their disappointment had been bitter at being left out at the last minute . . . .

Older now, Jethro Quimper knew and understood that Ivo didn't want Paul's sons to join in. Still, from a young man's perspective, the disappointment had been cruel. That led to anger and the search for something else to amuse while the moon was full.

That was when Geoffrey had walked across the courtyard with the water-buckets for the night's cooking. Unaware of the other three perched on the loading-platform of the barn, he had his dark head down, frowning as he studied his way through another thought, and was as quiet as he always was. In the dying light of the evening, he'd looked so much like the woman that had tricked his father, Jethro had suddenly seen a brilliant solution to his boredom and his father's betrayal.

One thing had led to another, and what had been a lifelong game of tormenting the youngest brother might have culminated in a very final way that night . . . but the ersatz victim had managed, just barely, to outwit them. Jethro hadn't thought it a loss, really. Jeanne Potier-Lestrade had sent her son across the Channel to her father to spend the rest of the summer. He was out of their hair for a few glorious months. But when he returned, things reverted to their normal status, which continued unchanged until the boy was old enough to strike out on his own, and strike he did, picking the filthiest city in five countries to live in.

Their lives were twisted together, re-merging every so many years. Circumstances and their opposing professions made avoidance impossible. This was the latest. He wanted it to be the last. Lestrade had information he didn't even know he had, and if they didn't pry it out of him, that Padderzon, Sherlock Holmes's newest pet, would have completely won against the *Kelenner*. Moriarty's Empire, hard-earned, exhaustive, and *stable* . . . would crumble like a sand-house.

War within the ranks would follow.

Quimper's thoughts suddenly lifted disturbing questions. Lestrade was an idiot, but there was nothing wrong with his *memory*. Had he learned anything useful when he was living here? How mobile had he been with a broken foot?

Had that information been enough to let him slip the dogs the other day?

The agent drummed his fingers on his desk, and stared hard through the window, but the forest was not forthcoming.

Potier's Croft:

"Get those potatoes out, now!"

Potier-*kohz* leaned on his shovel, while a handful of friends from the glory days applied gardening tools to the ground. There had been a sudden snap. It had frosted a bit instead of keeping to the usual thirty-five degrees of Brittany's early spring. The brutal pig – in pieces-roasted on a greenwood spit not far away. A wreath of sweet tobacco danced around his cold-pinked face. Underneath his beard, the old man's eyes gleamed with a fire his *compadres* had not seen in years.

"You are such a *sklav*-driver, Tri," Jean Kerbol grumbled without fire. The tip of the shovel struck a thin plank and everyone, including the men who were overtly tending the fire with sticks, meat-glaze, and bottles of rotgut, drew inside themselves. Ploudaniel's brother was playing the small-pipes, but at least he was good at it.

"Poor old man!" Potier roared. "Ploudaniel! Gabriel! Sein! Give these rickety old men a bit of help with those vegetables!"

A universal groan of complaint floated up, and several men exaggerated lumbago and aching backs, but it was Potier's party, after all. A crowd of old men in dark clothing circled around the root cellar and began working the loose plank that served as a door against the sheltering layer of earth. Potier pulled the cork off his flask with anticipation, and the flickering firelight opened up the small pit. His *douaren* had the time to grin and hold an arm up before he was yanked to the surface. Someone tossed a light-weight pea-jacket over his shoulders. Ploudaniel quickly began excavating large potatoes in his wake for the roast.

Surrounded by a constantly moving swarm of men his own size and similarly dressed in dark clothes, Geoffrey was as good as invisible to any spies crouched far off into the cover of the tiny lip of forest on the hill.

"Time to grow a beard, boy." Potier said under his breath. "You've put it off long enough." He grinned at his grandson's grimace of resignation.

"What have I missed?" he asked in the same voice.

"Ah, the usual." Potier-*kohz* rolled his eyes. "They've sent the Gendarmes after you on the excuse that a dangerous criminal is impersonating a Scotland Yard Inspector. That the impersonator *killed* the inspector and is not to be considered right in his mind so to please call the authorities as soon as anyone sees anyone suspicious. He has bruises on his wrists from the police-manacles he broke from, and a wound on his head from a fight with *poliser*."

"*Oh, that's clever.*" Lestrade said darkly. "That *has* to be that Quimper's idea."

"Well, they don't call him *Quimper* now. He's operating under the name of *Galliou*. We all know who he really is."

"That being the real authority around here." Lestrade accepted the bottle of water-cider gratefully. It wasn't coffee, but it would do . . . .

"Did you get any rest, *Mab*?" his grandfather asked solicitously.

"I – " An unknown assailant pounded him on the back in heavy-handed goodwill. "Didn't – really have much choice," Lestrade gasped out. He brushed straw out of his hair. Finally at a stopping-point, the stitches had stopped pulling. He hadn't bled in hours. It was a thing to behold.

"We're having a bit of a festival." Potier grinned. "The boys and I are celebrating our retirement . . . ." He drew Lestrade to the remains of the low stone wall and they sat while the chaos continued about them.

"Your retirement!" Lestrade took the bowl of pig-roast pushed upon him on reflex. Hunger had a strange way of going away whenever he looked at the mountainous hog roasting in the flames. He looked around. There had to be at least fifty men, *none* of them as young as ten years older than his own age.

"Aye, we're retiring from our farming and going back to the smuggling business." Old Kerbol leaned down to grin over his shoulder. "One last visit to the glory days, *Ermin*," he used the screech-owls' pet name for him. "We're smuggling you back home."

97

I should have expected this . . . Lestrade's reaction must have shown because his grandfather only continued to look ridiculously pleased with himself at the massively dangerous thing he was planning.

"Can we talk?" he said at last.

"We are talking." Potier smirked.

Merciful Mother of God . . . Lestrade searched frantically in his mind for an appropriate Anglican prayer that would fit this nonsense. *"Tad-kohz* . . . have you considered . . . ?" Words dried up. Asking a man who not only made his living in one of the most dangerous if not patently illegal forms of income in the world, asking if they knew what they were doing was simply stupid. He opted for the familial guilt. *"Tad-kohz* . . . Your daughter, who is my mother, won't be happy about this."

"I've been good for years," the old man sniffed. "I retired early to make her happy, I'll have you know. What is it your English writer said about dying in battle . . . It beats sickness, old age, and falling down the cellar stairs."

"That was Ambrose Bierce, and he was American!" Lestrade exclaimed. "A *mad* American. Even for an American!" Lestrade closed his eyes. "Oh, Good God . . . I think that's redundant grammar . . . ." Lightheadedness was making his mouth run where it shouldn't.

"Well, he wrote a good dictionary. I never understood a *word* of English until I read it."

"It's not really English, *Tad-kohz*. Bierce is American!"

"I fail to see the difference."

"You can say that in my presence, but please don't say that around one of *them*. They're rather strict about that sort of thing." Lestrade warned. Simply to keep the peace, he started eating. It was actually palatable. The cooks had basted the meat in some sort of melted plum conserve. "Do I want to know what the plan is?"

"Certainly. We throw ourselves into a memorial feast for my dead grandson, and take to the caves."

The "dead grandson" lifted a skeptical eyebrow. That was one thing Potier loved about the boy: Little affected him unless it was *spectacularly* outrageous. "Well, that's simple," he drawled. "But I hope you aren't going to try to convince me that we can walk underground from here to the port."

"Goodness, no. The biggest cavern system is only five miles." Potier missed the slight choking sound from his audience. "And it's not in a straight line . . . we'll have to hop the cave systems, moving slow, like the sea-turtles, coming up for air every so many hours or days, even." Potier suddenly had a thought. "Are you afraid of small dark spaces, *Mab*?"

Lestrade just looked at him.

Kerbol hooted. "You didn't ask him that *before* you buried him? You *are* getting too old for this line of work, Seagull!" Several of the smugglers collapsed into hysterics.

Chapter X - Baptism

"Eat," Old Kerbol cautioned when the laughter died down. "If we're to go under the earth, we'll need food. And it's easier to carry the food *here*," he rubbed below his ribs, "than on the back."

"Who'll to be doing the above-watch?" a man Lestrade knew as "Sein" wanted to know. Lestrade was trying very hard not to stare at Sein, but it was *difficult*. The man was partially unpigmented. Patches of ghostly white skin mapped over his face and exposed hands and lower arms like the colours of a dairy cow. With the smallest of his nose and round little dark glasses on his face, he gave the impression of being a human narwhal. If he was one of Potier's smugglers, the detective didn't know *how* the man avoided being seen at night.

"Kerbol, you're the quickest when it comes to running above the ground," Potier decided. He was also picking up a fork to eat, though he was more-or-less using it as a metallic stick to hold his meat as he chewed. "Can you meet us at the Old Depot?"

"Where the trout are?" Kerbol asked mysteriously, and nodded. "It should work fine. I told my daughters I would go see to their poor baby brother tonight . . . ."

"I wondered how those little pullets gave you permission to get away for the night!" a wag joked in the crowd, and Kerbol turned, almost absently spinning his metal plate through the air like a Greek discus. Lestrade heard a bell-like sound and contrite gasp.

"We'll have to be careful," another man murmured. He was smoking a pipe made out of a peculiar white-and-black striped wood. "There's no knowing if those fools discovered the *kev* or not."

"Here's hoping we don't find out the hard way," Potier answered with a frightening lack of concern. "We've run the Earth-gauntlet before, *Mab*. And the Earth is too old to be mocked."

That last said was a proverb with many layers of meaning, each depending on the context in which it was made. But it was nearly always used as a lesson against overconfidence.

They ate under the cover of the party, which grew livelier with the release of several large glass bottles shaped like onion bulbs. No one who was going underground took anything stronger than cider and coffee. Potier wrapped up food as it progressed, sticking to only a few items: Pieces of meat, dried fruit, a handful of hot peppers, a waxed bag of the grey-and-black salt of Brittany's salt-pans, raw potatoes without flaw in the skin, a packet of bread-charcoal, and a tiny bottle each of crabapple juice and live vinegar. Half of the things Lestrade didn't understand the point of, and the other half made him nervous for a very good reason. Potier wasn't underestimating the problems. That humble little field kit was comprised of the most common supplies for battle.

Potier had finished stringing shut the bag he planned to carry on his back. The rest of the goods were being spread among the other members of the self-elected party. In the bright firelight he glimpsed his grandson, staring upward into the star-clotted sky. The old *floder* wondered how much of that summer he'd remembered. Geoffrey appeared to be searching for something.

"Watling Road," he murmured once, and fell silent.

There was no mark of civilization in this part of the world. No lamps, no gas, no low rumble of the furnaces. Instead of the casual and callous power of Industry tinting the skies with orange and sulphur, there were only spills of ink and diamond dust above their heads. It was unnervingly quiet. A barn owl screamed once, upsetting a flock of geese. In the darkness, Lestrade heard the old man chuckle. Nothing could get past a flock of geese, he remembered. They made wonderful watchdogs for that reason, and they were easy to take care of.

Walking on grass was something one never did accidentally in London. Outside of the few parks, the lawns were privately owned and jealously guarded. Outside the *ton* it was different, and then it meant re-learning to walk all over again, like getting one's sea-legs back.

This close to each other, Lestrade made out the features of the men just in front of him. Sein's discolouration had extended, it would seem, even to his hairs. Odd patches glowed like fungus where it peeked out from beneath the edge of his knit cap. Three other men were in front of Sein. One was Potier-*kohz*. Three other men, Ploudaniel was one, followed, their slightly heavier packs making them slower and more deliberate as they navigated a winding path past the acres of animal trails, and the occasional stump of a boot against a limestone outcrop.

The darkness was complete.

There was no moon.

It wouldn't have mattered anyway.

A famous poet once said that the caves of Egypt were full of the *dead*. In Brittany, they were full of the *living*. They always had been that way. There were *always* reasons for a man to hide.

Still . . . Lestrade took the pause at the lip of the forest. He smelled the evergreen and there were tree-shaped holes cut out of the Milky Way. His sense of direction suggested they'd gone somewhere close to two miles, but as it had been in a looping, criss-cross of a trail. He wasn't certain of the crow's-eye distance.

Still . . . One gaping black hole looks much like another. For Lestrade it made the difference to see someone in front of him drop into a void no larger than –

"We call these the *keyholes*," Potier panted. Despite a full meal, he was exhilarated and flushed with excitement. "You have to turn to the side to make room enough to pass through." He then proved it. The earth swallowed the old man as easily as a man with a meal.

Silence. A faint call of approval crept out of the earth at their feet. There was the scent of disturbed, damp earth, sweet with alkaline clay and hinting of mushrooms.

Lestrade *knew* he was out of his depth. There was no sense in pondering fearful what-ifs. He followed suit, slowly, knowing others were behind him. His hands held on to the cold, wet blades of coarse grass with both hands and he turned as he'd seen, reminding himself that if Potier could do it, he was small enough too. Inch by inch, the earth slipped past his legs, then his waist . . . He felt it press his ribs, just slightly, and forced himself to breathe. The cut throbbed in his skull. He lowered one of his shoulders, making more room while saving his hands for the last. He just didn't want to let go . . . not until his feet caught some sort of purchase . . . .

The last time he'd been underground, it had been in the company of starving tin miners in a decaying shaft with rising black water. They'd nearly drowned to a man, and all to prove by infiltration a mining company was cheating the Crown of its ore tax. He'd sworn never again. Being below the earth had been too much like walking into the gaping maws of ancient monsters. Ogres, earth-spirits. Life was strange. Now he was going underground to save his own life.

Only a few seconds were needed to bring back decades of memory. Soft, wet rock brushed his elbows. *Bisclavaret* ran to these dark hollows, hiding his mortal's clothing before running out to feast on human flesh. Korrigan slept in giant kingdoms beneath the sod, emerging now and then to trade a human baby for one of their own. What was a sleeping dragon if it wasn't a cave, resting but full of silent dangers? All those old fairy stories his sisters had loved so much – a love Martin inherited, but *he'd* never felt for the embroidering of the story. Want to *truly* scare yourself? Simple. Don't bother with telling ghost stories, or camp out in the graveyard on the Night of the Dead.

Go underground.

Something slippery scraped the tip of his shoe. Firm clay. A harder stone pressed against the leather. His grandfather's large hand closed at his foot, reassuring with a squeeze. A sharp stab of yellow light erupted like a volcano beneath, and Lestrade remembered the tiny dark lanterns the old man had looped to his belt like an odd set of keys.

One last breath above the ground, and he turned his head straight up, making as much room as he could. The stars glowed like the holes punched in a dark lantern. Watling Road burned overhead, a cold track of fire across the sky. King Arthur's Chariot, the Big Dipper, hung in the firmament on invisible threads of physics. The planets twinkled. Stars never did. Ironic. Potier-*kohz* never tired of talking irony to his grandson.

He let go, and the cave swallowed.

Potier held the lantern up with his better hand and drew his grandson to the side. To do him credit, his *douaren* was taking it all rather well. In the thin glow of the lantern Potier saw him look up, taking in the height of the rock-ceiling above their heads, and the long length of slippery looking clay that one had to slide down more then jump.

"How do you get back up?" he whispered. A pack was tossed down without ceremony. Potier moved it out of the way quickly. A new set of legs were coming in.

"Well, we used to just stubborn our way up, but now that we're older and wiser . . . we just take the back route out." Potier grinned. "It's only three miles from here, and you can get there in three hours or less."

"Is *that* where we're heading?" He had that calm demeanor of a man who is resolved to be mannerly about his fate.

"Probably." Potier admitted. "I haven't decided which way to take yet."

Ploudaniel dropped, grinning through a thicket of beard that looked like a cluster of sheep's wool. He caught his mate's pack in his arms before it hit the earth and joined the other two against the cavern wall.

"We really should do this more often," the younger smuggler commented. "I always breathe better in these caves."

"It's the dampness." Potier said knowledgeably. "Look out, here comes Mad-Mab Malvo."

Sooner than seemed possible, the stone bubble – Lestrade devoutly hoped it would never burst – was filled by a total of seven men. Their bodies steamed in the cool air of the cavern. After the brisk walk the air felt stuffy, hot . . . enclosed, despite the fact there was a black opening by his grandfather that was twice the size of the literal double barn-doors. The detective stared at it, unashamed at the knowledge he was already developing something of a personal relationship with this element. From it a cooler flow of air fanned his face. It smelled like the silt of old floodwater, a cold stream, and slowly decaying wood, like the sort that is drifted ashore on a riverbank. Lestrade counted in his mind and judged the depth of the chamber was close to Quimper's sadistic silo. He was glad it was too far from the Ocean's Table to be affected.

It's always been too late to turn back. He listened to the good-natured chatter with half an ear. They were dealing with nerves, no different from a troupe of constables before a large raid. His eyes settled on strange little knots of twig and skeletal leaf, brushed up against the corners, shelters for some sort of rodent. *Dormice?* The Romans had brought them here, too, along with the grape, and carp, and stinging nettle.

Something made him look back at his grandfather. The old man was just as silent as he was, letting the others talk out their surplus of energy. Bright, dark eyes twinkled like polished obsidian.

"You have that look about you," Potier murmured. "It's touched you before."

Lestrade shivered slightly. "What has?"

"Something larger than yourself." Potier shrugged. "It's a touch of death what keeps a man alive, like a dose of cowpox against the smallpox."

Packs were returned to the appropriate shoulders, and – this was truly the defining moment – Potier went to a small pile of neatly stacked torchwood in the corner and began rationing out the "alternative" source of illumination. "For when we truly must use them," he explained. "Pine has a stink to it, and uses up oxygen."

And then he marched into the deeper darkness.

An hour-and-a-half later, Lestrade was wondering who in the world first came up with the brilliantly flawed belief that with age came debility. He was about ready to go out and fight the next person who said such a thing in his hearing. He was also quite willing to thrash the next yokel who uttered that tripe, "Age is but a number."

The cave looped and twisted inside and out much like one of the surface trails the smugglers used. Carved of water, much of the rock was worn smooth by that power, and short stutters of hard, dark chert speckled the softer stone like so much ornamentation. On occasion, some of these flint nodules were simply missing, like someone had pulled them away from the calcium matrix.

"When we're climbing, don't trust those nodules," Ploudaniel either read his thoughts or it was the right time for instruction. "They can just fall out in your grip. Always have more than one thing to hang on."

"I won't forget." Lestrade vowed uneasily. Who could forget something like that?

The light colour of the limestone itself aided in the illumination a bit. Its shade reminded him of warm eggshell, and sometimes tiny seeps and streams dissolved the soft mineral, carrying it elsewhere and leaving it behind as it evaporated, something like a child's dribble-castles built on the beach. Unlike the raw materials it drew from, these creations sparkled like diamonds. The older ones were tinted in yellows, dull oranges, blue-blacks, and browns from the trace elements in the water.

It was just like looking at the way Nature shaped ice . . . only this ice never melted and took years to form. The deeper they traveled in the dry passage of a dead underground river, the more elaborate the shapes grew. It twisted, like curtains, draperies, and formed soft clouds. It grew in straight lines like arrows, and hollow tubes dripped clear water down, drop by drop, into quiet pools of silver.

"This is one reason why we don't use torches," Potier said softly. "The smoke, it gets into the rock itself. If we were ever being tracked, the nose alone could tell our pursuers the paths we prefer."

It made sense. The air did move, but it moved quite slowly. "How long can the odor stay?" [1] Lestrade wondered. He knew he was speaking softly, but being here . . . in a world of abstract art designed by inhuman hands . . . it had that effect on him.

Potier grinned wryly. "Centuries," he said simply. "There's a room you'll see tonight . . . discovered it quite by accident when Ploudaniel here . . . he was just a boy at the time . . . was burying a few items in the earth. He picked up a rock and found a passage on the other side. Of course *he* crawled in. What he found was another sort of wealth . . . arrow-heads, axe-heads, spear-tips from the ages before metal. The smoke was still in the air." The footprints of the artists still in that soft, damp earth." He paused. "It must have been much colder back then," he said thoughtfully. "They wore fur boots."

The calm way Potier stated this sent chills up his grandson's spine. The concept of a moment preserved in Time like so many preserves was an unsettling one. And astounding. But Time *wouldn't* follow the rules of the surface. He reasoned. Time was marked by the sun's clock, and the sun was separate from this strange, silent world, so silent that when they stopped to rest, the blood sang in their ears like the ocean.

"We're going to have to stop here," Ploudaniel piped up from somewhere to his left side. "I'm not going past the Crevice without protection on my rickety knees."

"Time to rest a moment anyway," Potier agreed. He had replenished his lamp-oil twice so far, and with various grumbles of relief, everyone found places to settle on slightly damp stones piled in a loose jumble about the chamber.

For the first time since descending, Lestrade had a chance to truly look around while a skin of water was passed around with a handful of food – the pig had already been walked off. He was glad for the dried fruit. This room was small but almost spherical. The floor here was hard-packed earth, softened by the wet spots of water-drips from the stone straws slowly growing their way down. He looked up, not wanting to see anything large and ponderous growing out of the rock right above his head, but there were only the thin, white tubes, quietly forming a ring of stone with each passing drop.

They were very warm from the exertion. Heat rolled off them like a cooking-pot. Malvo, the official risk-taker of the group, wiped his face with a cloth frequently, and drank his water with relief. His eyes were blue and mischievous upon everything he looked at.

"Not long now," he beamed. "The Crevice and the stream, and we'll be at the Old Depot. We haven't lost those hot-peppers, have we?"

"I never go underground without them." Potier sniffed. He explained as an aside to Lestrade: "It isn't the cool of the *kev* that can kill a man. It's when a man gets overheated, and then he stops to cool off too quickly. He gets too cold to get warm again. It happens quickly, especially when you're tired, so if you start feeling anything like a chill, let us know."

"What do the hot-peppers have to do with being cold?" Lestrade had a feeling he already knew.

"A few bites of those, and you'll be right as rain." Potier scowled at Malvo. "Except for *him*. He eats them anyway."

"He'll *never* be all right." Sein sniffed. He took that moment to pull off his glasses. They were fogged to silver. Albino pink eyes blinked at them as he held his glasses away from his face, letting the glass acclimate. He cocked his head to one side. "Ah. I hear the River. She must have risen from that squall."

"Good thing she never gets very high." Potier was satisfied. "She'll be back above the ground in a few days, and wiping out more of our trails. Good for her."

A few minutes more passed while Loic and Winoc handed out strips of rag with rag-pads sewn in the center. They wrapped easily around the knees, protection Lestrade had no doubt they would need. The last man, a sun-blackened farmer named Roparzh who fretted incessantly about his twelve daughters under his breath (Lestrade decided he was entitled), gathered up all traces of their passage and tucked them away or buried them under the stones.

"I don't see what you're complaining about, Rop," Sein finally sighed. "They're *daughters*. It's not like they're going to go join the French Legion – or worse, the Navy." He jerked his thumb to the man for Lestrade's benefit. "It's a long-standing problem, Ormin," he explained. "All his *beulke* neighbors have gigantic oxen for sons, and worse, the girls have their Tad's brains and their Mam's looks. Poor Rop has to threaten someone with a shotgun at close range about every week."

"It's your own fault for not taking them to chapel more often," Lioc teased. "If you had, maybe a few of them would have joined the Convent."

"Then they'd have to worry about priests!" Roparzh sputtered. Lestrade was just starting to feel sorry for the man when all attention shifted his way. "What about you? Any great-granddaughters for the Seagull to worry about?"

He shook his head quickly. "Two sons." He held up his fingers to correspond ages with names: "Martin and Nicholas."

"They don't look like *him*, do they?" Loic pointed at Potier.

"Ah . . . ." Lestrade thought quickly. "Martin's a Potier in all ways. Nicholas is just as thoroughly a Cheatham. It's just as well they're devoted to each other." Otherwise, there would be turmoil that even the London Fire Brigade couldn't handle . . .

Potier had been about to say something. A strange expression came to his face and he rose, turning to the black passage that sang of water. "I just remembered that new retaining pond they put up at the croft was leaking. We'd better cross over this and get it over with." His uneasy voice put a similar pang in his grandson.

Potier lit more than his lantern this time. He ensured all the oil was nearby and the waterproof matches in every man's pocket. "You may not have to use the torchwood, but they do make useful walking sticks." He cautioned. "Boys, you know the rules. We head upstream and then cut *straight across*. Loic, try to remember that this time." He stopped to frown. "Straight across. You're guaranteed to fall if you go any other way."

Just as quickly, they were out of the room and bending right. Three paces and Lestrade found himself on the sloping bank of an underground river.

It flowed past their feet, only the surface layers of the water catching their flames, like mercury mixed with oil. There was not a single spark of illumination anywhere else. Lestrade told himself that the softness of the river's sound meant it was *probably* slow-moving and fairly calm. Probably. He watched Potier step upstream, moving as carefully as a suspicious goat on the muddy cobbles, until his lantern ran out of void. The light threw back on a ceiling of calcium that was less than a yard above the surface of the water. Oh, Good God. How long did it stay that way? And that was where they were headed . . . that was where they were going to cross.

Surrounded by water by two angles, Lestrade nevertheless felt his throat turn to powdery desert.

"There might be a flock or three of bats hanging off the ceiling," Potier called casually. "Try not to kill any. Their bodies could get washed to the surface and someone could notice."

"I'll . . . keep it in mind." Lestrade assured him evenly. He had decided in his mind to just disturb everything as little as possible. It seemed safer. Not thinking would help too.

Walk straight across. He made the motions of swallowing and stepped down. The river was cold as snowpack. How long had it traveled underground to cool off so strongly? Mist rose from their bodies as their temperatures compensated almost instantly. A false sense of warmth crept in. The level rose past his waist with the fourth step. Lestrade froze for a moment, concentrating on his balance and not about to drop the lantern in his hand. The torchwood splinter touched the bottom with its tip. Reassured on a faint level, he held his breath, kept his eyes on his grandfather, and kept going. The old man bowed slightly, his grey hair brushing the top of the stone ceiling, and then he was gone. The flicker of light on the surface wrinkled like a phosphorus trail in his wake.

Other men might take the imitation security of being able to do anything an old man could do. Lestrade had never made that sort of mistake. Potier was a man in himself, survivor of shipwrecks, epidemics, snakebite, corrupt officials and even a strike of lightning. Lestrade could face his own mortality before he could wrap his mind around the concept of Triaged Potier falling to earth.

Straight across . . . Lestrade understood the scientific principle of this advice the moment his path stepped out of true. Straight across minimized the water tension against his balance. Even a slight alteration increased the pull of the water around him. He felt the current dig underneath the pebbles at his feet, undermining his weight. *No. Undertow.* He hurriedly twisted his body back to face forward as well as he could as he bent his head down, eyes on Potier's lantern like a lighthouse, felt something bat against his legs but managed not to react. The rock brushed his head, worn smooth and ponderous. He tried not to think of the trillions of tons above his head at that moment, reminded himself this was too large a place to even notice his mark.

It's been here before man was even in this land . . . it will be here after. You're just a small element, a single cell walking inside a blood-vessel of a stone giant. You're used to being small. This is no different . . . no different . . .

Potier had reached the shore. He turned around and watched as his grandson took another step forward – then reached out with his stick and caught Sein as the old man slipped on a smooth rock. For a moment both men vanished. Potier's heart calcified before his lamplight and the glow of Loic's candles caught two dark heads – one patched with glowing white – emerging back up. Sein spat a curse. Geoffrey merely spat water.

"A man like you needs a regular baptism anyway, Sein." Ploudaniel expressed his relief in a taunt.

"I lost my – " Here he shared a fine string of swear words. " – glasses!"

"You'll be fine. We're traveling underground, and then keeping to the night." Potier reached out and gripped his grandson's icy hand. He was pleased to see the boy was only using him as leverage, using his own strength to climb up rather than risk pulling him in. Sein continued to swear as he sat down on the rock.

"We're almost out." Potier told his panting *douaren*. "Fifty feet of crawling and we'll be out."

"Sounds wonderful." Geoffrey breathed.

Everyone piled to the other side, Sein subsiding but still very, very prickly, and they adjusted the pads around their knees, donned winter-weight gloves. Sein tied his now-worthless lantern to the bottom of his pack and joined the procession.

Lestrade was by now used to the deceptive quality of cavern space. What appeared to be a gaping hole often was only a slight scoop in the rock in their lights. In this case, Potier led them to a small hole in the rock, straight up a good six feet and accessible only by a single foot-hold.

I can't believe I used to complain about following Sherlock Holmes across God's Great Earth, the detective thought. In hindsight, the folly was stupefying. *Sitting around in a fog-wrapped hollow by the bloody Great Grimpen Mire waiting for a glowing ghost-dog to run up . . . On the other hand, I don't have to keep up with his bloody bean-pole legs, and neither does anyone else here . . .* He filed away this latest in a long string of grueling challenge, determined to tell the Amateur about this particular experience once he returned to London. *Dr. Watson would just love this.*

Potier turned his body to the side, put his outer leg on the tiny spur of rock, and hefted himself up with a single grunt. He twisted around from long experience, bent, and held out a hand. Lestrade copied the movements as well as he could, but was relieved when he was safely inside the channel.

"There you are, all over but the singing!" Potier beamed.

Incorrigible leprechaun, Lestrade thought. Well, there were no leprechauns in Breton. Korrigan was more like it. Potier fit the description of a subterranean dwarf rather neatly . . . .

This channel had been used in the past. At first Lestrade thought the cavern had grown even darker. Then he caught on the old smell of pine smoke. The rock was blue-black, smeared with smoke and soot. Travel had smoothed portions of the limestone like dark glass. Long cuts gouged the rock at the sides like tallies. Lestrade recognized it was some sort of record, but he didn't recognize it.

Without warning the channel dropped. Water splashed over their knees and hands. It was warmer, and flowing downstream.

"Watch out for any salamander eggs," Potier warned. "You get that slime on your hands, you won't be able to get a purchase on anything."

"I'll bear that in mind, *Tad-kohz*."

"Ha!" Potier called over his shoulder. "Starlight!" Lestrade was just catching a breath of fresh air – very fresh air. "Get ready for the drop. It's a good one!"

"Keyhole in," Ploudaniel panted, and Lestrade could hear him grinning. "Keyhole out. Let the old man go first. You can always land on him and break your fall."

NOTE

1. The old smugglers are using methods of caving that are applicable today. They have to keep alive, and the first step is safety. In effect, I'm describing modern cave protocol in terms a Victorian would understand. Also, yes, one can smell odors of human passage in a cave over a hundred years past – and then more. When I worked as a tour guide, the spring winds always brought the stench of the Civil War into the tour cave in which I worked.

Chapter XI – Out of the *Kev*

Two conflicting sensations struck as Lestrade squeezed through a keyhole that wasn't much larger than the one he'd used to enter the underground. The air had *changed*, as if it were generated from another machine. It even *felt* more electric than the subtlety of the cavern behind them. Lestrade took a deep breath, realized his lungs weren't large enough for what he craved. What had happened to him? When he was underground the slow, shallow breaths had been natural, something he needn't bother to question, the way a tortoise did in winter's sleep. Now he was alive again, and every nerve hummed as if he'd been rolling in brambles.

In the starlight, his grandfather's small, wiry form was bending forward in the narrow sluice of water and rock. Moss feathered his passage. His head vanished behind his shoulders and he was sliding off what appeared to be a cliff's-edge. A splash flicked spray in Lestrade's face – warm in comparison to where he'd been.

Starlight filtered isinglass through the small opening in the thick forested canopy. Water splashed under his hands and flowed past his padded knees. The path dipped forward like an otter's slide on the riverbank, and the small man's left hand slipped in a patch of moss-clad clay. He went down on that arm, and a small dart of pain went up the bone as he slipped through the weak matter and downward a full storey into the cool water of a quiet pool. After being in the caves, one more dunking didn't seem to matter. He rose to his feet with more resignation than alarm. A small fish leaped into the air, sinuous as a snake. Lestrade remembered Kerbol's comment about "trout". Were they inside a glorified fishing hole?

Water lapped at his chest. He felt grasses waving against his feet. Large stones ringed the pool. In their height they had been tall and proud menhirs, but now they were worn down to nubs, the way Time did to teeth. The moon was beginning to rise over the peak of trees. It threw a peculiar light over the world, like the way a mirror reflected a single candle into a room.

Tad-Kohz was just wringing water out of his wool-knit cap into the reeds that girt the side of the pool. "Over here's the easiest way out," he breathed slightly quickly. "I'll give you a hand, boy."

Lestrade sighed at being called a 'boy' again, but at least he would outlive it someday . . . should he actually live so long. It was being called "*bihan*" – "little" that he knew would never leave. *Ah, well . . . .*

He gave up fighting the wall of water and just stroked his way ashore. His grandfather was kneeling, leaning backwards with his hands stretched out to pull him up. Soft mud gave way under his sodden shoes. He gripped hard and winced slightly as the faint throb in his head returned. The water gave him up quickly, and he stretched out on the thick grass, glad to breathe with his eyes shut.

Sein emerged from the water next. His albino-pink eyes were dark red in the night, small and close-set. With his vastly receding hairline, it only added to his impersonation of a human whale. He wrung his knitted cap out before he even accepted Potier's hand for help, and climbed out with a distasteful expression.

"It feels like winter's come back," Lestrade admitted, pulling his arms about his chest for warmth. The thin mat of dead grasses created a sort of air pocket between his body and the chill of the true ground. Above his head, another splash as a bulky form oozed out of the narrow keyhole – a slit water-cut out of a sheer grey rockface. Puzzled, he lifted his head, realizing the rock was no higher than three storeys or so. Stingy trees struggled to grow out of the thin crannies of the rockface.

"Here," Potier was rummaging in his pack, and pulled out a thin cotton sheet boiled in linseed oil until it was yellow and waterproof. It crackled faintly as he wrapped his grandson inside it. "It's too easy to cool off," he reminded him. "Ploudaniel, for the love of God, this isn't a bathtub!"

"Not all of us kept the webbed feet of our childhood," Ploudaniel snipped back. He needed Sein's assistance in getting out.

The partial-albino sighed, his vision perfectly suited to the brilliant astronomical illumination above their heads. "No sign of Kerbol," he announced flatly. He of all people, would know.

Potier nevertheless, blanched around the workings of his pipe. "You're certain?" He breathed.

"Certain as my last name's Gwennard," [1] Sein answered grimly. He ran his long fingers through his remaining hair and squared his shoulders. "Give me a moment." The man advised. "I'll take a look about the paths."

"You be careful." Potier managed to snarl at him without raising his voice. "Quimper has used the night-sighted before." Under his hand, his grandson flinched at the unwelcome memory. The old man sighed, not liking himself much at that moment. "Get warmed up, *Douaren*," he advised. "Once we all rest a bit, we're heading to the next *kev*."

Some people would have taken that news rather badly. Lestrade merely took it with a sigh. Potier supposed that came with living around the English for so long. Inevitably, their stoicism leaked into the brain-matter.

"What is this place?" Lestrade wasn't normally awed by the inanimate.

112

"Bormanus' Meet." Potier spoke with more pride than superstitious respect. His dark eyes gleamed. "His name has altered, much like ours has over time. I think now they call him Borvus in the newer lands. Lord of the hot springs and healing."

Lestrade knelt, still holding the oilskin about his shoulders, touching the misting water with his hand. The remaining smugglers were piling out, with a quiet mixture of curses and speculations as to their fellow man's virility against hardship. Another liquid shape slipped through the water. A trout surely. "It's hardly a *hot* spring." He pointed out. "It feels as chilly as the rest of the waters we've traveled through."

"*Nann*, it's because the water never freezes that it gets it name." Potier settled down with a satisfied expression. With his own light oilskin, he was warm and cozy as a steamed clam. Loic and Winoc were sharing a single skin the size of a small tarp – the makeshift shelter in emergenices, Rop explained in passing.

Lestrade let the water swirl around his hand. "It never freezes?" He echoed. "As chilly as it is?"

"*Never*. The fog will freeze, and settle a coat of milky glass over everything it touches, *but this water never freezes*. No one knows why, so it made sense for our ancestors to name it after a Hot-spring God. I suppose they missed the one back on Britain?" He mused thoughtfully. "Or perhaps because of *that*." He nodded, old-fashioned style, with his head to point, instead of rudely using his fingers. Lestrade followed the line to see that Ploudaniel had re-lit his lantern to warm his hands. Softly reflected in the glow was a very badly proportioned scratch in the old menhir: A woman with stick-thin limbs and a skirt, a serpent looping about her waist.

"Sirona, the Star. They say she was Bormanu's mother, but he took over her springs and healing skills in a great war." Potier had finished his pipe. He puffed once, deeply, gratefully, and handed the instrument over to his grandson. "When I was a boy, you could still see the star-diadem about her head. But the rock melts, like the earth itself, and she melts with it. You can see she has a shallow dish in one hand, a scepter in the other, but only when the sun is bright overhead. Even in the morning, the dawn is too weak to show the lines." He puffed again. "In my grandfather's time, you could see she there was a clutch of eggs in her dish, and the snake had spots. So I'm told."

"You call it a *Meet*, though." His grandson sounded for the entire world, suspicious, like Potier was deliberately with-holding information. "What is the Meeting Place?"

"See that *taol maen*, [2] off to the side that faces the sun – well, the sun if it would be up?" Potier nodded with his beard. "That's what they call the Rock of Litavis . . . the Lord of the Forge. There's the notion that *he's*

113

the reason why the water never freezes . . . ." Underneath his beard, his teeth gleamed. "But if you ask me, I say we were never *that* romantic and feather-headed. I think it's the motion of the water that keeps the ice from forming on the water, and that's why it never seals up."

Lestrade had not completely forgotten his grandfather's love of small jokes. "That wouldn't explain the part about the healing." he pointed out. Steam was rising off his warming body. It was only a coincidental reflection of his frame of mind.

"No." Potier chuckled deep inside his beard. "No . . . it would not." He took his pipe back and blew a double ring. "But we'll get to that. My words fail in translation. Best to show you in person."

"Hmm." Lestrade had heard variations of *that* theme before. For his own sanity, he would withhold judgment. *Time to rest, anyway.* Keeping mentally abreast with the likes of Potier would keep anyone in a state of perpetual exhaustion.

Minutes passed, long and slender as the blades of grass under his arm. Kerbol's absence was an unspoken worry. Sein's abrupt exit adding to it. Lestrade didn't for one minute think even Quimper could compete with the night-sight of a blooded albino. It was a matter of being patient and accepting the fact that so much was out of their hands now.

I have no idea what to tell them when I get back, he realized. It was the first time he'd accepted the possibility of his survival in all of this. *There's a definite fine line between telling what happened and letting Clea know what happened . . .* Tolerant as they were of him, her brothers wouldn't hesitate to take a brick to his skull if they felt he'd put their sweet little sister through any grief.

Oh, Good Lord. Martin will run away and join the smugglers as soon as he's of age. Lestrade closed his eyes, wincing at the very real possibility. *And poor Nicholas will follow along to make sure his brother's all right . . . .*

"Hsst!"

Faster than Lestrade would have thought possible before the trip underground, the troupe of old men pulled out an alarming collection of weapons. Knife blades, an ice pick, several small hand-guns with carved grips . . . .

A warble of a sleepy-sounding owl rippled through the undergrowth, and the men barely relaxed. Lestrade caught his grandfather's gesture and rolled behind a fallen menhir.

"There they are." Potier breathed his relief. He lowered his own ugly-looking revolver, a large chunk of metal that looked like it should be quelling riots on a Navy ship somewhere. "Kerbol, you had us worried. I thought the high road meant speed."

114

"I had to be more careful than I thought." Kerbol leaned forward, hands on his knees as he rested a bit. He wasn't much larger than Potier. The two could have been relatives (and knowing Brittany, probably were somewhere). He took a deep breath as Sein dipped to a pack and began a quick meal of cold meat and a bottle of water-cider. "Some of the gendarmes showed up not long after you left." He took the bottle gratefully and took a single swallow, breathing a moment. "They thought I was you, old man. I suppose I'm going to get even uglier when I get your age."

"Yes – six months." Potier snorted. "Go on."

"I passed myself off as you, and it worked, thank God. My sons-in-law weren't in the group." He wiped the sweat off his wrinkling forehead. "Kemper is calling a Wild Hunt." Kerbol said tightly. "I heard it with my own ears." He cupped them as if in alarm. "I stopped by my house after the gendarmes satisfied themselves that the Seagull was in appropriate mourning . . . My daughters' husbands like to talk."

"*That ass!*" Potier hissed. "That ass! I'll nail his better part from the highest oak! No one's going to be safe from a Wild Hunt! It's been too many years since the last!"

"When was the last?" Malvo blurted. "We were *much* younger!"

"Ivo Quimper kept his monstrous hunts going for years up until he 'died', but that wasn't in Brittany." Sein growled. "The last Hunt on this soil was back in the year your first grandson was born, was it not, Triaged?" The dead had no names.

Behind him, Lestrade was hurriedly throwing the thin oilskin off his shoulders. "We've got to warn the Tinkers!" He exclaimed. "They won't be able to defend themselves against that kind of onslaught!"

"How? I don't even know where they are – I only know where they were *last*."

"Padriac's folk keep to the higher ground close to the boar-thickets of the forest. If they hear the least thing suspicious, they'll jump deeper into the cover. But they won't be ready for those *dogs*." Lestrade whispered, appalled. "The *maer-kohz* have dogs, and they'll have rifles, and they'll be in disguise, so they don't have to worry about being identified!"

"They'll probably paint their horses too." Potier growled. He was very pale in the moonlight, but it was uncertain if it were from anger more than fear. "No one's going to give a description of a horse in the daytime if they see it at night, glowing from phosphorous."

"No . . . ." Lestrade combed his hair back with his fingers, thinking. "Quimper's going to wipe them out. The survivors won't report a crime." No good deed goes unpunished. "We've got to get to them first."

"That could be what Quimper *wants*," Potier pointed out. "You're falling into a trap."

"It's not a trap if you *know* it's a trap!" Lestrade shot back.

Kerbol grinned, poking Potier in the ribs. "Sounds like Surcouf right there."

"That's as much a blessing as it is a curse." Potier sighed. "Everyone gather 'round. We need a plan . . . and Sein, do you still have those finely woven canvas sacks about you? Good. You're going to need at least three of them when you go out again . . . ."

NOTES

1. Breton word for albino. *Gwen white*. Sein literally translated himself, turning a handicap into his personal identity.
2. The original Breton word that the newer word, *dolmen*, comes from. It means literally "*stone table*".

Ch XII – Running

"En nos e kemerer ar silioù, dale a ra vad a-wechoù."
Translation: *"At night one takes eels, it is worth waiting sometimes."*

Lestrade had no idea what was so important about those sacks, but *everyone* patted down their pockets and kits for more of the same. Mad-Mab Malvo had a sack that had begun its days as a finely woven pillowcase. This was hailed with glee but with no explanation as to why this was so much more preferable. It was all secreted away with Sein who was about to go off without the rest of the smugglers and do . . . *something.*

The detective was beginning to get that disturbingly familiar sensation . . . He had it quite often when his superiors at the Home Office were being mysterious. It was similar to, but not *quite* like when Sherlock Holmes had him on a case. Holmes's worst failing was never telling anyone else what he was doing . . . but he was never as bad as the Home Office, which had a bad habit of throwing up sacrificial policemen in sticky cases.

"You're going back underground with us." Potier gnawed on a strip of dry meat as he pondered out the smaller details. "How do we contact the Tinkers without you?"

"There's a signal they know me by." Lestrade cupped his hand over his mouth and demonstrated the rising-fall notes. Sein practiced until he was satisfied he had it down correctly. "End it with two short bursts," he cautioned. "That way they'll know you're working on my behalf. Otherwise, if they see you and not who they expect, they'll head deeper for cover."

"Do you think they have *any* weapons at all?" Sein wondered.

Lestrade sighed. "They can go to ground in a heartbeat. They just can't get away from dogs. Their own camp-dogs are used to protect, not attack."

"Ya, there's a difference," Sein said glumly. He hunkered down and drew a map in the thin layer of soft yellowware clay at their feet. "If they're as secretive as you say, then they're smart enough to go into hiding anyway – after they smuggled you to the Seagull." Lestrade grunted his agreement of that. "And up *here* – " He made a splotch in the dirt. " – would be the best place to go. It's higher ground, and you can see for miles around. The biggest problem is getting there in time."

"The Wild Hunts begin when the Moon hits the apex," Potier reminded them. "It's possible he *could* be starting early – pup always was more eager than his father, long may he rot in his grave. [1] Sein, we'll have to change our initial plans just a bit. What's the state of the old store rooms?"

Sein made a face, its awfulness stretched by the poor starlight. "It isn't *bad*, but we'll have to dip into the stocks." This sounded like an absolute last resort.

"Well, we *did* put them there to be used," Potier pointed out. "There's a chance we'll be followed to the earth, so that means we're about to operate past our usual procedures, men." He lifted his hand up, a small man rallying a force of hoarfrosted warriors. Lestrade didn't know which had the brightest gleam – the whiteness of their beards or the whiteness of their eyes. "We're bypassing the man system of the Midwife's Cavern," the old smuggler announced. "For now we take to the higher lands, but when you hear me yell at you to turn turtle, I expect you to do so!" He turned to the sack-laden Sein. "How much time before we see you again?"

"I shouldn't need more than a quarter-hour to get them," Sein answered mysteriously. Something about the *vagueness* of this casual response just lifted the hairs on Lestrade's neck. "Give me a half-hour each to get there and back up to you."

"Then we'll take the Serpent's Path and head up to the higher ground. Keep calling for the Tinkers in case they're choosing to hide in the lower grounds. We'll watch for them on our end." Old Potier lifted his hands, and shaped them rather like two horns on a bull. "Pincer-movements . . . we ought to be able to find them soon enough."

"Finding them will be the *simple* part of this!" Kerbol muttered.

"Simple doesn't always mean difficult," Loic patted him on the back.

"No, it just means *simple*." Kerbol sniffed. "*Dysentery* is simple . . . Let's get going then."

They walked slowly from the gleaming little pool fed by the underground brook. Lestrade was surprised to feel a slight pang in its wake, and he wondered what about the experience he missed. He'd never looked backwards on his way out of an underground passage before.

After several hours below the earth, traveling above felt a little . . . *peculiar*. Almost . . . exposed and vulnerable. Lestrade's experience had been limited to dark, wholly *man-made* tunnels in claustrophobic mine-shafts until this point. No matter what happened, one never completely forgot that particular world of tin and coal had been the creation of Man. Man was the *intruder* in these dark, lightless pits. Under *those* earths, superstition had its place. For their own sanity, the miners left bits of their precious food out for the Knockers, [2] or small carved gifts for the saints that loaned their names.

Stone caverns were *different*. They were convenient to Man, but not shaped by his hand or *for* his hand. There was less of a sensation of trespass in that quiet place. Almost a feeling of a guest invited to stay a bit before moving on . . . but the vastness of its rooms were unsettling, to say the least. Human architects didn't know how to make such shapes or sizes without their collapse. That it had happened due to the inexorable drip of water against stone made it all the more humbling.

Caverns measureless to man . . . .

The quote was a fragment, a distillation of thought to the detective. He was fully aware of his limitations in education. Sherlock Holmes's many disparaging comments about his intelligence had a basis in fact and as much as it galled, it would never occur to Lestrade to complain about the taunts. As un-systemic as Holmes's education was, Lestrade's had been much worse, the product of a rootless lifestyle that had to justify each inch of space in storage. Books, rigid and unyielding, were luxuries as much as education in a classroom.

His brothers had been allowed those luxuries. What was left for the third and youngest anyway, if not the generosity of his elders? It wasn't as though there was much future awaiting the youngest-born. Armoricus would have inherited family's means had he lived. Paul would have picked it up in Armoricus' stead if he *hadn't* wound up in a prison for half-wits. The least son, the *tantony* . . . the smallest of the small in all respects, had no rights whatsoever. It was Lestrade's dark amazement that they *hadn't* named him after Saint Anthony, patron of the least and the forgotten.

They walked, single-file on the forested path with every third person carrying the dark lanterns tinted red. Large stone bubbles rested in the earth below their trod, secret voids that were shaped without particular plan, and their rupture from cavern to sinkhole was just as mysterious. No one knew what could prick those bubbles.

The movement gradually dried the underground river from their clothing and cooled the sweat as it formed on their faces. Once in a great while, someone would lift their lantern slightly, briefly casting a spill of light onto a wildly disordered word of jumbled path and knotted bush underneath a crazy-quilt world of tree and branch. Everything was black. Green-black, brown-black, or grey-black. Birds rustled in the branches over their head, disturbed by the light as it slipped through their roosts. Owls were calling in random pattern. The hunting cries chilled the air faster than ice. Ploudaniel would mutter "*Diwall!*" (Careful!) At least once every fifty paces.

Lestrade had not planned on re-entering the forest, especially so soon after his departure. But it *felt* the same in the night as it did in the day. It smelled of living roots and crumbling rock and damp carpets of moss, but other than sight and scent and sound there was nothing his mind was truly accustomed to other than the presence of the men with him.

The path wound upward before it straightened briefly three times, each time marking an upward scaling against an unyielding wall of solid rock. Kerbol, leading the way, stopped so quickly they had to struggle not to fall into him.

"Well?" Potier whispered impatiently.

"Something's frightened up a herd of deer," Kerbol answered just as quietly. "Over on the other side of the forest ridge."

They all fell silent then, save the blood that pounded in their ears and vibrated behind their ribs. Very faintly, dry sticks cracked with high, sharp, short sounds.

"They're in the pines," Malvo had nothing reckless about his features or his voice at that moment. "Are they the Tinkers?"

"They don't travel at night unless they're forced to it." Lestrade whispered softly.

"We don't know if it's friend or foe *yet*." Kerbol pointed out. "Can't be more than a quarter-mile away. But it can't be Kemper." He made a strange, thoughtful sound as he gnawed on his bottom lip. "Or can it? *Gouelanig-kohz* . . . How does he run the Hunt?"

Potier sighed softly. "I don't know," he confessed. "He hasn't had one in these lands in years, and I was never land-locked like I am now."

"He'll circle the forest." Lestrade spoke in a barely audible voice. The old men turned. His head was turned down slightly, dark eyes inward on memory. "All the way around first. That's how he did it when we were children."

"Looking for any leftovers and scraps," Ploudaniel nodded. "They'll be swept up before the Hunt truly begins."

"Once he's circled, the hot-nosed dogs will be given lead." Lestrade swallowed dryly. He was clutching his forehead as if in pain, the memories pulling all the buried anguish out to the fore. "They'll go for the strongest scent. It's the cold-nosed dogs he'll keep with him to the last. They'll be running through the forest in a loose pack . . . They'll be heading for higher ground, driving the prey upwards. Once the dogs get the quarry at the highest point, they'll chase them back down right into the mouth of the hunters."

"A *mechanical* approach." Potier murmured, stroking his beard. Lestrade realized for the first time (and with no small sense of shock) that his own habit of speaking slowly and deliberately when he was thinking hard made him sound like his grandfather. "That could be to our advantage . . . ." His voice trailed off as the thoughts overwhelmed him. "Mechanical thinkers do not always react quickly to a sudden change in what their predictions say will happen . . . ."

"Then what do you suggest?" Loic asked softly. His partner Winoc waited in the sidelines, content with holding the lantern and waiting for orders.

"We are running." Potier said simply. "As long as it is under our direction, we cannot truly be called the prey, *nann*?" His grin was tight and fierce under his beard, and Lestrade had another sense of shock – a worse one this time.

His grandfather *ached* for revenge against the Quimpers for what they did to his daughter.

Somehow, the Seagull would have a recounting of some sort tonight.

Triged Potier saw his grandson catch him in his thoughts. In the dirty lamp-light they met each other's eyes, neither apologizing. Potier nodded very gently, the rising wind ruffling the long hairs of his heard.

And finally, Lestrade nodded too.

For a charming week we wandered up the valley of the Rhone, and then, branching off at Leuk, we made our way over the Gemmi Pass, still deep in snow, and so, by way of Interlaken, to Meiringen. It was a lovely trip, the dainty green of the spring below, the virgin white of the winter above, but it was clear to me that never for one instant did Holmes forget the shadow which lay across him. In the homely Alpine villages or in the lonely mountain passes, I could still tell by his quick glancing eyes and his sharp scrutiny of every face that passed us, that he was well convinced that, walk where we would, we could not walk ourselves clear of the danger which was dogging our footsteps.

– Dr. John H. Watson
"The Final Problem"

NOTES

1. The Breton concept of Hell is an unresolved afterlife, quite gloomy and depressing.

2. *Knockers* were earth-spirits who aided the Cornish miners . . . if they were polite and never swore in their presence. A miner must be good and generous and polite and helpful. Only then would the Knockers let the miners know where the profitable seams of ore rested in the earth. Many people believe the stories of the Knockers are distilled folk-memory of ghosts or the earliest race of Neolithic miners who plumbed the depths for the metals they so badly needed. Their name is from their method of communicating, which was to "knock" on the walls of the mine to show where the seams were.

Chapter XIII – Hunting

The Dog is the servant of man, but the wolf is his master.
– French Proverb

The land was no stranger to men who acted like wolves.

It was in 1440 that the peninsula erupted in horror to learn a nobleman with ties to the Royal throne had been luring over two-hundred children from the peasantry and bathing in their blood. Gilles the Marshall, who claimed to become a werewolf, had believed a prophecy that would retire him to an Abbey when his years had ended.

Perhaps Gilles had took this to mean to do whatever he wanted so long as he retired to the priesthood. But when the arresting officer was shown to have the last name of L'abbe, he blanched. It was later that he sought to escape his execution by joining the Carmelites.

And perhaps he would have succeeded. Despite the uproar, he was connected by royal blood to the highest men in the land, and had fought long and hard against the English. But he insulted his peers when he entered the courtroom clad in white to pronounce his new-found spiritual purity . . . and about his waist he wore a belt of ermine, which only the feudal lords had the right to.

In his snow-white clothing and his carefully trimmed black beard, he resembled the Ermine's Spot with his whole being. But it was his beard that would be remembered, for it was so black it appeared to be blue, and stories of the monster Blue-Beard would be passed down for generations, fact becoming myth long after the executed predator's remains were burned to ash and scattered on the wind.

Ivo Quimper had confessed the story had been a powerful impact upon him as a boy. Wolves were his favourite beast, and so he hunted them every chance he had, even if he had to travel abroad to do so. He was a strong, powerful man, famous for his ability to command his dogs, and he knew how to make people fear.

For his son's part, Jethro admitted the story interesting and memorable, but the hunt itself was better than listening to some long-dead wretch who wept when finally caught.

"I *know* this is just paint and phosphorous, but it still gives me a shudder to see it," Grioux confessed, faint distaste in his voice as he watched the last of the shaggy pelts pile up on the selected horses and dogs.

Jethro Quimper nodded agreeably as he tapped a new cigarette into its silver holder. *That* would have to be left behind or hidden away once they started. "It's taken us quite a few years to perfect the technique," he pointed out. "As caustic as phosphorous is, we can't really keep it directly on the hides of the animals . . . Once I started painting loose skins and piling that on . . . Well, one might say it was even more effective."

Grioux had to agree. The dogs had stopped being *dogs*. Under the shields of glowing skins and pelts they were some sort of monster out of a colder, more primitive time. Half the animals were so well rubbed with soot they might as well be the blackness between the starlight. With only the whites of their eyes and teeth shining, they allowed the human eye to see movement, but no defining shape from which to draw comfort. The horses were no less intimidating. Quimper had colored them along the same plans, half-black, half-glowing with phosphorous-tinted pelts.

The riders and hunters finished it off. Oiled soot made them dark as the dogs, but the phosphorus barely tinted their bodies in single long, thin stripes – an implication of exposed skeletal structure that was something purely nightmarish. Wolfskin headdresses were only tipped by teeth and empty eye-holes.

"I know what I'm looking at," the little interrogator murmured, "but I'm still taken aback."

Quimper openly grinned. "A high compliment," he answered.

Grioux puffed a sigh into the cool dusk. Being forced to do without his cane always put him in a prickly mood. "What is the goal, Jethro? Is it to be just hunting L'estrade down, or punishing those who helped him?"

"Ha." Quimper pulled hard at the smoke entering his lungs. "A nice question, that. They are one and the same. L'estrade doesn't know the land well enough to have escaped us without help."

"The Tinkers. They *had* to have known something." Grioux was still disgruntled at the hindsight. "But I don't know how they could have hidden him."

Quimper had been wondering that himself. It did occur to his more-flexible mind that there might be a difference in this tribe between the cowardice of running, and the cleverness of stealth. "We'll have time to ask them, *nann*?" Quimper shrugged. "Can you pick out the leader of the troupe?"

"Easily. He had no teeth to speak of, and smoked a stone pipe. His hair looked like it belonged on a rain-soaked sheep that was in wont of shearing."

Quimper made a moue of distaste. "There'll be no hiding *him* in a crowd," he decided. "Has everyone arrived yet?"

124

Grioux overlooked his impatience. The Hunt couldn't begin until the dusk deepened a bit further. "I believe so. At least, we have the riders for the horses."

"Good." Quimper suddenly gnawed on the stem of his silver holder. "No one dies without permission," he said in a low voice. "And we're going to have to be as quick as we are clever. L'estrade doesn't even know the value of the information he has – He's a postman who can't read. If we're to find out who was helping Padderzhon, we need the names and faces of who he has in his head."

"Which has me puzzled." Grioux admitted. "Why can't we just have one of our men check the rosters of who was on duty for that case?"

"Because the names aren't matching up." Quimper slammed his gloved hand against the fence-post. "Not all of the men working for Scotland Yard that night actually *belonged* to Scotland Yard. Padderzhon had his own men there – his own version of spies! Names would be better if they were genuine – which I doubt – but it's the descriptions of the men on that raid we have to have!" [1]

Inspector Patterson never saw it coming. One moment he was walking to work in a pea-souper of a spring fog – the next, a large square hand filled his vision. The leather-hard man had a close-range view of some very familiar cufflinks and imported cologne before his back slammed against the rough brick-work of a building that formed a normally well-lit alleyway.

"All right, you dunce!" Tobias Gregson managed to be completely threatening without touching Patterson again. To his side, Bradstreet was scowling like a drumhead, arms folded over his chest. "Just how much of that story you gave the C.I. was a lie, and how much of it was an untruth?"

Patterson didn't bother with pretense. "Are you interrogating me in public?" he shot back, coldly and calmly.

No denial. Gregson and Bradstreet traded a significant look. "One of our men is out there, behind the lines of your Professor's army." Gregson bent forward and his blunt forefinger rested, ever so gently, over Patterson's breast-bone. "You bollixed this raid up, Patterson. You didn't factor for human error, and you most certainly did not account for what anyone else was saying. Even Sherlock Holmes didn't put himself above our statements." [2]

"And speaking of, where is the Great Detective?" Bradstreet asked in tones of clear ice. "He and Watson are nowhere to be found in London. The fire at Baker Street – you knew what that meant, didn't you?"

"Are you going to keep this up where anyone can hear us?" Patterson hissed, furious with fear and frustration. His light blue eyes were watery and sleepless-red in the thick grey fog. "It isn't safe!"

"And it's any safer at the Yard where someone can overhear us in the comfort under a roof with a hot teacup in their hands?" Gregson wanted to know. "Someone spies on *us*, man, they'll have to *work* a bit for it."

"I'd invite you to my house to continue this conversation," Bradstreet smiled like a shark under his mustache, "but my wife wouldn't be happy to see *you* much, Patterson. Did I ever mention her father was "Basilisk" Roane? You remember him from the old days, I'm sure . . . ."

Patterson gnashed his teeth. "Look here, you two! None of this was supposed to happen! Not any of it!"

"I'm *shocked*." Gregson said in his most infuriating drawl. It really was maddening. He often used it to provoke the reaction he desired from criminal or inferior. Patterson flushed from the tops of his collar to the roots of his scalp, but Gregson wasn't finished with him. "Kept your cards too close to your chest, you did! We were supposed to mop up what was going to be the Professor's main gang – only he never made it to the ship, did he? He didn't trust *anyone*, so he probably switched direction en route without telling anybody – kept his secret assistant with him for some protection, but that was it. In the meantime, you and your friends were controlling the raid and you'd convinced our Chief Inspector we didn't need anyone posted outside of the North Sea."

"Stop." Patterson was quite pale, but he lifted his hands up. His attackers subsided but they never dropped their angry gaze from him. "I worked with information that was good when I had it. I didn't know the Professor's plans had changed." He took a deep breath, still angry and in control of himself, but also in a mood to unburden. "It had to be that way. There was no choice in the matter. Some of my informants had family inside the Professor's gang. If we worked too deeply, it would make their role obvious. They would have died."

"What about us?" Bradstreet did not raise his voice, but it pushed through a fence of his clenched teeth. "What about the Yard, Patterson? We have families too! Lestrade has two little 'uns, Cooper is the main wage-holder for his family – You know Cooper, don't you? His father was killed by one of the Professor's gang back in the '70's . . . and Forbes? He supports a sick brother entirely on his pay. Just because we vow to serve doesn't mean we're your sacrifices!"

"*He had to be stopped*!" Patterson blurted, and it was so desperate and consuming the others stopped to stare at him. "My God! Moriarty had to be stopped! He's been in operation for decades – *Decades!* This was the first time we'd ever been in a position to stop him!"

"So now what?" Bradstreet shot in while Gregson remained silent. "Lestrade's missing. We're pretending he's dead, when in truth there's only a chance he's still alive."

"There's more of the Professor's men in the Mainland of France than there is on the side of the Channel." Patterson sighed. "And these partners aren't fond of each other. There's only two crime lords that hold any sway on the western side, and that's Quimper and his collaborator, Grioux."

"And you think they won't work together if it means they can salvage their *status quo*?" Gregson asked the question very very quietly. "Where are Holmes and Watson, Patterson?"

Patterson took a deep breath. "They've fled England."

"You lie!" Bradstreet choked

"I'm serious! Moriarty . . . He's *obsessed* with stopping Mr. Holmes. Holmes is the only one who's been able to crack into his network and break it! Holmes was supposed to . . . to cause a sort of distraction, as it were, and get as far away from us as possible so the Professor would be forced to divide his attention."

"Do *not* tell me Watson is involved." Gregson said in a terrible voice. "Do *not* tell me Sherlock Holmes would be selfish enough to take an expectant father on a death-trip and leave his expecting wife behind."

Patterson, if possible, turned even paler. "I don't think Mr. Holmes knew about that."

Bradstreet glanced once in each direction, then took a single step. His large hands picked up the other man – who rivaled him in size in all ways – and carefully smashed his spine against the rough bricks. Patterson choked as the air was forced painfully out of his lungs.

"Talk." Bradstreet commanded. "You can have me arrested for insubordination, and you can take my badge for not obeying my superiors, but you will not have me an accessory to murder!"

"My . . . my *orders* were to keep Mr. Holmes as safe as I could," Patterson snapped. He was far from defeated. He didn't seem to understand what he'd even done. "He has connections . . . friends and allies . . . in high places . . . and yet no one of any rank knows London's crime as well as he does. He had to be kept alive, don't you see?"

"So you hinted to him you had affairs well in hand, but he should serve his country by making tracks?" Bradstreet paused only to swallow bile. "Did you plant the idea of Watson in his head, Patterson? Or was that the idea of your precious superiors?"

Patterson shook his head firmly. "The plan gave Watson high odds. He's a perfect bodyguard: Loyal, follows orders, trained in the military, a dead-shot with medical skills for emergency situations! Look, you think of the case records! Watson is the reason why Holmes is even alive today!"

"Holmes would do nothing – *Nothing!* – to jeopardize Watson." Gregson joined in the pushing of Patterson against the slimy bricks. It would be hard to say who was the more frightening: The naturally intimidating Gregson, or the usually gentle and gruff Bradstreet who now looked like a fire-eyed griffon. "How is it Holmes didn't know of Watson's good news?"

Patterson shrugged. He was calm now. His lack of emotion was in his acceptance of the facts themselves. "Holmes was in France until he returned. It's a long distance. Wires get lost."

"My . . . God." Bradstreet said in wonder. "Patterson, you don't know what you've done."

It was sheer luck Lestrade's call was heard. They broke out of the clearing to find the Tinkers collected at the base of a small brook that was rather noisy. The dogs, trained to a high pitch, vanished into the darkness at a single word. If someone gave the right command, they would leap out and block the intruders from their owners with their own bodies.

"*Galvin!*" A large, hair-clad old man lifted a yard-long arm and waved. "I thought we'd left you in the lowlands!"

Lestrade smiled wearily as the bedraggled party tromped through the small field of grasses and forage. Long weeds whistled around their trousers, and not a few tried to hang on with their thorns. "We're returning the favour, I fear," he answered back in the *Shelta*. "Those parties I asked you to keep an eye out for . . . They're starting up a Hunt, and no one will be safe tonight."

Several of the children, who had emerged as soon as they recognized Lestrade, suddenly ran back to the wagons.

Winoc abruptly whirled, nearly colliding into Ploudaniel. "That's Sein!" He exclaimed to a signal no one else had heard.

"Go get him," Potier instructed. He moved to the side to make room and extended his hand to the old Gipsy again.

Padriac Dooley's eyes were dark under their woolly roof. He sucked on his pipe loudly. "This could be difficult," he said with great under-estimation. "We do not have the coffee to erase your smell this time."

"It's not as simple as coffee, Mr. Dooley . . . ." Lestrade closed his eyes for a moment. "They're looking for everyone. You're all in danger."

"We have a safe place." Potier took up the cue as the old Irishman's brows beetled together. "Please, come with us where the dogs and their gunmen cannot go."

Old Dooley rattled a question off to Lestrade. Lestrade answered softly but firmly in the same language. Dooley nodded slowly, turning his stooped-over back to face his clan.

Potier considered that these Tinkers were too far used to hardship to act like regular humans. They did not scream or protest or fuss or do any of the other things people were expected to do when their fears overrode their common sense. As one they filtered each to their possessions and picked up what they could easily carry.

"Can you trust him?" Lestrade asked Dooley. "This is my grandfather. His men will show you where to go to ground."

"What about the horses?" Dooley asked wistfully, but without much hope.

Behind them, a chuckle. They turned to see Sein walking forward. "Horses? How many?" He grinned. In his arms he carried large, bulging sacks. "Shouldn't be a problem, *nann*?"

Potier laughed. It was a surprisingly worrisome sound. "Sir, get your people ready and follow this man. My grandson and I will create a diversion to buy you some time."

Dooley nodded and they clasped hands again. "*Nus a dhabjon dhuilsha.*" They parted quickly.

"Come." Potier tugged Lestrade's forearm, his own full of Sein's mysterious sacks. Lestrade followed despite a growing sense of worry. The two men got their way back across the field but Potier cut downward. Loic was waiting for them inside the forest.

"I took a 'glass to the bottomlands." The man offered. In a group of oldsters, he was probably the youngest at the age of three-and-fifty. "There's movement in the outskirts. Glowing. I caught a bit of torchlight but I didn't look too long."

"Ya, don't burn your night-eyes." Potier approved. "What's your recommendation?"

"Take the higher path," Loic suggested. "It won't take you as long to catch up with us."

"My thoughts exactly. And remind me to give Sein a bonus." Potier almost giggled as he held up the sacks. Loic recoiled as if he'd been offered the kiss of a venomous slug. "What do you think, *Mab*?" He asked his grandson. "A nice gift for our fine Lord Kemper?"

One look at the writhing bundles Sein had brought back and Lestrade felt a strong urge to leap for higher ground. "You brought *pine caterpillars* with us?" He felt the threat of hyperventilation against his lungs. It was all he could do not to start screaming. "*Tad-kohz*, have you gone mad?"

"It's possible." The old man said cheerfully. "But, you *will* note I kept them under tight wraps the whole time."

"That's hardly any sort of reassurance!" His grandson broke into an icy sweat at the thought of what they were traveling with. Possibilities danced in his mind in full colour and vivid detail. Lengthy hospital stays and occasional funerals were the inevitable consequence of the things – and didn't he know it!

Loic made a weary sound. In the poor light he was all stick-lines, like a stork afraid to fly. "*I* don't blame you, *Mab*," he told the detective. "I lost a Guernsey Golden [3] to those things one year – and *before* I'd finished paying for her, mind you."

"Well, let's not get them stirred up any further." Potier noted. "It's wretchedly hard to find them this early in the year. If it weren't for those small pockets of warmer weather on the other side of the ridge, we wouldn't have any at all." He failed to notice the expression on his grandson's pale face. "Let's head to the higher earth, Geoffrey."

NOTES

1. Victorians had a great skill in verbal descriptions that we ironically have lost.
2. Holmes does not search the body for himself in the Lauriston Gardens, taking Lestrade in his word that there was no mark to be found on the dead man. Had he been particularly suspicious or contemptuous, he would have certainly done so.
3. A goat native to Guernsey . . . nearly driven extinct, it is beginning to recover in our days.

Chapter XIV – Pine Caterpillars

"Anduriñ so red, med karoud n'eo ket"
(*To endure is obligatory, but to like is not*)

Quimper's face set in a grin as he lifted his gun. The rounded hoops of the painted caravans shone in the light of brilliant campfires, but even as he thought there was something wrong, a dog barked.

A *single* dog – not one of his own. It had to be a Tinker's dog.

Not right, Quimper thought. *There's never just one dog . . . .*

"They're gone, sir!" Craddock announced sharply from the other side of the painted wagon. "There's no trace of them anywhere!"

The clearing was empty.

"Where . . . where *could* they go?" Griox wondered under his breath. He paced his horse out the milling knot of fellow cultists with a scowl to Quimper's side. Sweat runneled marks down his painted face like ghastly tears.

"Craddock!" Quimper snapped. "I know I heard a dog somewhere! You set your pack after it! Grioux – circle the dogs around the clearing! As soon as they pick up a scent, follow them. They've caught wind of us somehow, and they're trying to get away." Quimper gripped his reins tightly. "We didn't take them by surprise. They knew we were coming."

"That settles it," Craddock grunted.

"Yes." Quimper smiled taut as a bowstring. "They *had* to have helped L'estrade. If that's the case, he could still be with them!"

"What will you be doing, sir?" One of the little town *maers*, loyal and almost intelligent, wondered. Of the twelve men on the Hunt besides Quimper and his men, he was the only one who asked questions. It saved time.

"I'm going to double back." Quimper retorted, his quick mind already on probabilities. "There's a chance the Tinkers are clever enough to play the *louarn* – we'll see if there are any worthy of the title!" [1]

"Heh-heh-heh! Here they come."

Triaged's low and darkly amused observation, made from a good thirty feet straight up in the shelter of a knotted wolf tree [2] that stank of tannic acids, was met with the silent doubt it deserved.

After setting the traps, Potier had scurried up the ancient oak by the simple matter of *walking* up the lowest branches that scraped the ground like a ladder. It had not yet leafed its full green for the spring, but Lestrade, who was truly in it for the entire length of this mess, raced up the branch after the old man without thinking.

When it came to people like Potier, thinking was a waste of time.

Lestrade was once again glad he was small enough for the unique demands of survival in this situation. He stretched flat on a gently curving branch, not unlike the way a large cat would enjoy the day, and rested his chin on the backs of his hands as tiny bits of fire and phosphorous glittered and flickered through the forest path.

Having just watched a tiny brigade of grizzled old smugglers make an entire clan of Tinkers vanish underground with their dogs and horses – the horses had been quite a trick worthy of their own category – Lestrade decided he was *probably* up for whatever happened next.

The pistol at his side was just further reassurance . . . .

A dog barked, once. Lestrade felt the weirdly silent pack only added to the visual horror of what they were – an excuse for anarchy and murder was bad enough on its own.

He probably had his dogs muted, the little detective thought. As always, he wasn't fond of dogs, but he hated the idea of torture, and that was about as callous as it got. He remembered how Paul would be ordered to not speak at him for days on end. Only Armoricus had the right to talk to him, as if he was worthy of the honour.

Just one more reason why Lestrade had been glad to not have the attention of the Lord's son. That came all too soon when they grew older and more territorial.

The glow stretched further out. The dogs broke up, split across the ridge. The sound of their eager panting wetted the night air. It made Lestrade shiver uncontrollably. Without their ability to bay, they sounded like something that had never belonged on the earth. Sticks broke under their paws. Horses trotted, heavier and slower but much, much stronger, getting closer and closer. The glow of their costumes was utterly demoralizing. Lestrade knew what he was looking at, but it was still . . . he couldn't help his reaction. It was simply . . . *wrong.* Wrong on an instinctive level.

Did that wretch Stapleton ever come across someone's drunken story about the Wild Hunt over here? There was no way of knowing. Stapleton was dead with his secrets, drowned in the trap of his own making. Another death Lestrade would not have permitted had he allowed. After seeing what the monster had done to his own wife, he had shown himself to be as terrible as anything Quimper could have conjured up. Lestrade had wanted so badly to see the man before a jury and its judgment, with the noose no less than three weeks after verdict. Dying alone in a mire, drowning by inches in the darkness was not how anyone should have died . . .

The dogs found their trail. A high-pitched whine. The pack flooded through the undergrowth, straight as an arrow down the trod, aiming to the base of their tree.

Lestrade flinched and turned away from the carnage resultant. The dogs had raced *straight over* the path of poisonous insects. Within seconds they were yelping in agony. He wasn't fond of dogs, but he hated the idea of one of the animals was suffering simply because it was doing what it was supposed to do.

Pine caterpillars (no matter what their name) were about two inches long, brown, hairy and plentiful in the nests that weren't discovered and burnt out by worried fathers in the spring. It would be inaccurate to say they "bit" or "stung" – the effect upon contact was actually a severe chemical burn – and small animals could easily die from them.

But the dogs had only gotten the *light* dose. The trip-wired sacks of bulging, living toxins were triggered by the horses, and down they went upon the riders. In the awful clarity of the moon-drenched night, Lestrade saw a clot of the vile things fall right down the shirt-front of a man clad in ragged skins.

"Goodness," the Seagull sniffed. "A man shouldn't give such a high pitch when screaming. It's not the *least* bit manly."

Oh, my word . . . .

Despite that said high pitch, Lestrade recognized the owner as his soft-spoken tormentor by the silo. "That's Kemper's partner, *Tad-kohz!*" He hissed. "'*Illiz' Grioux!*'"

"Mr. Church?" Potier didn't look the least bit impressed. "Well . . . So it is," he noted as the man flung himself off his saddle, dancing like demons were clawing over his body, and screaming like the possessed. "I didn't recognize him without his applewood stick."

Lestrade struggled to swallow. "Is that going to kill him?"

Potier looked surprised in the moonlight. "That matters to you, *bihan?*"

Lestrade sighed. "*Tad-kohz* . . . I am a policeman. Torture was made illegal in England quite some time ago, and I'm glad for it."

"You're right . . . It isn't as if he's the one I really want." Potier agreed. On the ground, pure chaos was not only erupting, it was *multiplying* as the sky rained defensive, near-sighted poisonous insects. Although they were well out of the range of fire, the men tucked their collars up as they scurried down the other side of the oak.

"He probably won't die," Potier answered the burning question after they'd gotten a few hundred yards of running out of their way. The yelps, screams and outright swearing in a conglomeration of languages mercifully died in their wake. "But let me tell you, he won't be pleasant to

133

live with for a while!" The old villain chuckled beneath his beard, his large, dark eyes shining like a nocturnal creature's. "I once fell into a ball of those things . . . When I finally got out of the hospital, I was willing to rip my own arms out of their sockets to find some sort of relief. And it makes you very irritable," he warned. "It could be because of the scarring."

"*Tad-kohz*, at this point this is all moot," Lestrade panted as they kept running, "but you need to take better care of yourself!"

"I saved my youth for my old age, *Mab*." Potier skipped nimbly over a fallen log, noting his grandson did a fine job with keeping up. "Have you thought of joining the family business? You'd be quite good at it."

"Much as my sons would revere me . . . ." Lestrade slowed slightly. He was fast outrunning his ability to see in the path. "I would have to say no, Grandfather."

"The offer stands." Potier promised – it sounded threatening to the other man. Without warning, the cave they had been searching for loomed up. It was small, like a bee skep or rounded bake oven, girdled with thorny bushes and trees.

Inside it was more like an Esquimaux's igloo, the second chamber being much deeper and higher into the earth. After the brisk night air, the stillness of the little cave was uncomfortably warm and close. Hard-packed earth was at their feet instead of hard rock. It gave a musty smell, and a sense that wild animals occasionally used it.

But above their heads the slightest slip of an opening existed in the rock – a bolt-hole, long and lean. Moonlight filtered through at an angle, sliding pale grey paint across their faces. A bat flitted over their heads, lit on the rock and crawled out, awkward without the use of its wings.

"We'll have to . . . wait here . . . a bit," Potier paused for a moment, equalizing his breathing. He pulled a flask of watered-down cider from his jacket and handed it to his grandson for the first sip. "I want the moon . . . to cross over *there* – " He pointed with a nod to a spur of rock on the other side of the round chamber. " – before we head out."

"Fair . . . enough." Lestrade handed the flask back and wiped his forehead with his sleeve. "What is this place? It's like some sort of mad monk's cell?"

"A mad monk is redundant grammar." Potier sounded as though he spoke from experience. "But yes . . . we think it was used to mark the calendars. On the longest day of the year, the shortest, and on the quarter and cross-quarter days, the sunlight settles on notches cut into the rock."

"Huh." Lestrade wondered why they didn't just watch the stars like everyone else, but shrugged to himself. Humans weren't exactly the easiest things to understand.

They rested in quiet for several minutes. Their warming bodies curled slow plumes of steam into the moonlight, and the fine motes of dust their passage had stirred. Potier listened as his grandson's breathing calmed, and finally evened out.

"Can you tell me about my grandsons?"

Lestrade felt his throat swell up at the proud old man's quiet request.

"We named them from their birthdays," he said slowly. "Martin was born on November 11th, the old date, and Nicholas, the following year at December 6th. I think you'd like both of them. Nicholas has . . . ." Lestrade, as always, stumbled at the attempt to describe his second son. "He's possessed of a strange sort of luck," he said at last. "Sailor's luck."

"St. Nicholas was patron of sailors," Triaged pointed out.

"True, but . . . ." Lestrade heard himself laugh, self-conscious. "He nearly died at birth. His mother nearly died. I really did think I would be burying them both in the churchyard . . . but they pulled through and they haven't had any trouble since then. Nicholas takes after his father-in-law . . . Big as a house, I swear. For a long time he didn't seem to grow, but honestly, I think he was just growing *on the inside*, because this past year he's getting as big as his older brother. Unlike anyone in our family, the boy doesn't worry about anything! I've never seen anything like it."

Potier grinned. It was somehow conveyed in the darkness. "And Martin?"

"Martin is a Potier." Lestrade didn't know why he was embarrassed to say it, except that the family never would win any prizes in beauty. "He . . . *Tad-kohz*, he can't sleep when it's a MoonCurser's night. He looks like me, mostly, but he has his mother's gorgeous lapis eyes. I've never seen anything like the Cheatham eyes. They're shaped like mine, but they're coloured like Clea's. He even has the thin stripes of gold within them."

"Well, once in a while, there's a Potier in the family that's easy to look at." The Seagull put his back to the wall comfortably and stretched his legs out. "I would like to see them someday."

The comfortable silence drifted by degrees to darker waters.

"How is *Mam*?" Lestrade made his voice sound like he didn't care one way or the other.

"Still with your father." Potier answered similarly, as if he didn't care one way or the other about his son-in-law. "Her hands hurt her at times. Marcus assists her." There was another long silence. "Do not seek them."

"I wouldn't dream of it."

Potier sighed. "This sad world," he judged. "We are often in the hells of our own making. I believe that."

"Then I hope that will suffice." Lestrade answered softly. He was too tired and, he suspected, too old to devote any portion of his life on resentment against his own family. Quite willingly he felt his eyes grow heavy, and he shut them in sleep.

NOTES

1. The red fox of Europe, which likes to double back on its own trail, confusing the less skilled or suspicious dogs.
2. An oak too old and twisted to be harvested for lumber. Murderers were often executed on them.

Chapter XV – Soldier On

The moon had risen to its highest point when Potier nudged his grandson awake. Lestrade stirred quickly, his dark eyes large and round in the near-perfect darkness. Potier was rising slowly to his feet, the tiny dark lanterns clinking at his waist.

"Time," he whispered softly.

Lestrade stretched cautiously to make sure everything was still in an ignorable state of complaint, and stood, making certain the candle stubs, his loaned pistol, and his field kit were still in his pockets.

While Potier checked his own materials, Lestrade spent a few moments getting familiar with the French double-action revolver. It was made for dark work. A blue patina mixed with the brown on the metal, throwing off its ability to be seen in poor light. He didn't like that it was only a five shot, but the walnut grip was tight and firm, and fit easily enough in his hand.

Just make certain whatever you do will be solved in five shots or less, he sighed to himself.

Potier grinned at him as he passed over an extra handful of bullets. "Are we ready then?"

"Ready enough," his grandson answered. "Where to?"

"We'll be meeting up with your friends underground through a *kev* we call, the '*Kev* of the Dolmen'." Potier went to the back of the little cave where a small stockpile of supplies rested, and lifted a woven splint basket up, checked whatever contents were inside it, and tucked his own gear bag inside its confines. With a quick click of buckles he shrugged it on, satisfied with its weight. "As long as we step lively, it shouldn't take us too long to get there . . . Then of course, there's the chance Kemper will poke his aristocratic nose in our humble affairs." He made a considering stroke of his beard and reached into a deep crevice, pulling out two long alpenstocks with leather loops on the top instead of a knob.

Lestrade swallowed hard and looped the stick through his left wrist. It fit perfectly. Potier had cut them for men of his own size. They came just to the ear. "If you get yourself killed – " he began.

"Not my intention, *Mab*," A large hand clapped his shoulder. "There are many more funerals I wish to attend besides his."

That was cool comfort, but at least Lestrade could understand it. "We can't let him get hold of the Dooleys," he repeated. "They have no one to speak for them. If that monster hurts or kills them, there's nothing they can do."

"I understand completely." Potier said quietly. "Monster indeed."

Swiss Alps:

The lamplight was warm but weak inside the confines of the Tudor-styled chaplet. Dr. Watson weakened it even further by gently lowering the wick inside the globe, until the flame was all but a single ember. It was one of his many skills – to know exactly how far to manipulate an instrument, and go no further. And yet, he never thought of his particular delicacy, or even saw himself as being remarkable in any way.

He had never *planned* to be remarkable. That was the thing.

The doctor managed to push away from the small writing desk without making a sound. He did not pick up the lamp, not just yet. His body cast a weird shadow against the whitewashed walls, bent over and stooped, although he himself was still as erect as a day in formation.

In a few months he would be just a year shy of his fortieth year. No grey touched his temples yet. His hair and mustache was still thick and dark as ever. But his desert-tanned skin was a shade paler than normal, and his brown eyes cast thoughtfully at all corners, crannies, and windows of the small rental cottage.

He would feel safer if only he could find darker shirts, but getting a change of clothing after Canterbury had been met with erratic results. Holmes only cared about clean collars and cuffs, but Watson disliked having to buy his dry goods blind. His bad shoulder ached often in this damp air, and the wound chafed against stitching seams his tailor knew to circumvent. A pair of braces and sleeve garters were helping him make do, but he worried that the small annoyance would turn to a fatal moment of distraction.

Not that anything would get past Holmes . . . .

Watson crossed into the main room, noiseless in the night, and carefully fed the fireplace from the side instead of straightforward. Holmes never even moved from his spot on the other side of the stonework, so deep was his exhaustion. Watson was still a little surprised that Holmes trusted him enough to let him take over while he slept, but there was no denying that Holmes's personality was a new and troubling one.

They were running for their lives, and yet Holmes had never seemed more at peace.

A challenge was what he was made for. It was in the very stuff that made him what he was. That mind was so far above the rest of mortal men he could not be fully happy unless he was at his utmost stimulation. Strange to think that only stimulation could soothe him – contradictory,

138

even, but Watson had noted something of that behavior in the few men he treated who took cocaine to *calm* themselves.

Watson understood that no matter what, this would be the last case for Holmes. This was his personal crossroads, with only two possible paths to take. He would have argued that there were still years of good left in his friend, if only his friend could believe him, but even a faithful friend could read the signs before him: That restless, brilliant brain was weary. Moriarty symbolized years of his struggle to do some good in the world – and there was no imagining the anticlimax after the battle had ended.

It was war, and only one army would win. Watson intended it be theirs.

He quietly settled himself into the corner opposite from the bed where Holmes was resting. It was a minute's work to put out his Adams where he could reach it, and from there his hands rested in his lap. Despite the warmth of the room, he retained his dark coat. It hid the stark whiteness of his shirt. His collar and cuffs were removed, along with his waistcoat.

Silence outside the quiet chatter of the fire as it ate the fuel. He was comfortable with the lack of noise. Holmes had appreciated that quality in him since their first meeting. It was not safe to divert his attention, so for now Watson merely composed his letter to Mary in his mind.

He hoped she was well. She was certainly safe enough visiting her old schoolfriend in Surrey's version of the Outback . . . the only threat to her health over *there* would be in the nature of an angry honeybee or a stampede of sheep.

Himself was another matter.

The time for running had passed days ago. Watson was now able to think.

He did not like what his own observations were telling him.

"How long were you in France, Holmes? I thought you would be on the Continent much longer. I even sent you a wire when you were in Nimes."

"Indeed! Nothing earth-shattering, I hope?"

"Compared to our current events?" Watson had to laugh at that. *"I had hoped to find you,"* he said slowly. *"I suppose you had already left –*
"

"I left Nimes on the last of March," Holmes's grey eyes flickered curiously as he reached for his pipe. It was a new instrument, a battered amber that had been part of his disguise as the old priest. Even the tobacco, sweet and light, was against the detective's usual preference, but added to the alternative identity – and there was really little choice but to

139

smoke it all up. *"I dislike the notion that we missed our communications, Watson. That is an intolerable inefficiency."*

"Think nothing of it, Holmes."

"I will not for now, but neither will I forget. It makes me question my previous belief that Moriarty was overlooking me while I was in France."

"But still, a simple wire mislaid?"

"Perhaps and perhaps not. It is possible to hold both options until one is confirmed or denied." And he turned to his pipe, brooding through the smoke and silent.

Holmes asking for his companionship was unusual enough since his marriage. He was brusque and impatient when the subject of women came up – but never when it came to the woman who was his closest friend's wife. Indeed, he appeared to have a bit of wondering admiration for Mary, who resolutely ruined many conventional attitudes of the Victorian Ideal in her support of his strange friendship.

And few enough men understood Holmes – even fewer women. Often, Watson wondered if Holmes's contempt was rooted in a carefully built-up previous experience – as if he understood on a *logical* premise that Woman was every bit as capable as Man, and thus, should prove it at every opportunity. But Holmes did not understand the *emotions* of class divisions, or the rights of the peers, or why he should be his own judge and jury on a case . . . Perhaps he also did not understand the full sorrows of a woman's lot, or why they did not chafe harder at their bonds. It would fit very neatly into how Watson suspected Holmes operated. If Holmes felt he was being treated unfairly, he simply did something about it. But alas, he was too intelligent for his own good, and he did not understand why the rest of the world did not operate under his codes.

Mary Watson held her husband only by the bounds of love. She did not use the shackles of manipulation, guilt, or jealousy that so many of her type used upon their husbands. Be it from her own unconventional upbringing abroad, her many sorrowful years, or the fact that she held Sherlock Holmes to be largely responsible for her happiness, the fact was he could do little wrong in her eyes.

In return, Holmes did his best to keep her husband out of danger.

He does not know about Mary. And what would I tell him? That she has low odds of carrying our child to term in view of her recent illness? He would insist I leave him to his certain death. I cannot.

John Watson had never been forced to choose between his wife and best friend before. Nor had the two people closest to him ever made it so. If anything, Mary and Holmes were satellites in his world, each orbiting with mutual respect. He loved them both. They both needed him.

What, then, could he do?

A soldier must continue on. And fight for victory.

Brittany:

The hunting horn sounded faint and distant. A long, low moan that ran through the forest from the higher ridge. The men froze for a moment on the murky path.

"They have our scent!" Potier hissed. "*Hurry!*"

And he took off running as though the *true* Hell Hounds were chasing them from the sky, King Arthur at the head of the pack in his search for a rascal's blood.

Lestrade pressed himself to keep up, knowing his old wound was a liability when it came to speed. The old man's pack basket bounced on his back, a pale spot that helped him see where to follow. As one they kept their staffs level with their waists, trying not to run into anything.

A signal gunshot – sounded like a bloody *Springfield* – on the other side of the hollow. It couldn't have been more than a quarter-mile away. Lestrade was bewildered that the sound was traveling so well before he realized it was bouncing off the limestone outcrops, ricocheting like bullets from wall to wall as they raced through a geological alleyway. Potier wasted his breath saying something *absolutely* vile through his beard.

"Further up!" The old smuggler panted. "We've got to take the high route!" He thrust himself pell-mell into the bracken and brambles. Thorns like elfin knives stabbed into their legs and sleeves. "It'll be hard for us, but harder for their horses! They'll have to go around the long way!"

"And the dogs?" Lestrade hissed.

"Worry about – *that* – when – they get here . . . ." For good measure, Potier pulled something out of his coat. Cold metal blocked the spotty starlight filtering through the broken canopy. Satisfied the safety was on, he stuffed it back in.

Lestrade remembered berry brambles could not thrive in shade. They were suddenly exposed and in the open, heading straight up a slope that was forty-five degrees if it was fifteen, hanging on to lumps of limestone and hanks of stubborn long grasses that slashed at his supple leather gloves. His legs burned. The staff seemed to sway in all directions at once, blocking his movements. Water filled his chest as he gasped for air. As the throb in his bones spread upward and into his skull, a too-familiar sensation of heat gathered at his temple. *Oh, Good God, not now . . . Don't start bleeding now . . . .*

141

Potier was gasping for breath – another source of fear for Lestrade. He didn't know the land like the old man did, and if he needed help there was no solution outside of an inglorious end. He glanced behind his shoulder, and the blood went from hot to cold in his veins.

A good five storeys below, glowing riders were galloping to the base of the sloping outcrop. Glowing dogs milled at their hooves. One second was all Lestrade needed. Six men total – one more than he had bullets. And none at all to count the dogs.

The leader pulled a horn cut from a strangely warped seashell to his lips and blew an eerie sound – short and sharp and High *C* – and half the dogs spilled away from the melee of horses and hides and collected in front of the leader. Two blasts lower, Middle *A*, and the cold-nosed dogs were milling at the bottom of the slope, trying to whine with their muted throats as they tried to climb up.

They couldn't climb up – not with those enormous feet and legs meant for running, but they could block the quarry from coming back down. And in case they wanted to try their luck, two of the Riders were sitting put on their mounts.

"*Hurry!*" Potier sounded as though breath was something he had lost forever, but his wiry body still moved, still found the foot-and-hand holds and his grandson followed suit. In the corner of his eye, the hot-nosed hounds were running further up the forest path. The long, winding way to the top of the escarpment.

Without warning they were off the side and on to the top. Lestrade wasted a moment of astonishment – *Made it!* – before stumbling to Potier, helping the old man get to his feet in the wash of silver grasses. They leaned on their staffs, panting hard as the earth spun before their eyes.

Long ago, humans had discovered a spring flowing through two tightly bound rocks standing upright in the top of the tiny land spit that thrust out of the ridge like an odd finger. The spring had flowed straight into the massive bowl of a collapsed cave adjacent to the forest and into the gaping black hole at the bottom. Somehow they had commemorated the earthy mystery by capping the bound stones with a large stone table. It was big as a country house . . . but nothing like a fortress. Like the serpent woman's spring, there was a ring of standing stones, but these were larger, older, and rougher, like a giant child's building blocks left to collect nocks and chips.

Potier groaned aloud. "They're too close!" he swore as he panted. "We can't take the *kev*! They'll follow us inside and straight to the others!"

Lestrade saw what he meant. His pulse plummeted. The sinkhole was between them and the Riders. Someone shouted – he fancied it was that damned Craddock.

The detective gnashed his teeth together. They could hear the chaff breaking as the dogs and riders approached. There was no place to escape, save for the forest on the other side of the racing dogs, the side path with its demonic Riders . . . or the sinkhole itself, and it was large enough to let anyone use it. Potier was right. The Dooley clan was half children and the other half were old. They couldn't be risked like this.

"Head up, Potier!" he gasped. "I'll take a bullet before I take another bloody dog bite!" The two staggered to the massive dolmen, Lestrade pushing his grandfather up on his shoulders until he scrabbled a purchase on the top. He took a deep breath, took a running jump, and managed to just grab Potier's rough-skinned gloves. Large teeth snapped the air behind his left foot. They spilled over the surface of the stone table, gasping for air in lungs that had grown too small for the purpose.

The dogs couldn't jump as high as the lip of the table. Lestrade pressed himself as flat as possible, blocking his grandfather from the vanguard Riders. Behind him, Poiter was making angry little noises as he struggled to shrug out of the little pack basket strapped to his back. He finally rolled on his side and began frantically working to get separated from his bundle.

The Riders had the advantage of height. They milled slowly, not able to reach the top of the stone table either – Lestrade wondered belatedly how the devil *they* had just managed that trick – nor were they able to get a clear shot without some luck . . . but they were *perfectly* capable of preventing their escape. Lestrade experienced a wave of frustration that made gnawing on the rock seem like an attractive prospect.

Someone rattled a quick witticism in a heavy northeastern dialect.

"Ha, you think so, *d'Armor*?" Potier bellowed at the top of his lungs. "I'll be sure to tell your *very* pretty mamm all about that, next time I sell her some of my *special* wares!" Lestrade's mouth, which was already open in order to breathe faster, collapsed the rest of the way. There was a choking gasp from below. "Ya, she's still quite the sprightly little *intañv* . . . but then, *you* ought to know what widows are like!" As an explanation, Potier added, "Takes after his father, thank god. Got the brains of *seaweed*."

"The bloody *hell* are you doing?" Lestrade thought about throttling him, just to save his life.

"Mental." Potier sniggered. "Now he has to kill me. We'll see how Kemper feels about that."

"So we're throwing chum to the sharks now?" Lestrade swallowed and let his head rest on the stone.

"Well, we'll just see." They listened to their hearts drum beneath their bones as the Riders finished collecting around the table. Lestrade could even smell the weird heavy scent coming off the ragged pelts, and the sort of sweat man gives off when he's doing something pleasurable.

Over the lip of the lichen-crusted grey rock, Lestrade could see all too clearly the way things rested. There were six Riders in all – eight counting the two guarding the bottom of the slope. With these Riders were at *least* twenty dogs. Half were scenthounds, but the other half were dismayingly large mastiffs, designed for damage.

The leader was dismounting and striding on long, athletic legs to a spot where the dogs were milling about. Lestrade found him all too familiar. He sighed to himself, feeling just about every mixed emotion under the moon as the tall figure knelt to examine the ground.

Jethro Quimper lifted a smiling face up to the moon, to the figure lying just out of gun aim on the dolmen.

"Bleeding already, L'estrade?" He drawled. "The night's a bit young to finish the game."

Swiss Alps:

He knew.

The Great Detective saw so much in the small details, that there *were* no small details.

Mary's absence meant nothing by itself. But when Watson asked about the telegram . . . .

Possibilities had factored in his mind over the amber pipe. The impossible ones were quickly discounted.

Watson dropping the subject neatly, to all appearances not wanting to disturb his friend – and how like him to be so unselfish! But in the outskirts of Meiringen, while they played the tourist, Watson had sought out the dry-goods shop for thread to bring home to his wife – something he always did, for she enjoyed the romance of other lands and villages stitched into her creations . . . but he lingered slightly too long over the palattes of white. Eggshell, ivory, cream, the tint of guernsey, stark-white and silk, the sort used to create fine Ayrshire embroidery . . . the sort of embroidery used to create christening gowns.

Call him an ass then, and call him a fool three times over. Watson was never one to refuse a friend who asked for help – and Holmes had asked for his aid fewer than he had fingers on one hand. Nor was Watson the man who spoke of his own worries. It never occurred to him to do so, wrongly thinking that his problems were of no interest and an unwanted burdening on people.

But . . . .

Holmes opened grey eyes to the darkness of the ceiling above.

144

What if Watson was honestly afraid to say something? He and Mary had already lost their prospective children three times since their marriage. Holmes's mind was logical and even, but even so he saw no sense in a world that would torture the only couple he knew that were suitable for parenthood.

Did Watson see this as a relief from his past sorrows and his still-tender hopes? As dangerous as Moriarty was, he was at least a tangible enemy. One he could battle. John Watson preferred to tackle his obstacles head-on, but when it came to illness and the loss of children . . . It was no enemy that could be fought for a clear outcome.

Holmes devoutly hoped that lost telegram hadn't been by artifice. If so, he would make a point of learning where its source was. But that would be later . . . if there was a later.

For now, he had to think of how to save Watson from himself.

Brittany:

Bleeding already? Only Lestrade's hand moved, reaching up to brush against the coarse stitches at the rim of his scalp. His glove-tips ran over a cooling slickness by his ear. Congealing pulled at his skin, like a light plaster.

"It always *was* a game to you, Quimper," he said through his teeth. Behind him, his grandfather had finished unburdening from the pack. "I suppose that's the lot of the advantaged. Is it a game for your Professor, I wonder?"

"Hmm . . . ."

There were too many of them for Lestrade to shoot – the temptation was fast approaching venomous levels. It was nightmarish beyond his limited imagination. The milling Riders were grinning, anticipating further amusement before they satisfied their cult's desire for business. "It's true he does not share our sense of amusement . . . but then, we hardly share his. Dry old books and numerical columns are not exactly the stuff a sporting man is made of." Quimper flashed white teeth as he thrust a perfumed cigar between his teeth. "Now then, how are we going to get you down, both of you . . . I assume that is your redoubtable grandsire behind you? *Allo, Amezeg.*"

"I'm no neighbor of *yours,* you lipous predator," Potier snapped with full spirit. "Come a little closer, and we'll discuss your ancestry." He rapped his stick against the rock.

"Tsk." Quimper laughed out loud. "We'll make this simple, L'estrade. We don't need your *Tad-kohz*. But if you come down, we'll not kill him."

"Oh, *really*." Lestrade gave that statement the scorn it deserved. "And what are you going to *do* with him, offer him tea and pancakes?" Behind him, Potier snorted.

"Nothing so falsely civilized." Quimper held the reins of his horse lightly. "We just need *you*. Your grandfather is superfluous to our business. Come on down, and we'll send the Seagull back home to his family. I'll bring him to his daughter myself." He lifted his voice. "It's been a long time since you saw poor little Jeanne, your favourite daughter. Why so long? Wouldn't you like to see her again?"

"You think I'm so old and decrepit I can't any time I want to?" Potier snarled. "How about I just shoot you between the eyes?"

"I wouldn't recommend that," Quimper said sadly. "You see, there's the matter of the *dogs* here . . . They only respond to my commands. Permit me to demonstrate . . . ." He lifted that strangely shaped seashell to his lips again and blew, a low *G*. It was electric. The hounds galvanised into action. As a living, teeming mass they began throwing their bodies at the dolmen. Lestrade shrank back slightly, horrified at the sudden change. They had gone from silent to slavering.

"They can't jump up there, it's true," Quimper noted casually, "but they can keep that up all night. And no matter how many bullets you have, old man, I guarantee you you *don't* have enough." He blew again. "That should bring the remaining pack up here, as well as the other two Riders."

Potier muttered something, stroking his beard frantically. "That's only half the story, you filthy killer! What do you want with my grandson?"

"Oh, it doesn't matter," Lestrade said wearily. "*Believe* me. I'll wind up dead anyway."

Quimper sniffed. "You used to *appreciate* my speeches when we were younger, L'estrade. A pity. Well, how will it be, then?"

That question was suddenly rendered moot, as an enterprising hound actually *leaped* to the top of a boulder lying half-swallowed in the grass. There was barely time to react. It flew through the air with its teeth gaping open. Lestrade saw a black gullet and froth and bone-coloured eye-whites as it arrowed to his grandfather. He was on his feet too quickly to think. The dog's wind blew out of its ribs as the staff struck it, but it scrabbled for purchase before he could finish swinging it to the edge of the rock and its teeth gripped the wooden pike like a bear trap.

Potier came up from behind, using his staff like a harpoon and struck between its eyes. The hard skull of the beast made a dull cracking sound but the dog let go only from momentary surprise. Good enough. Lestrade pushed it over the edge but was not surprised to see it back and leaping with the rest.

146

Jethro Quimper laughed out loud, delighted. "Good boys," he praised his dogs. "I always say an intelligent dog is never a waste of breeding!"

"What do we do, sir?" Mr. Craddock breathed.

"'Do'? We let them wear themselves out. They don't dare use their guns. They need to save them for the enemy that can shoot back." Quimper puffed rapidly, his eyes never leaving the growing melee piling upon the table. "We won't have to do anything but watch and take them when they're exhausted."

Chapter XVI – War and the Dogs of War

"Restachoù mad so mad da gaoud"
"Good remains are nice to have."
(The Breton version of "Leave a good-looking corpse.")

Triaged Potier was no stranger to desperate situations. Thinking in them was always a waste of time. A battle was up to the Fates as often as not, but he wanted his grandson to survive this nightmare.

After the first hound caught on with using the fallen menhirs as step-stools, the others had followed. There were menhirs all over their dolmen, like the numbers around a clock-face.

Damn calendar stones. Lestrade was not the least bit impressed with hoary old architecture, and he felt justified.

The large dogs were their most vulnerable when they were in the air. If they could get them fast enough, their staff could just sweep the brute back off the table and possibly – just possibly – get them hurt enough to slow them down.

Not all the dogs could make the leaps. But there were plenty who could.

The old smuggler shouted in his mother's dialect a curse worthy of Surcouf and put his back to his grandson. Geoffrey was a Potier more than a Lestrade. Indefatigable, but his reserves were thin. Truth to tell, Triaged had started to feel his age a few hours ago, and would no doubt feel all of it – should they live to see the light of day.

They had been holding back the impossible for almost an hour, and it made it all the worse that their hunters were treating this all as some sort of diverting garden party. Through a curtain of sweat in his eyes, the old smuggler could see they were passing flasks around, smoking, and giving critiques on the skill of the combatants. Bets were changing hands on who would fall first. Potier was devil enough to feel slightly flattered at the strength of some of the opinions he was hearing.

At least there was one thing. *One thing.* Geoffrey took after his father, Thomas Lestrade, in his *utter* single-minded determination, and that meant he would *not* lose his temper on a whim. Potiers were impulsive dreamers, and Triaged had been at his fifth decade before he had learned to simmer himself down. Despite the finality of their situation, Geoffrey's face remained coldly concentrated on the other side of his honest fear. He used his *chausson* kicks wherever he could, but they were risky. Overbalancing and falling was a very real danger, as was the chance of getting those large teeth sunk into his foot or leg.

While Potier was striking at one dog, another came up to his side. Geoffrey shouted and struck it back, but a third hound had spilled over the side of the table and was leaping for his arm, planning to drag him down. Potier saw his grandson fall to the stone with a gasp, the large jaws wrapped around his forearm, and had no choice but to yank out his precious revolver.

A glowing white beast leaped over his grandson and went for his face. Potier put a bullet into its own. The slug went out the back but the momentum kept the dead dog going, knocking him two steps backwards. He wrestled to get it away from him in time to save his legs from the latest monster clambering up the edge.

Quimper made a thoughtful, amused sound as Potier's gun went off. "First blood," he announced. "Although I'm sure I don't know which one it is." The Wild Hunt had pulled back to the higher earth that ringed the sinkhole. It gave them a better overall view, even if it limited their ability to aim any helpful bullets.

"I want that old man," d'Armor pleaded. "*Please*, sir. You heard what he said about my mother!"

"Yes, I *did* hear." Quimper didn't precisely concede to his partner's desire for revenge . . . yet. "Be assured, I'll let you know when it's time to get that old MoonCurser." He never took his eyes off the sport in the centre of the ring as he spoke.

"Sir," Mr. Craddock spoke on his other side, very quietly. Quimper never took his eyes off the fight, but leaned to the side to listen. "What do we do with the old man?"

"As I said, no one dies without permission," Quimper answered in the same voice. "There could be some use out of him yet." Not the least bit being the means to hurt the old man's family. Just the conservative possibilities were madly tempting. "But keep an eye on d'Armor. I don't want him trying anything outside of my orders."

Craddock nodded knowingly. To hear was to obey.

"I doubt there's a single gossip on the peninsula that doesn't know about that man's mother," he muttered to the big thug. "Except for d'Armor . . . and I truly do *not* wish to deal with the aftermath."

Lestrade was serious in preferring a bullet to another dog bite. It was more luck than design that the hound had caught the loose sleeve of his over-large coat in its mouth. From the instinct borne of nightmares, the detective made his gloved fist into a ball and twisted inward, grabbing the thick leather collar with his free hand for purchase. The hound gagged as it felt itself being choked as the fist pressed down its throat. It tried to back away frantically but Lestrade was stuck with the problem now. He tucked his shoulders in as a nearly all-white hound leaped into his side vision and a bullet went off close to his ear. He got his leg under the spasming animal and pushed with everything he was worth, letting go quickly enough that the dog wasn't prepared and slid right into two of its comrades as they were just getting to the edge of the table.

Just enough time to grab up his staff again and face the newcomers head-on. They were over the edge well enough, but it took him longer than it should. He paused for breath in the sudden lull as the dogs fell back, thinking. His bad foot ached all the way up to the base of his back, matching every dent Craddock had put into his body on the *Athene*. Griox' bruising, he noted in clinical graveyard whimsy, were still fresh and sharp. *I wonder if Mr. Holmes ever did a study on bruising the* living?

The dogs paced, eyes on him. They could smell his blood. It was no wonder they preferred him over Potier.

"You're starting to slow down, L'estrade!" Quimper called out. "Perhaps you need a rest?"

Lestrade glared icily in the direction over the sweep of grass where a Demon Incarnate rested.

"Still afraid of heights, I see!" he shouted back. "And *you're* the tall one!"

Quimper roared, richly amused. "That's the stubborn little *mevel* [1] I remember! Never *were* good at taking orders, no? Always a battle with you."

"You would know." Lestrade gripped his staff. He was soaked in sweat. It stung the oozing stitched at his head. No matter what, he didn't see any way out of this. His blood trail was as good as a flare in the night to these monsters, and Quimper could track in moonlight as well as day. "Anyone ever thought for themselves, you made certain to punish them for it. *Margodenn* [2] or *sklav* – no one else exists in your world." That taunt was made specifically for the ones who were giving Quimper such pleasant company. "How is your friend doing, eh? Did he have to make an early night of it?"

"Who, Mr. Griox?" Quimper shook his head from side to side, almost the way a serpent does when it can't decide where to strike. "I had to send him home. A shame. He would have liked to be here. We can let you tell him all about it tomorrow, *nann*?"

"*You* can tell him all about it tomorrow, boy!" Potier roared back. "As rich as *you* are, surely they'll let the two of you share a hospital room!"

The cry of a *large* dog split the air. It was like a ship's horn in the fog.

"Mother of God!" Potier turned as white as his beard tips. *"What was that?"*

"Padriac!" Lestrade couldn't believe it. "That big fool came to see about us!"

Some of the smarter dogs had hesitated at that sound. Lestrade couldn't blame them. The howl was unearthly and demoralizing and . . . *hungry*.

Below Quimper's men were suddenly alert and primed for battle. Guns were pulled out of their pelts and hurriedly checked for their load.

As if that would help them . . . .

Lestrade felt a grin like a Hallowe'en lantern clench his face. Irish wolfhounds were *sighthounds*, bred and trained for war in an era when it was completely honourable to disembowel the enemy with a barbed speartip. For centuries their job had been to attack *weaponed* humans outright, leap up and drag them out of chariots and saddles. In the last battles between the Irish and English, they had pulled knights in *full armour* right off their gigantic mounts in ease. They were the largest dog the world had ever seen. At seven feet tall when they stood on their back legs, they dwarfed the tallest owner. They *had* to be large. They only fought in pairs or singly. *Never* in packs.

When told only the royalty could own wolfhounds, Dooley always smiled as if someone had told him a *particularly* rich joke.

Like a demonic ark, the *kev* at the bottom of the sinkhole disgorged six ice-grey adult wolfhounds, leaping two by two out of the dark hole in the earth.

Padriac Dooley had trained his dogs for gentleness and to protect his children. But there was a lot of war left in their blood. And the glint of new, spike-studded collars gleamed around thick necks.

Cu' Faoil, Padriac had called them. *We brought them to Caesar on his request and the Romans saw them kill the lions in the arena. After that, they could only look at them from behind the bars of a cage.*

Lestrade had always thought Dooley was bragging just a bit.

Not anymore . . . .

The detective back-pedaled in haste as a team he recognized – Padriac's best, Phorp and Luath, – *bypassed* the stepping stones and leaped straight up from the grass to the stone table. Gigantic bodies slammed on top of the no-longer large hounds, giant jaws clamped on necks and crushed spines. Lestrade realized in dawning horror why that massive boar in the forest had looked so . . . *battered* on the back of its neck. It had been killed by a single bite. The other wolfhounds were tearing through the swarm of chaos, knocking the beasts over as lightly as croquet balls.

Muted or not, Quimper's dogs were screaming.

Lestrade had a feeling he would never forget this experience, try as he might.

A bullet went through the air over Phorp. Went wild. The shooter was panicking. Lestrade had his own gun at that point and fired, pushing his grandfather down to the stone on his stomach. A Wild Hunter shook like an epileptic. A wolfhound – Babh – merely leaned up and neatly pulled him to the ground by his head. Lestrade didn't let his eyes linger there.

The old man cursed fondly at being protected and took aim with his own revolver. His free hand scrabbled to the side, seeking his pack basket.

"Gentle when stroked, fierce when provoked!" Padriac Dooley himself stood at the lip of the cavern entrance, and by his side, the faithful Ploudaniel poised with some sort of *large* shotgun. By the looks of things, it was something designed along the lines of a punt gun, but the detective devoutly hoped it *wasn't*. Things were terrible enough right now without bringing something like *that* into the fight.

"Phorp! Luath!" Lestrade yelled at the top of his lungs. Recognizing him as "family" the giants paused in their bone-crunching. *Ree-meeder!"* He leveled his finger at the wildly plunging horse that Quimper was trying fruitlessly to control.

"What did you just say?" Potier gasped as the dogs took off straight for the agent.

"I told them that was the chief devil." Lestrade gasped back.

"Oh . . . ." Potier was not often taken aback. His voice was strangely meek. "Good."

What happened next was perhaps inevitable.

In the murderous rout, d'Armor arrowed through the crowd of panicking men, dogs, and horses that had no memory that they had been trained for battle. In his right hand a gun gleamed. Craddock, following orders, let go of his own horse's reins and took off after the younger man just as he reached the bottom of the stone table.

Contrary to Potier's comment about his intelligence, the man was decent in a fight and possessed some small gift in tactics. He marked his target from the ground, swung with his free hand up the lip of the stone table, aimed, fired, and dropped back to the ground under the stone table in a heartbeat.

"*Tad!*" Lestrade all but screamed as his grandfather grunted in pain, falling backwards with his body drawing up like an insect. He fell almost across his precious pack basket with a mortified gasp. Lestrade dropped again to the stone, throwing his arm across the old man's chest. Somehow he lost his gun – it skittered over the rough-textured stone and with it, a good bit of his hopes. Potier swore and groaned and the moonlight revealed a dark smear of blood on the grey lichen.

"Basket!" He groaned. "Where's my basket!"

"*Forget the sodding basket!*" Lestrade exclaimed.

"Give it here – !" Potier rolled to his side in an effort to get it.

"For the – " Lestrade sealed his lips shut, dangerously close to showing a temper, and grabbed it up. "Here's the bloody thing!" A shadow fell across the moonlight. Lestrade looked up at the upside-down hulk of Craddock, blocking his world. "Oh, no . . . ."

The big man's left hand held a desperately large-looking truncheon of *gutta percha*. Lestrade hadn't known they still made those. He rolled away from his grandfather, reaching for his staff at the same fervor Potier had reached for his basket. The pistol was too far –

Craddock simply pulled him up using his shirtfront the way another man would lift up a bit of luggage. Lestrade gasped as he grabbed at the man's tree-trunk of a forearm, and did his best to find the nerves under that thick hide. Craddock merely smirked, the moonlight bouncing off a single silver canine. The truncheon lifted and Lestrade knew full well from hard experience what would happen would be a skilled, single tap and then lights out –

"Conan! Etan!" Padriag was shouting to the nearest duet of wolf hounds. "*Tae* Galvin!" The dogs heard and began leaping across the field, but Lestrade was fairly certain it *wouldn't* happen in time. And if he tried to block the blow with his better arm, a broken bone would result . . . .

Behind the thug's legs, a long white arm was clutching at the rim of the table. D'Armor was aiming for another shot.

"Leave him alone, d'Armor!" Lestrade shouted for all he was worth, and distracted Craddock just long enough to cause a blink. That blink was met with the hardest kick Lestrade had ever given anybody into the thigh, and a furious howl was the result. The detective hit the rock. Spun on his last chance and – *Hang it, this was war!* – put a *coup de vache* into d'Armor's head. The man was dead before he finished falling to the ground, but it didn't stop Craddock. Thrusting forward on his uninjured leg he reached for Lestrade, who was still on the wrong side of his gun.

"Down, *Mab!*"

Lestrade barely heard it in time, and it was a tone of voice no one would disobey. He moved on instinct, throwing himself backwards as a woven cloth sack flew threw the air, the throat-cords ripped open. It slapped Quimper's henchman in the face and he gave the single most loudest scream in the battle.

Numb with shock, Lestrade stared through a film of sweat running into his eyes as Craddock collapsed in stages across the stone. The asp vipers in the sack writhed furiously across his face and neck, seeking a place to hide.

I didn't know he even had a scream like that in him. Lestrade couldn't quite believe the evidence of his senses, but Craddock was undeniably dead.

NOTES

1. *Mevel*: Servant
2. *Margodenn*: Puppet
3. *Sklav*: Slave

Chapter XVII – Collecting the Pieces

Conan and Etan had finished their leaps to the table. Lestrade turned quickly, forced by circumstance to see canines as companions, and put his hands up in a peace sign the big things understood. They must have caught his scent on his grandfather, for they paused and circled them, pausing in guard positions. The detective hurriedly kicked the asps off the edge of the table with the toe of his foot, trying not to anger them more than he had to. They flopped awkwardly off the side to . . . where God knew where.

Potier was huddling up to his knees, bent half-over and clutching at the meat of his upper arm. Judging from the size of the bullet rend in his coat, the wound must hurt like the very devil. Close enough range to scorch the flesh, the stink of the powder rang in Lestrade's nostrils as he pulled open the fibres to look inside. Part rip of flesh from the passing missile, part obnoxious bruise, it glistened black-and-purple in the pale light, and his grandson yanked out a blue handkerchief from somewhere in his pockets, pressing its folds over the injury to seal it from the open air.

"He's actually dead?" Potier craned his neck to see around Lestrade to the prone hulk by his ankles.

"Isn't that *supposed* to happen when one takes a face-full of poisonous snakes?" Lestrade tried not to sound like a smart-arse, but the conditions were compelling. "Easy, Etan," he told the large bitch sniffing at his ear. "I'm fine." *Although I can't say for how much longer . . .* Around them the last of the death hounds were being routed. A few dead horses and not a few dead Riders were sprawled like so many plague victims across the field. A thought struck Lestrade – a most worrisome thought – and he counted the large silver shapes loping under the moon. *Two, four . . . six. All accounted for.* He breathed his relief. He didn't see Quimper, but Phorp and Luath were all right. Phorp limped heavily, his war mate licked his face consolingly.

"Careful!" The little detective had caught on that Ploudanial and Padriac were cautiously stepping their way across the battlefield to the table. "There's poisonous snakes in the grass!"

"Shouldn't have killed him," Potier was still protesting. He sounded put out, as if Craddock had died merely to spite his elegant plans. "He must have been allergic to the venom. It's quite mild, you know."

"*Tad-kohz*, you threw a whole bag of the things at him! What did you *think* would happen?"

155

"They hardly ever bite venom on the *first* strike." Potier protested, still trying to find the flaw in his scheme as his grandson wearily lifted him to his feet. "And they don't have that much."

"So the point *was* – ?" Lestrade wondered.

"Scare the devil out of him, and perhaps cause some rotting bite wounds where it would hurt him a few days later," Potier explained without a bit of upset to his voice. "Don't get me wrong, *paotr*, I'm not really upset that he's *dead*." The wide old eyes had turned into hard stones, just like that, as he looked at the corpse. "We've heard rumors," the old Breton said under his breath. He looked about for the first time, and took in what had been a disaster for the *maer-kohz*. He whistled faintly. "Where is Kemper?" his voice hushed.

"That's what I'm about to find out." Lestrade limped to the rim of the table, sucking his breath in as something, some muscle somewhere above his knee, decided it didn't like him anymore. "Ha, Padriac," he rasped. "Got a hand?"

"Got two, *kam a'kena*."[1] Dooley grinned and lifted his long arms up. Potier made an insulted sound, but deigned to be lowered into the large man's grip. With a gentleness that gratified Lestrade, he and Ploudaniel got his grandfather to the grass. Potier gnashed his teeth, but made no complaint to what had to be a very painful wound.

Lestrade sighed and slipped off the stone table and trotted across the sinkhole to the worst of the carnage, hand resting in his gunpocket. Now that the battle was indubitably over, the big wolfhounds were back to their normal sweet-natured and mischievous selves. Phorp even looked up at Lestrade and whined slightly, his injured paw holding up in the air. Lestrade smiled weakly and patted the dog on its massive head. True to his form, Phorp let him examine the wound. It looked like some sort of cut or stab into the meat of his paw. He hoped it didn't infect.

Why was it dogs liked him anyway? It was one marvelous mystery, considering how he felt about them.

Tired to the bone, the detective went to the edge of the clearing where he'd last seen Jethro Quimper. Other than a scatter of skins and a few effects, there was no sign of the man.

Hunting and tracking was a *gentleman's* sport one he had pointedly not been trained in. He thought of how Holmes could read a blooming atlas off a single footprint and wished for the infuriating man again.

Something clinked against his shoe leather. His fingers recognized the object even as he lifted it up. The strange seashell gleamed chill and remote in his hands. Something like a conch shell, but *dark*, its calcium affected by some mysterious influence of the environment. The leather gritchel that had carried it sprawled on the grass, its strap loosed.

Something hard and rectangular was inside. Lestrade shook it out onto the grass rather than risk touching it. His eyebrows shot up as a glass-tipped calligraphy pen, ink, and pencil fell out along with . . . .

Of all the things an ordinarily clever mad, multiple murderer would take with him to a cultish killing spree, a notebook would have *never* been his guess . . . .

Evidence of a sort . . . .

As quickly as that, Lestrade stopped being a fugitive and began thinking like a Yarder again. It felt good.

The others were waiting for him. He rose slowly, stuffing the bag into his much-battered jacket and limped his way back to the informal palaver, the dogs following him in long, slow lopes. He had the whole collection by the time he reached their side.

"When you failed to show up at the Healing Pool by a half-hour, we realized something was up." Ploudaniel offered a rolled twist of tobacco lit from his little dark lantern. "Even allowing for the fact this old smuggler drags his heels with his old age . . . ." He smirked as Potier used his good arm to smack him. "It was just going to be me, but this old Gippo wouldn't have anything of it. Said his dogs had taken down enough of the wild pigs, and they needed a bit of a relaxer . . . ."

Lestrade shook his head at the old Tinker. "One of these days, Padriac . . . ."

Padriac only chuckled. "A war dog needs a war at least once."

Ploudaniel's cigar tasted so strong it *had* to be locally grown, and the detective drew it in gratefully. Potier's colouring was fast approaching normal, but his eyes were overbright with questions.

"He's gone." Lestrade let the smoke slide through his lips as he spoke. "But he's been wounded. He left a blood trail into the woods, and I don't think we should follow." He held his glove close to the flame of the dark lantern, and they could all see for themselves. Quimper's blood was still bright and thin, an arterial cut as opposed to the dark sluggish blood out of a small, low-oxygen vein. "Phorp hurt him badly enough," he decided. "Quimper wouldn't have made such an odd wound in a dog's paw if he wasn't trying to . . . ." Here a long-buried memory rose up, and Lestrade gulped down.

" . . . get away," he finished faintly. Another dog, long ago. Another quarry in a place known as Plymouth, where the Wild Hunt ran with dogs painted to look headless. And the King of the Wild Hunt drove a hearse coach, all the better to hide his human prey. But Plymouth hadn't had these sorts of forests. And a small boy had been forced to hide in the heights of a barn, not an ancient stone table.

"Never chase a snake into the grain field," Potier agreed with a nod. Disappointment at Quimper's (apparent) survival warred with the delight of getting a *very* good coup back upon him. His dark eyes were pained but worried for his grandson. "Are we ready to go?"

Padriac had been wrapping Phorp's paw with the swift ease of many years of practice. "We are ready here," he announced. "Shall we?"

Lestrade took a deep breath. "We shall," he agreed. "I'm even looking forward to going underground, *Tad-kohz*."

Potier grinned at him from around his curl of smoke. Sweat still shone at his face. "I think we could all do with a bit of the healing waters," he said mysteriously. "Ploudaniel, how's the moon milk crop this year?"

"Excellent, thank God." Ploudaniel said reverently.

"What did you just say?" Lestrade was fairly certain he'd heard wrong, but with moon cursers . . . .

"You'll see, Grandson." Potier's head bobbed, he was so tired. "Ploudaniel, you lead, if you would. I'm not in the frame to pay close attention right now."

"Here, we can hold each other up," Lestrade offered wryly. He caught Padriac's approving smile from behind as the old Tinker heeled his dogs to circle them, using Ploudaniel as a lead. Together the two entered the cave.

"At least *this kev* entrance doesn't make you suck your breath in first . . . ." Ploudaniel said cheerfully as they reached the running water.

"Still straight *down*, though . . . ."

Brother Jerome's Anglican Chapel, London:

Gregson looked about, but even London was fair emptied this far past midnight. At least in some areas. He slid into the pew at the back, not looking at Bradstreet, who was facing forward in a strangely reverent position.

"I'm not accustomed to this," he said for the record. "I'm a Methodist." He glanced uneasily at the false images decorating the plaster walls. "My ancestors only came here to lop off the heads of the idols."

Bradstreet chuckled lightly. "Some of mine did too. The way I see it, we were all Catholic in our history at least once . . . ." He leaned back in his part of the pew. "Did you find out anything?"

"Yes, and some of it was actually useful." Gregson knotted his hat between his large hands. "To begin with, not all of those constables who came in with Patterson were actually constables." He nodded as Bradstreet gave a start of surprise. "Could have fooled me too. There was some time

158

spent training them up. Wouldn't be surprised they think a bit like policemen now."

"Very well. Where are they from?"

"Good question. Patterson worked undercover for years, right?" Gregson did not wait for an answer. "He passed himself off as someone who was a lot more rotten than he really was. Not that I'm complimenting that fool. But I had to ask myself, how often did he run into useful people in his work that were of a . . . shall we say, similar mind?"

"People that were willing to bring down the Professor, in other words."

"Exactly. Mr. Holmes was trying to get justice against the Professor in legal ways – and thank God for that – but why did Moriarty escape our justice for so long? Because he was using the people who either couldn't be touched, or didn't have a voice." Gregson devoutly wished for a smoke. "D'you think Brother Jerome would – ?" He sighed. "Never mind."

"I thought about that myself," Bradstreet said softly. "He uses murder and its intimidation to get what he wants . . . We all know that the garroter and the bludgeon man will stand his term in jail – even face the drop – before he'll tell tales on Moriarty. So what's left when someone can't get justice through the courts of law?" He shook his head. "The only thing left is revenge. There's enough of it amongst the clans. Enough of it that this is why I live here, and not in the ancestral grounds." The big man rubbed at his jaw. "A promise of revenge would be the only way Patterson could pay back the people who was helping him."

"I'm impressed." Gregson said truthfully. That's a downright elegant piece of thinking there, Bradstreet."

"Not really. Not if revenge is what you grew up with." Bradstreet did not look at the other man as he spoke. "Lestrade's not the only Yarder who found some sense in Law and Order."

Gregson could well agree with that. He didn't have to comment. "Patterson literally impostered them into this raid to bring the Professor down. The names he used *weren't* the ones that added up."

Bradstreet caught on. "The gang'd want the descriptions of the 'policemen' with certain names . . . descriptions that would match up with people they knew."

"Any one of us inspectors would have done for interrogation. It was just Lestrade's bad luck who was on that ship." Gregson mashed his fist into his leg in frustration. "Damn that Patterson! He was so desperate to bring down that gang he didn't think of the costs to the rest of us! No wonder he was ready to fight instead of negotiate! He probably thought we'd belly-up like a fish and give the gang all the names and descriptions they wanted, and burst the whole thing wide open!"

Bradstreet rubbed at his temples. "It's spilt milk now. The important thing is . . . What can we do to keep this from getting worse?"

"Now *there's* a question." Gregson brushed his fingers over his face. "Off the top of my head, we've got to keep our people watchful. Forget Patterson completely in all of this – Forget the rest of the Yard. We know who we can trust without question. We need to take 'em aside and give them a few words. If Lestrade is out there, he's going to try to get word to us – to one of us."

"And hope we see something before the wrong person does." Bradstreet agreed. "I just wish we knew who he would try to contact."

Paddington Street, London:

Clea Marie Lestrade *née* Cheatham had taken the day to go back to their apartment off Paddington. Mrs. Collins had proven herself beyond the usual call of a landlady and pitched in her help as soon as she understood what was going on.

"I was hoping you had a moment to spare before you headed back." The dignified old woman remained in the doorway where Clea had just lowered her husband's letter out of the safe and into her lap. The watery shine in the younger woman's blue eyes was to be expected.

"I . . . I don't see why not, Mrs. Collins." Clea hesitated, and tucked the paper into her skirt pocket. She paused to wipe at her face as she followed her landlady down the stairs and through the small pergola they had fashioned in the small alleyway between buildings.

The two women had walked outside to the precious back gardens choking with sleepy herbal growth and neat piles of street sweepings to be used for the spring planting. The first bed was already in place. Clea could see the flush of tender young growth rising from the soil, speckled red lettuce and the edges of what would be the delicate yellow radishes Martin adored so religiously.

Just seeing them and being reminded that Mrs. Collins was so fond of her tenant's children made Clea's eyes sting again, just a bit. She kept her lips shut and followed the slender woman to the end of the brick wall. Hops vines slept here, and a few rambling roses along with two *extraordinarily* hardy figs that went into the most coveted jam in London.

Mrs. Collins brushed her withered hand into the brown matting, where the vines grew like vegetable warp and weft. A tiny wren's nest fell out. So *that* was where the little thing had nested all summer. Clea automatically reached, knowing Nicholas would like to know the answer to this particular mystery. He was great friends with the birds.

160

Clea's hand faltered at something just behind the spot where the nest had fallen out.

"I imagined at first it was one of the boys," the old dancer admitted.

"What . . . ." Clea murmured. Set deeply into the stonework was a stout peg of terra-cotta, stained and fit carefully to blend into the colour of the brick as well as the carpet of vines. Further up, there was another just like it . . . and a third at the very top.

"Something boys do," Mrs. Collins said with perfect confidence. "Ram a bit of wood into a wall where the ivy is thick, and use it to climb in and out of their bedrooms. Helps 'em sneak out with their folks none the wiser."

"If my brothers ever did it, I never knew." Clea felt oddly . . . cheated.

The dancer chuckled softly. "Perhaps they were too heavy?" she offered kindly. "I've *seen* those brothers of yours. Circus elephants, aren't they?"

Clea tried not to be distracted. "This is careful work, Mrs. Collins. A boy couldn't do this. Not unless he'd been apprenticed to a brick man early on."

"You're right. A man did this." Mrs. Collins agreed. "A man who knows a little bit about masonry and brick."

Clea was thinking hard. She lined up the proportions of the terra-cotta pegs set into the wall in her mind. She turned around and looked at the other collection of vine growing up the wall of Mrs. Collins' stately house. The vine in question was slender but very sturdy – if imported – River grape. The vines stretched all the way up to what had once been Geoffrey's old bedroom. It was now the little library room but . . . .

Mrs. Collins was smiling to herself as she picked out a thin stick of licorice root from her apron pocket. She chewed on it lightly as her little tenant walked across the building to where the vines clustered the thickest.

These vines were far better established. It took Clea nearly five minutes but she found the same terra-cotta pegs set deeply within the mortar of the building. They *did* lead right up to Geoffrey's old bedroom.

Clea collected her voice in stages. "How long have you known about this?" she asked.

The old lady shrugged. She was *much* less proper when she was around the equally libertarian Clea. "He stopped most of his dangerous work when he married you. A man likes to settle down when he has a reason to come home."

Clea was still thinking. "You never told me. Nor did he."

"He never intended on going back to the old ways, my dear. Too many of his friends never came home from those sort of cases – well though they paid. Leaving you a widow would be to, well, *fail* you if that makes any sense. That's how men think. They're not like us."

Clea nodded. The letter in her hand was proof enough. "He . . . he used the pegs recently, didn't he. That's how the nest was loosened in the first place. And . . . The night he left that letter . . . he knew something felt wrong . . . He would have used the window to slip out and they weren't there to know about it." Men weren't so different, were they? Fathers, sons, husbands . . . .

"Men never change, not really." Mrs. Collins' lined face looked wise as it smiled at her. "And that's just as well."

NOTE

1. "Son of the House"

Chapter XVIII – Drums of Stone

J ean "Illez" Griox rode with excruciating slowness back to Quimper's estate. It was difficult to say which stung the more – humiliation of having to leave the Wild Hunt, or the poison of the pine caterpillars. The wretched things would have been a useful tool in interrogation in the past. The oversight rankled like the rub of each burning, swollen body part against his clothing at every step of his horse's hooves. Even the cool of the night air could not quench the fierce gnawing sensation on his skin. His party of five rode slowly back through the forest, his teeth set deep in his jaws, diverted slightly from his way back to Quimper's estate.

That was when the low whistle – made with difficulty, through parched lips – caught his ears through the knot of undergrowth.

This *kev* opening, large compared to the last and with plenty of room for the trickling spring water, had been traversed easily. The water flowed little more than twenty feet to the bottom of the passage below, and there were plenty of hand-holds in the lumpy rock. Lestrade felt a sigh of relief once they were back under the surface – a sentiment that would make his wife check his forehead for a rising temperature.

It was as damp as he remembered . . . but it gave an impression of warmth now that they were out of the winds of the surface. As good as it felt to the rest of him, it pulled every bruise to the surface of his skin and began a too-familiar throbbing.

One moment under the ground they were walking. The next, Potier's legs gave out and pulled Lestrade down with him. Lestrade aimed so they sprawled against the walls of the damp rock, wincing and holding his breath as his grandfather swore softly.

"Don't, *Mab*." Ploudaniel offered. "You're just as hurt as he is . . . ." The wiry smuggler knelt carefully on the cold floor of the passage and eased Potier upright while Lestrade tried not to panic. "Have to carry you a bit, Triaged," Ploudaniel said without apology. "Or rig a travois once we get to the crossroads."

"Whatever you have to do." Potier agreed faintly. "I'm just so damned tired right now. Can you believe it – ?"

"What about blood loss? We need to fix that before they try to bring another dog in here."

"*That* won't happen any time soon." Old Dooley broke into the conversation. As they twisted to look at him, the elderly Tinker was in the act of pulling out a small waterproof bag, about the size of his fists with the drawstrings taut. He grinned – Lestrade decided it was more like a smug gloat than a grin – from around the stem of his stone pipe as he held his little lantern up to show his prize. "One whiff of this, and anything smaller than a Wolfhound will run screeching in the other direction."

"Do I want to know what that is?" Potier, drained as he was, still perked up in interest.

"Oh, a little this and that . . . and a few things the London Zoo wasn't needing . . . ." Dooley knelt, joints popping like party snappers as he scattered the dark-looking substance here and there between their bodies and the *kev* entrance.

Lestrade caught the faintest, barest scent of the powdery stuff. "Ah," He cleared his throat. "Not that I'm prying into your little secrets . . . but by any chance, would that be powdered lion dung I'm smelling?"

"Yes. From the London Zoo," Dooley said sternly. "The London Zoo is the best. None of the other zoos work as well." He shrugged as Lestrade groaned out loud and sank his head into his hands. "Sorry, lad."

"You mean other zoos won't let you take dung home with you?" Ploudaniel wondered.

"No," Lestrade groaned as the little waterfall dripped around them. "It means that all those complaints we've been getting about the lion keeper feeding stray dogs to his animals have a basis in fact . . . !" His shoulders shook with the despair of hopelessness. "Oh, *God*. I wonder if I could hire Mr. Holmes to take this one on . . . ."

"Mother of God!" Griox swore. As bad as he felt, Quimper fared little better – and looked much worse. The agent was bleeding slow seeps out of clothing that looked to have been mauled by heavy machinery more than something living. "You look like the sabot in the factory!"

Quimper groaned slightly, huddling his hand up close to his chest – and it was that admission of weakness that stunned his hardened partner more than anything else. "Damn that . . . ." He stopped talking to shudder a breath inside his ribs. He held it a moment, his face grey and sickly in the light, before letting it out. His soot and make-up ran eroded sweat marks down his face like tears. "Damn him," he said at last.

"Who?" Griox had a feeling he knew. "Damn who?"

"Both of them." Quimper answered, but faintly. His light-coloured eyes rolled up in their sockets, and he pitched forward in front of his horrified men into the grass.

"We need to look at that arm," Lestrade said in a raw voice.

164

"Let's take a moment . . . ." Padriac offered, and pulled out his little leather-bound hip flask. The old Tinker took a first courtesy sip and passed it on. Lestrade let his grandfather go first – he knew what was in it.

"That's *not* cider from Normandy." Potier said once he got his breath back.

"I don't think even the Normans would claim that horse spit." Lestrade admitted. It was quite the backhanded compliment. "Padriac, is it true you keep it in a glass flask because of what it does to all metals?"

Dooley smirked, which was a little difficult to do when one was missing all but eight teeth, and *those* were deep in the back of his gumline. "It works quite well," he pointed out. "We can rest if you wish – there's time."

"Can't do much against the tides anyway," Potier murmured.

Lestrade took his word for it, easily. Inside that battered head rested infinite maps of the Channels, and each map was different according to the time of the year and the tide. Let the experts take over . . . He sank back into a less-rigid portion of the cave and drew his arms across his chest while Ploudaniel saw to a very annoyed Potier's arm.

It hit him then, in the hot, close air of the cavern while his tired mind drifted.

Craddock was dead.

Accidental, but none the less terrible for what it meant.

Lestrade couldn't feel *sorry* for the man, bad though the death was. At least it had been *quick*. Craddock had helped Jethro Quimper murder by torture unknown numbers of victims – many *members of his own gang* – workers who had betrayed his trust or simply *disappointed* him. And for what? Much as he didn't want to, he could see the man in his face whenever his eyes shut.

And . . . that look in his eye while Griox pressed him for answers at the old silo. Flat and dead as if nothing he saw was even real.

Getting the drop on the man in the middle of that storm had been one of the worst things Lestrade had ever experienced. Had it not been for the terrific sound of the thunder and rain and the steady rings of lightning, he never would have made it. But it had been just enough to climb out of the well while Craddock struggled to keep warm and dry. He had been thinking of Griox' treachery, and not on the odds of Lestrade climbing out.

And then the scream. Those *snakes* . . . .

"Are you sure about this?" M. Judicael wondered. Griox overlooked the questioning of his orders. The man was a bit of a rogue. His name was proof enough of that. "I'd feel better if we could get you to the doctor too, sir."

Griox held in his temper. "I'm well enough," he said coldly. "It's M. Kemper you should be worrying out." The younger man looked at the ground at that. "Get him back to his house and see to his needs. I'm going to go find his dogsbody."

"I haven't seen Craddock *anywhere*," Judicael pointed out. "Perhaps he didn't survive the fight at the Stone Table."

"We won't know until we look. And in either case, M. Kemper needs to be treated now – he's bled half-white as it is." Not that Griox didn't plan on turning that into his advantage. The *Kelenner* would get *his* report before it got Kemper's. "I trust my confidence in you is not misplaced?" Griox spoke like an arrow.

"No. No, it is not." Judicael assured him. "I'll see to him myself." The young face abruptly grew hard and rock-like, cool and callous. "You needn't concern yourself."

Griox nodded at that and, rather than bother with speaking with sore face and lips, he wheeled his horse about and began his way down the path, the remaining five members of the Wild Hunt following with the very last of the dogs. Six in number. Whatever happened, Griox was confident they could take it. These dogs were not the faster-running and impulsive scenthounds that had run afoul of the pine caterpillers. These were full-blooded mastiffs, slower, trained to hold close to the horse, and ready to attack at a moment's notice.

Padriac Dooley was building himself the thickest cigarette in weeks – the situation rather called for it, and hang the expense of the tobacco. The old Tinker manipulated the thin curls of tobacco and the transparent folds of paper, one-handed, while the other rested at his belt.

Ploudaniel, who had donated part of the tobacco, suddenly frowned. "Are you rolling a smoke out of the pages of a Bible?" He demanded.

Dooley looked at him like he was mad. "You pray your way," he suggested. "I pray mine."

Ploudaniel decided it wasn't worth the candle. He shrugged. His people were well used to the holiness of the Word of God, and for all he knew, Dooley was praying with the paper. He was certainly *adopting* a prayerful attitude. "We won't have much further to go," he said under his breath while the other two, slumped against the rock, tried to rest. "I just don't know how much longer *they* can go under their own power."

"I haven't been underground in a while, but my lungs remember. It feels good."

"Just don't do this without one of us as a guide." Ploudaniel warned. "I don't want you to get lost in the *kev* passages here and die, especially after you helped us like that . . . ." He was trying not to look at the quietly

166

panting wolfhounds piled at the old man's feet. (Even for one of Potier's crew, Dooley qualified as "old".)

Dooley did not mention he had played games of blindfold chess since childhood, and he already knew how to get back to the rendezvous. "I don't want to die either," he assured the other man. "At least, not that way. I promised my mother I would send her off for a proper burial when she died."

Ploudaniel nearly swallowed his smoke. "Your mother is still alive?"

Dooley chuckled. "She always swore her elderberry wine kept her years long . . . Perhaps I should start taking some, eh? Save myself for the days of my forgetfulness?"

Ploudaniel's mind barely comprehended the notion. He cleared his throat instead. "You think they'll be all right?"

Dooley didn't have to look at the grandson and grandfather resting in the dry spot of the *kev*. "It's probably just the fight." He tried to sound like he knew what he was talking about. Tinkers didn't kill. They weren't good at it and couldn't live with the consequences.

Ploudaniel accepted this with a sigh. "You're probably right." They smoked in silence for a moment. The air took the fumes straight up. "My God, blood is a strange thing, is it not?" He asked suddenly. "He looks just like his *tad-kohz* . . . just more cautious. Thank the saints . . . I'm sure the world couldn't take another Triaged. Would have counted his teeth against a shark's in his heyday . . . ."

Dooley laughed softly. "I'm not very good at judging you people. The boy has promise, though. Well, he's not a boy any longer. I should stop calling him that."

Ploudaniel looked at him askance. "I should say not. What's adulthood to your people?"

"A man isn't an adult until he marries." Dooley answered. "That's all."

"But what if they never marry?"

"Then they stay children forever."

"You don't look well, Geoffrey." Potier gingerly patted his grandson on the shoulder – probably the only unbruised three-inch spot on his body. "The water's going to be cold further in. We should rest a bit before we keep going."

Lestrade didn't want to say it, but Potier had shared a part in what had happened. He needed to be warned. "If Quimper's alive, he'll be furious to find out about Craddock."

Potier made a spitting motion.

167

"This will be the third time I've taken his 'sergeant' from him." Lestrade ached all over. He closed his eyes for a moment. "Armoricus," he whispered, though the name had begun to finally lose its ability to hurt him. "And Paul . . . and now, Craddock."

As Griox had suspected, firelight leaped against the light clouds over the Seagull's home. The MoonCursers were still there, still drinking massive amounts of liquor over the pit roast and raking steaming potatoes out of the ashes.

At the edge of the forest, Griox waited, watching. His swollen face, taut as a drum and blistered, twisted in his bile, adding to the pain that inflamed his temper. A single word, a gesture to his men, and the dogs was all it took. As one they trickled down from the cover of the forest and swept upon Old Potier's farmhouse. They were less than halfway down the grassy slope before the field of snowy heads turned to see their attacker.

"You are saying he will take revenge on me for Craddock's death?" Potier wondered.

"I *know* he will." Lestrade closed his eyes. "The only reason why he hasn't put a reward out for my death is his has some feelings for *mamm*. But he's always waiting for his opportunity . . . and as for you . . . ."

"Odd . . . I didn't know his slaves meant so much to him."

Lestrade flinched all over, as if a bolt had struck.

"Geoffrey, they were *my* grandsons too. Why do you think so many of us stayed away?"

"I never really noticed." Lestrade said quietly.

"Well, you were the youngest." Potier sighed and examined his hands. "Understand, *Ormin* . . . ." He deliberately used Lestrade's nickname from early childhood: "Ormin" because he couldn't pronounce the word correctly in his youth. "Armoricus made his choice long ago, before you were born and he realized Jethro was rich and his parents were poor. And Paul . . . ." He shrugged in a Gallek fashion. "Paul followed Armoricus in everything. The two were never without each other."

"But Armoricus was never without the Master's son."

"It was also true that Jethro was never without Armoricus." Potier sipped from his little bottle. "The bond they had was quite strong, Geoffrey. Quite . . . quite strong. And no one had the power to break it."

"Did they really want to?" Lestrade asked with no little bitterness. "It was what the Master wanted."

Potier did not run from the question. "Yes, it was what the Master wanted. Ivo Kemper had never lost in anything before, nor had he ever been bested in anything by your father. It would never occur to him that his . . . Well, his largess and feudal attitude would be so poorly received by the daughter of such a rich and important man." Irony and worse things slid through Potier's voice. "The Quimpers have forgotten themselves," he added as if it had just come to him. "We had money, and we had our power, but we were never more than what we wanted to be, *Mab* . . . Thomas was far more suited to Jeanne than Ivo was. But he couldn't conceive that a poor man who spoke to horses better than his own race would be better at him in something."

"Why didn't they just leave?" Lestrade wondered. "I've wondered that, every day for years. Why didn't they just leave?"

"I didn't know that answer myself . . . not until I learned, quite by accident, that Jeanne turned over *so much* of her sea-silk dowry to Ivo in trade for their lives." Potier sighed. "I *could* have called Ivo Kemper to war, but I would have been alone. The Lestrade and Glenan families were too few from the epidemics to side with me, and my brothers were dead from the storms. Their sons were all infants and their women-folks, deep in mourning. Kemper would have wiped your family all out, piece by piece, "accident" by "accident", for they were landlocked while I was as free as the oceans. Ivo was satisfied at the blood-money to his insult by taking the sea-silk . . . Your parents did not have much to escape with after that . . . and, I'm afraid, your mother was soon weakened with her succession of births. That's how she first started to grow ill. It wasn't long before the dowry was *all* gone . . . and they had nothing to flee *with*."

"Couldn't she have asked you for help?" This was a terrible night for questions.

Potier did not look at him. Perhaps he couldn't. "Even a flea can have some pride," he whispered. "And Ivo Quimper owned a piece of your father, as surely as his son owned a piece of your brother. I don't know what that dreadful bond is, and I *don't* want to know. It's none of my business. But Thomas is a man between the pincers." Potier closed his hand upon the air. "It was bad enough when you were a boy, Geoffrey. It was even worse in my day. I helped them escape the first time, you know."

Lestrade hadn't known, but it made sense. *Something* had driven Thomas to rescue his mother from Ivo Quimper's dubious "hospitality" at the Plymouth manor, and it had probably been the one impulsive movement of his life. Had his mother asked him for help? Most likely. And later, when they realized Thomas' family was still within the grasp of Quimper's bitter vindictiveness, Jeanne, warm and generous person that she was, had offered up thousands of pounds' worth of her family's sea-silk in trade for Ivo's forgiveness.

Only Ivo had had the final revenge after all. In Armoricus. It was a peculiar twist of anyone's fate that Geoffrey, the only L'estrade that was purely L'estrade in his loyalties, was born to be the outcast of the lot.

"It was Feudal." Potier murmured. "Completely feudal back then. The Kemper family has lost some of their power now, but back then . . . Men and women could do nothing without the word of their master. A single act of defiance would mean repercussions upon the entire family. A boy stands up to a Lord, a baron, a squire, a duke, even if it's only to correct a mild error . . . I *guarantee* you, that entire family will be the only one who misses their share of the harvest in the fall."

"Well . . . it's not so different in England." Lestrade picked at a loose thread at his sleeve. "Not so different at all. I suppose that's why there's so much contempt for the working class . . . because that independence couldn't be made unless they were either kicked out of the estates, or they ran away." [1]

"It's a fearful thing, to break all ties." Potier murmured. "I dislike your father, but I also pity him. There was a terrible burden upon his shoulders. To be free of the Kempers would also to be free of your other grandparents, and your cousins . . . your aunts and uncles. And they depended on *him* to hold them all together."

And that he did. He held them all together. But he could not hold on to a single son.

"But *I* had to leave." Lestrade knew. "I had to leave before they killed me or I killed them."

"Ya. *You* were strong enough. When they exiled you, it made you free from all of it, though it hurt like the Devil's teeth. Sometimes the only way to desert the ship is to cut the mainmast." Potier, oddly, made a sound of amusement.

"What?"

"Family is a strange thing, you know. My Jeanne takes after her mother. Adventurers in the blood, and yet . . . Utterly brave when it comes to the truth. Never once bothered them that there were those out there who could do something they couldn't do. My family, *we* were known for being willing to just leap into the breeze, or sail with the neap tides, and take a risk because we knew it was the right thing. Terrible tempers. Some of us disguise it in wit, I'm sorry to say.

"Your father was known for his amazing will. Always said he could wear out a *rock* in a fair fight . . . *His* parents were known for brains – languages on his mother's side, and there was the ability to make the *oddest* friends with his father's. And here *you* are, Geoffrey. Friendly with Gipsies, speaking their tongues, stubborn as a glacier, determined that no one ever hang *you* for the crime of false pride . . . A strange mix of us all,

170

a little of this and a little of that. I see *all* of us in you, unlike the others. They all took after the Glenan or Potier or Lestrade, like ymps off a graftling tree. Not you. You have a little legacy from everyone. Fitting then, that you were the one who could break away. I suppose you had no choice – all that combination of qualities, good and ill, inside you."

In retrospect, what Griox did was somewhat foolish. He had spent most of his life pretending to be something he was not. He should have considered he was not the only dissembler in the world.

The old *floders* were old for a reason, and carelessness was not it. The first row of bullets cut down the vanguard. The second shots for the leader of the remaining dogs. And the third ones were for him.

Gabriel and Pierrick, the tapped leaders for the group, observed the remains upon the wet grass as the dogs milled their confusion. The horses were little help. They had galloped off in a panic, possibly back to their stables but Gabriel doubted it.

"Now what?" Gael wondered. He was still chewing on a mouthful of dinner as he spoke. His half-brother Mael (they shared the same unimaginative father), was already cleaning out his guns for the next potential sally.

"Do what we always do." Gabriel shrugged. "We clean up after ourselves." He shook his head and poked at Griox, but the man remained dead, his blistered face turned to the gently waning moon. "Strange," he murmured.

"What is, friend?" Mael asked softly. It had been a long time since they'd had to kill anybody.

"I've waited two-and-twenty years to kill that man," Gabriel murmured. "He broke my father's back with his damned walking stick." He lowered himself to one knee and rifled through the pockets of the corpse with absent skill. "And suddenly he comes straight here."

"Life is like that." Mael offered gently. He tucked his cleaned gun back in its place.

"Let's clean up," Pierrick's son Per sighed. "I don't want the Seagull to come back home to a sight like this . . . he'll never have us over again."

"Seawater or sinkhole?" Per wondered.

"Seawater." Gabriel said after a moment's thought. "No garbage down the sinkholes if we can help it, men. Egypt's caves are for the *dead*, but ours are for the *living*."

"Ah."

Potier stopped and pulled a slow, relighting breath into his body. The faintest blush of soft salt air sank inside his lungs, soaked into his blood vessels, suffused his entire being. "We're close."

"Two miles is close," Ploudaniel smiled. "I did tell the others to meet us at the depot. With luck and no delays, we'll be there before midday. How's the arm?"

"I'm glad the moon-milk is coming up." Potier answered. "You said the crop was good this year?"

"Plenty of it."

Dooley poked Lestrade with his pipestem. "What the devil is moon-milk?" He glared at the little detective's shrug. "You aren't any help at all, are you lad?"

"I never claimed to be, not *now*." Lestrade snapped wearily. He got a friendly slap on the back for his troubles. It hurt terribly.

The past two hours had been spent in a shambling sort of haze, and Lestrade knew he had no intelligent clue as to where they were at this point. Cavern systems were unlike animal trails. They followed the paths of water, which in turn followed only the weakest points in the stone matrix that held up the land itself. And who could tell by looking where the weak points were? His normally excellent sense of direction had been thrown to the subterranean winds as they felt like they were climbing upwards, bending backwards, returning to one direction, rising to another level, sliding down another through a slick clay ramp, and splashing through infinite tiny streams.

Frogs and a few fish met the haze of their lanterns. Their unblinking gaze chilled the detective as they passed them by, but they seemed to feel – and dislike – the heat from the flames.

"They've gone blind," Ploudaniel told him. "It only takes a few days. Sometimes they can live a long time. The fish especially."

"What do they live on?" Lestrade strangled.

"Whatever they can." Ploudaniel was looking at the faint, drifting swarms of spring-hatched insects washed from outside, but Lestrade knew what "whatever" meant, and he shuddered without any sense of shame.

They grew warm again. The fog slowly crept up from their bodies and hovered over their heads and shoulders in a warm mist. The cold water of the streams began to feel good as they passed through. Unbelievable as it was, they were sweating. Ploudaniel doled out dried fruit, mostly meat plums, and raw bacon with hardtack crackers. They ate as they passed a softly shining white city of calcite crystals, complete with towers and minarets and odd lumps like the Russian onion domes. More water slid down the delicate sculpture, collecting into pools so clear they were magnified. The pawprints of a cat walked in the bowl of such a pool. Its

172

pads were as large as a lion's out of the zoo. The small crumbs fell from their hands to the bottom of the cave but there was no need to worry about a trail of breadcrumbs in this fairy tale. Anything that could be eaten, would be. In a matter of hours. Small crickets scuttled away from their lamplight, returning at their departure.

"Get ready," Potier's voice was rough from exhaustion. "We're about to walk on the Drums. If anyone's following us, this would be the time to find which passage we took."

"What are the Drums?" Once in a while, that damnable Potier curiosity took control. Being around other Potiers must have a lot to do with it.

Potier, leading the way, took a step upward, knocking the faint traces of sand from his soles as he did so. They were on a narrow path, but instead of sand or silt or earth or clay at their feet stretched a long expanse of dull orange and blue-tinted stone, smooth as the water-worn rock that faced their sides. Up, down, left and right, it was nothing but a passage gently covered with an opaque layer of cave rock.

The old smuggler tapped the toe of his thin wooden boot on the path.

Lestrade felt the hair on his neck stand up and salute as his spine congealed to ice. A low, musical throb had echoed throughout the cave from that single step. *Hollow.* There was air beneath their feet, beneath this layer of stone.

"A long time ago, this was all a quiet, still pool." Potier murmured. "The minerals that make these underground cities and shapes and straws and spirals . . . they had no place to go. So the minerals began to grow *over* the top of the water. Finally, the stone closed up and the water died away. It's all a big stone bubble, strong as bedrock . . . but I've heard people play these dead pools like a musical orchestra."

"Interesting." Dooley murmured. Out of respect for being tracked, he chewed on a cold pipe. "I'm not too old to learn something, I see." His green-blue old eyes were shining, and Lestrade knew the rascal was *enjoying* himself.

"We'll stop to check on everyone's hurts at the end of this," Ploudaniel said sternly. "Let's go . . . and walk quietly."

Lestrade didn't have to be told twice. Or even once – not after hearing that hollow echo vibrate under their feet.

NOTE

1.   This feudal system lasted especially strong in the country, even during World War II.

Chapter XIX – Idle Cop
Nets Arrests

The box of wax vestas scattered across the smooth stone floor. A tobacco tin followed, its ring dull and sharp as loose gunpowder rolled out in a black stream.

Potier cursed under his breath. "Of all the luck," he swore again as they stopped, single file, and Lestrade knelt to help him sweep it all up. The powder grains were the worst. Dooley produced a goose-feather, scissored neatly across the top like the world's smallest whisk broom, and they managed to get most of it off and on to a flat piece of paper.

"Padriac, why are you carrying a *feather* around in your pocket?" Lestrade began, and then caught that particular expression on the old man. "Never mind," he assured him quickly. *He's probably using it to forge antiques or something . . .*

Potier rose slowly, reassured that as many possible traces had been eliminated. "Not much longer," he told them. Ploudaniel nodded confidently. He was looking brighter and more alert now that they were getting closer to their goal.

Lestrade was glad for it. They had not just walked. They had *crawled* too, and inched sideways, making the length of the (comparatively) short cavern passage feel three to four times more its actual charting. There were places that the wolfhounds had found unpleasant, but to do them credit they hadn't actually complained other than giving their master a look that was disturbingly human and personable. Had they been walking on two legs, Lestrade was certain they would be lobbying the old man for extra portions at mealtime. But never a whine. Not even from Phorp. The limping sight-hound still had Quimper's dark blood on his fur. *And they saved our lives. They're entitled to at least a good meal.*

They continued on, slowly, and more cautious. The tiny dark lanterns were being rationed out carefully. On occasion the little detective renewed an aching part of his leg, sides, or arms with a brush against a sharp jut of rock inside the pale matrix of the rock. By degrees the air slid past their faces, fresher and smelling of the sea.

"How far are we from the coast?" Lestrade finally murmured.

"Hmm, not far . . . probably three miles as the crow flies." Ploudaniel calculated. "We're lucky it's springtime. In winter, the air flow reverses and it smells musty." He abruptly hopped straight down, no warning, his bootsoles clicking on grey rock. He turned and held up his arms, guiding

Potier to his side. The hounds merely hopped down, once they saw where it would be safe.

Long ago, an underground stream larger than a London sewer culvert had washed downhill at a fifteen-degree slope. It left in its wake a jumble of stones the size of carts, and a pile of soft clay riverbank against the walls. Small shapes huddled up at the top. Bats, Lestrade realized. He wondered if they were waking up yet or were they still asleep?

But the water had not completely become extinct. A lively hum of a small brook vibrated somewhere by his ear, and he turned to watch the old smugglers carefully picking their way down the rock. He switched out Dooley's lantern for him as the old Tinker paused to check his own precious tobacco supply.

"More fun to smoke it than chew, let me tell you," the grizzled elder said.

Lestrade laughed wearily. "I think I'd fight Quimper as-is to have my pipe back," he confessed. "I'd even let him keep his wretched walking stick."

Dooley's woolly eyebrows floated up to a spot somewhere close to his scalp. "Do you think he's alive?"

"I don't know, but Phorp gave good. I'm no stranger to getting mauled by a dog, but I've *never* been attacked by something as serious as a wolfhound." They made their way after the *floders* with a great deal more caution. "The fact that Phorp's got a stab in his paw and not a bullethole tells me he was completely taken by surprise."

"If he's alive, he'll be hurting for a good long time," Dooley said with confidence. "Gipsies can't murder, Galvin. You know that. We fight in wars once in a while, but something like this is different. That's why we have dogs. Mostly, the *sight* of them keeps people away, but when that's not good enough . . . ." He shrugged, oddly sweet and matter of fact.

"I'm sorry about your wagons and supplies." Lestrade admitted.

"I wouldn't worry about that either. Ploudaniel and the others promised to keep an eye on them until we could return for them . . . which I suspect won't be *much* longer."

They fell silent, neither one needing to talk – and even thinking wasn't that good of an idea right now, with so many possible things to slip and fall on. This wasn't the surface world. This was the deeper, older world beneath it, and a broken bone could take days to address.

They turned a bend. The rock had been water-carved into a shape strange and elusive, like a flattened frog with stretched-out feet. They turned inside the curve of the shape and found themselves in another grotto. Something brushed the now-worn leather of Lestrade's boot. He looked down in reflex. A stone spearhead glinted back at him.

175

"Just kick them aside," Potier suggested. "They're all over the place."

Lestrade took in the fact that this was quite true. What he'd thought was the mixed colours of the stone floor was in reality a long-forgotten flint mine. Shards of flint points, broken points, failed points, and creditable pieces were littered across from where they were to the small pool glimmering in their lantern-light. He recognized arrowheads, longer spearheads . . . something like small barbed fishing hooks, but there were some items he quickly gave up on. They were for functions or uses that he didn't have any background to recognize.

Something caught his eyes, an alien shape. He paused to pick it up while the others moved to the pool and drink their thirst away. A small arrowhead. He turned it over in his hand, puzzled at its shape. Something like one of those strange German Yuletide trees, and the suggestion of a serrated side. A crack in the centre of the tool gave the reason for its abandonment.

"I always liked those," Potier had come up to his side. "They remind me of the tips I would find in the fields when we were in Cornwall. I used to wonder if it meant we weren't the first wave of Bretons fleeing one invasion or another . . . Perhaps we were fleeing a particularly annoying Roman despot, ya? Or perhaps someone learned the design over there and liked it so much he kept it."

Lestrade smiled despite himself. "What if the Cornish design came from here?"

"Ha! Good thought!" Potier chuckled. "I wish we had the time to teach you, *Mab-bihan*. I'd take you to the *kev* where the crystal rock devoured the bones of a great bear. Or show you the *kev* paintings. That's something to see. But that can wait for a better day. For now, drink. It's easy to run too far on too little water."

Lestrade put the stone tip back on the floor, but with a faint regret and not understanding the mystery. Martin would burn to know . . . He drank like the others, feeling the ache in his teeth from the sheer coldness. Tiny balls of crystal rolled in the bottom of the pool like pearls, stirred by that slight action of the water as he pulled it up in his hands.

Is this where the stories of underground cities and treasures came from? Once prodded, the thought held a fierce life of its own and would not be easily buried. Small people, the earthen dwarves . . . they would have fit in these strange, tiny passages. These glittering white domes of silver and crystal and silk and pearls would have been turned into incredible spirit realms with only the least amount of imagination. Spirit realm indeed. The living resided here . . . but never for long. This was a place to visit, never to claim. It was haunted by the remainders of lost centuries.

Lestrade was rarely hindered by imagination. He far preferred it that way. Imagination was not something he trusted. It could too easily take control of its owner and lead to incalculable failures and errors. He still didn't understand how Sherlock Holmes could do what he did without working inside the boundaries of what was known and *proven* investigative procedure. [1]

Still . . . he was beginning to feel a slight sense of . . . perhaps *guilt* was the word . . . or trespassing into a dead man's house. He knew the owner was dead, and yet . . . it was disrespectful.

"Here we are! Hold still." Potier did not explain himself. One minute Lestrade was staring at tiny pearls rolling in the bottom of a cave pool. The next, he was shoved firmly into a stone bench that still had the tool cuts of its Neolithic owners in the sides. His grandfather lightly recleaned the stitches at his scalp – and by his grimace, Lestrade suspected it did not look very pretty.

"Now. Nothing like a salve of moon-milk." Potier then leaned backward and scooped up with one fingertip a runnel of pure white ooze slowly edging its way down the wall of the cave. It came off like thick cream. Before Lestrade could ask what he was doing, the cool, wet stuff was liberally plastered all over the stitches.

"That should do it." The old man beamed and quickly stripped off his jacket to give his arm the same treatment. In the lantern glow his miss-shot bullet wound was ghastly. It gleamed black and charred from the close-range strike, the rest of it ringed in swollen plum-purple and fading to a nauseating green the colour of a frog's belly. Lestrade was too busy trying not to say anything to the sight, and so he remained wordless while he dressed up his wound with the same stuff that was on his head.

"We don't know what this is, or how it forms, or how it even does what it does," Potier managed to give the least reassuring explanation Lestrade had ever heard in his life, "but it does seem to help you heal up from wounds."

"I think I'll stick with acorn mold," Dooley lipped his pipe stem. "No offense, but seeing as how I'm not in need of it . . . Phorp will take a little, though . . . ." And to show his polite curiosity, he indeed dressed the dog's paw with the soft stuff.

Lestrade frankly had far more faith in the acorn mould, as well as the absolutely vile and bitter yellow tea Dooley's wife brewed up for everyone at the slightest hint of a bad illness. He rubbed the back of his neck and rolled his head, testing the joints for their ability to move. "How much longer until we're out? And for that matter, where are we going to show up?"

"Our end goal is the patch of sea caves." Ploudaniel looked as though he wanted to smoke too. "The whole Dooley tribe is waiting with the rest of the *floders*. Once we check and see who won what from who in the cardgames I'm sure Loic started up, it's just a matter of getting one of Sein's grandsons to let us get into one of their boats and head on out."

"Then it's almost over." Lestrade breathed.

"Ya." Potier grinned. He looked almost regretful. "But how are we going to send word home to your folk, *Mab*?"

Lestrade furrowed his brow. "I'll think of something."

Clea Lestrade leaned back and wearily wiped her forehead with the back of her hand. Her thoughts were in a turmoil – quite the usual of her standard calm and sensibility. There were too many things to think of. Geoffrey's trouble – surely a disaster worthy of a Biblical rendition. Martin was drooping like an ivy – and was being about as talkative as one too. Of all the times to act like a Cheatham. Nicholas was burying himself into his thoughts and spending rather too much time with his older cousins – which wouldn't be so bad if they weren't complaining that he was so good at beating them at the stickball games in the back of the garden. Clea fancied she understood what he was doing. She was starting to do battle in the kitchen, and poor Elizabeth had seemed to understand her need to cook out her frustrations and angers.

But there comes a time when you either run out of bread dough, or flour, or sugar, or salt. Eventually the dishes pile to the top because you've overworked the limits of the kitchen. You can no longer run to the butcher's or fishmonger's because you've fed your family to the point of stupor and if they eat *anything*, it's because they're trying to spare what's left of your feelings.

That left the teapot and solitude.

Clea poured herself the first of what would no doubt be many successions of a smoky twig tea and stirred until she wondered what the point was. She hadn't even put the sugar in yet.

I should have started sewing again. Her fingers itched, but only from habit. She was too tired to do anything with a sharp implement and a delicate piece of cloth.

Her eyes burned wearily, or from the residual smoke in the kitchen. Even her *hands* were sore from all the lifting and pulling of cast-iron tools and pots and pans. She drew the cup up and sipped lightly, taking a grain of comfort in her surroundings. The sunlight of dawn was beginning to show itself through the layers of delicate linen and lace of the breakfast room window. Grey and sad though it seemed from its spot at the canals, she was glad to see it.

178

The toy blocks were still spilt across the little table. She could only look at them, her eyes unfocused slightly, thinking of the night Geoffrey had brought the whole lot home. Beechwood and milk paint, letters, numbers and simple shapes carved along the sides. It had been a typically generous gift of Hazel. Some women would have held on to the items like misers, waiting optimistically for the day they could hand them down to their childers' childers.

For several weeks, Martin had merely fascinated himself with the potentials of a career in civil engineering. For a child, he was most particular in what he wanted to do and how he wanted to do it. (Geoffrey professed ignorance of family knowledge, but Clea was fair certain she knew to blame his side of the tree for that trait.) Walls of blocks were built, slowly and carefully. He learned how high was sensible, and how long a low wall could stretch.

Then one evening Clea (pregnant with Nicholas and half-mad with boredom) ran down the street for some of the fall grapes. She returned to find Geoffrey by the fire, reading the newspaper with his feet out. Martin was lying across the tops of his father's slippers and frowning as he created three separate rectangles of blocks, each one separated by colour: Red, Yellow, Blue. The black ones he was simply ignoring. Clea still remembered the humour of the sight, and how grateful Geoffrey was to have her distract the solid little weight off his numbing ankles.

Clea smiled again at the memory. It always made her smile to think of that, and many other memories. They had few quarrels, but then, there'd been quarrels *enough* during their courtship. Neither of them actually pulled their work home with them. Their household was supposed to be a place of refuge. By unspoken consent, Geoffrey kept his work to the one office nook in the rooms, and Clea made a place for herself in the lower kitchen away from Mrs. Collins' maids. Otherwise . . . that was that.

Movement caught her eye through the pale shimmer of fog. Her heart leaped in her chest, driving out the cozy thoughts. A messenger in full uniform plus a muffler against the damp was leaning his bicycle against the low stone wall of the Cheatham House, pausing only to check his clothing for any flaws before squaring his shoulders and marching forward. Clea almost laughed out loud at the boy's concerns. The laugh died in her throat. It was a telegram missive in his hands. He was just clearing the front porch when she thought to put her teacup down.

Reg Song
Play for charity supper
If may clear stop
Safety not issues stop

Clea's jaw dropped at the paper in her hand. Seconds later she was racing out the door and screaming for a cab.

"It's *Geoffrey!*" she panted. "I know it is!"

Inspector Gregson looked at her in mild shock across his desk.

"We came up with it one night." Clea cleared her throat, willing herself to calm. "We were playing a game with anagrams using the children's toy blocks. Geoffrey took 'Inspector Lestrade' and came up with '*Idle Cop Nets Arrests.*' I had 'Clea Marie' and I came up with *Maie Clear*, but he said I was cheating for using the Old Spelling for the month of May . . . ."

"'*May Clear*'," Gregson supplied. His beefy face was slowly clearing in a look of anticipation. Gregson whistled shrilly. "And he sent the telegram to you because you played the game with him, and we're no doubt being monitored . . . ." His lips set in his broad face. "'*Safety not issue* . . . .' I'll just bet that means he's sneaking in underneath the weather. Trust your husband to bull his way through *that* china shop." He glared at the mark on the paper. "I know this telegraph station," he sighed. "Man's worthless." A square finger poked it. "What does this charity supper mean, you think?"

"I have a charity to cook for the day after tomorrow," she answered, just beginning to shake. "I turned it over to my staff . . . but Geoffrey knew it was a job that was weighing on my mind."

"What's Reg Song – oh." Gregson blushed in embarrassment. "Pardon me, I didn't recognize my own name there." He cleared his throat. "So it's addressed to me, translated through you, sent to your father to keep anyone from overtly noticing . . . to let us know that he's coming home the day after tomorrow . . . ." The big man rubbed his jaw. "The question is, *where's* he coming from?"

Midday, Brittany:

"Lovely beard you're growing there, Galvin."

Lestrade paused just long enough from what promised to be a frantic digging along his face and gave Dooley a terrific glare of contempt. "At least it's clean," he snipped. "How can you tell when a dishwater beard is dirty, anyway?"

"Ooh, I'm hurt." Dooley slapped his knee and laughed. He would have slapped the inspector on the back of his shoulder, but decided not to.

The man was a walking medical lesson as it was. "We Tinkers are naturally clean folk – as well you know."

"Well I know." Lestrade agreed. Tinkers were more than clean – obsessed might be the real word. They didn't even wash male and female clothing together.

The reunion of the Tinkers had been heralded by the wolfhounds. Dooley took pity on their straining eagerness and gave them permission to "go home" and the pack loped with that frightening speed and inhuman grace through the opening passage to a wide-open chamber, large enough to play a game of rugby in. Children swarmed right back, climbing over their elder with the eagerness of birds upon a very thick chunk of suet.

Potier paused only to laugh, and took stock of the situation. "How is it?" He lapsed into the older Breton dialect of his youth for expediency. Lestrade understood it only because he'd once lived with the man for an entire season. Not feeling ready to talk again, me merely leaned against a bundle of sea-tack and closed his eyes in complete weariness.

"Griox tried to attack your house, Old Man." Lioc spoke. "They were all cut down. Don't worry about the mess . . . it was taken care of."

Potier smiled without any humour whatsoever. It thickened his voice. "I warned that one years ago. Did he think we were being falsely prideful? Well, it will be a bit of a safer land. Don't tell my grandson. He might have to act like a policeman someday."

Yes, Lestrade thought. *Please do not.*

"Anything else?"

"We had a report that Kemper is alive, but only just. He's got no less than four doctors working over him, and rumour has it he won't be the same ever again."

"Nor would anyone be. I'm satisfied with that, but I'll keep my eyes on the horizon. Sometimes a dog is more dangerous when it's wounded." Potier slapped someone's back. "When can we head out?"

"We've got a bit of a delay." Sein spoke roughly. "The ferry *just* borrowed the better boat to deal with some heavy traffic . . . Seems there's been some sort of strange death the British *poliser* want to deal with."

"A death they didn't want to deal with when they thought my grandson was dead?" Potier asked in a voice like a freshly forged bear trap. "What death would this be?"

"Someone important, that's all we know. Someone working with the English government. An entire day-party was moved to an hour's delay, and the whole lot of them – Parisians, those complaining babies – *insisted* they would have their sailing with our without the usual methods. So they pushed a handful of money at my grandsons, and of course they took it."

Sein sniffed. "I hope the man was worth it, that's all I can say. We might be sailing across the Channel with his coffin."

NOTE

1   This is, of course, before the events of "The Bruce-Partington Plans" in 1895, and Lestrade doesn't know that Holmes operates well outside the boundaries of the law. It's this lack of knowledge that fosters a good bit of his suspicion and skepticism (in my opinion).

Chapter All the Difference

The big man was leaning upright against a slightly grimy pier post that had once moored a French pleasure-craft along the dock of the Channel ferry. A dusty newspaper folded and refolded inside his hands as he read from page to page and started over constantly. Against the dark blue wool of his coat, a brightly polished badge gleamed. Such a sight was almost unheard of – plain-clothed policemen chose to dress like the ordinary fellow at every opportunity. Lestrade couldn't believe it.

Triaged Potier couldn't believe it either – especially the way his grandson was running through the crowd as heedless as a billiards ball on the wrong end of the cue.

Just in time, the big man saw who was about to greet him. Like the sun coming out of a cloud, he dropped all pretense of acting casual and whooped. There were enough French out there that they didn't even notice strangely acting Englishmen.

"Geoffrey Lestrade! And here you swore to never grow a beard unless we headed back to the days of the hairy elephants!"

"Roger Bradstreet, you blooming idiot, what happened? Did the raid succeed? Where are Cooper and Forbes? How did you know to find – " Lestrade abruptly answered his own question. "You took the address off the telegraph station. But how'd you get here so quickly? We've been waiting to cross for hours!"

"Oh, we were waiting for *you*. Especially since we decided not to trust that moronic Patterson after the way he practically set the three of you up – The lads are fine, Geoff." Bradstreet held up a hand. "Both of them are just fine, but worried sick about you. I took the liberty of letting them know where I was going and why before I headed out of London."

"Thank God for that." Lestrade closed his eyes. Over his shoulder, Bradstreet was goggling at an older, even smaller version of his old friend. Then another part of Bradstreet's statement came back to him. "What's all this about Patterson? Moriarty's gang seemed a little concerned about him."

"Oh . . . I can see that." Bradstreet said, taking in Geoffrey's bruises with a slightly perturbed look. "It's a long story, but worth the telling. We'll just wait until you're back among your family first, right?"

"Bradstreet . . . Did you lose your temper with Patterson?"

"Well, not really. Gregson was there to see it not get out of hand. And Patterson never told me to *stop*."

Lestrade closed his eyes again. "This is the part where I tell you that I'm not at all curious as to the particulars," he said wearily.

"But that's the best part," Bradstreet protested. "Don't you want to hear how I smashed him into the wall and used his spinal column for a masonry mallet? There're Patterson-sized outlines in the Frazier alley building now where all the bricks have been knocked into place." Bradstreet suddenly gulped for air and a second later, Lestrade yelped in pain as powerful arms clutched.

"*Ouch!*" Lestrade exclaimed, and he did not care who heard him. "You sodding dimwit! Bradstreet, if I wasn't beaten to sand grains right now, I'd – "

"Thank God!" the half-Scot breathed. "Geoffrey . . . just . . . ." He searched his friend's face, eyes trembling with emotion. "Thank God."

"You were *that* worried?" Lestrade wasn't ashamed for staring. Bradstreet had faced the deaths of his parents, his baby sister, and three of his own children. He didn't react like this in public . . . .

"My God, it's been a disaster." Bradstreet said brokenly. "You have no idea. It's going to take years to straighten this out. Even before Moriarty killed Mr. Holmes, it all fell apart. Patterson had friends all the way up in the Foreign Office! The – "

Lestrade clenched his arms tightly enough to bruise. "Mr. Holmes is dead?" he gasped. "When? *Moriarty killed him?*"

Bradstreet nodded bleakly. "Or he killed Moriarty. There's no telling which. Mr. Holmes took the doctor and they fled London while the raid went down, but *Moriarty followed him.* They caught up in Switzerland. Dr. Watson was sent on a blind case and when he came back, Holmes was gone at the edge of a big waterfall and there was a note he'd left behind to read." Bradstreet held out the newspaper he'd been pretending to read. "Watson sent us a wire. And . . . it talks about it here," he said softly. "For all of twenty-five words." He looked down. "After I see you to your folks, I'm going to the train station. We're all going to meet the doctor when he gets off. Not right for his poor little wife to be out there late at night . . . ."

Sherlock Holmes was dead. It wasn't real.

Watson. Lestrade staggered back, the newspaper falling through his fingers page by page to hit the deck. Potier yelped faintly and dove for them, hungry for the news of the outside world. Lestrade let him. His eyes were glazed over from this one last shock.

Dr. Watson was coming back by himself. The newspapers – He was alive. But Sherlock Holmes was dead. Lestrade tried to consider it, but nothing happened. No insight broke through the wall of cloudy ice in his world.

"What is it?" Potier wondered, stunned by the way his grandson had survived all, only to go grey and waxen at the sight of a newspaper.

"It means," Bradstreet murmured, "that London is changed."

"Just . . . We're going to the station with you." Lestrade rasped, his voice faint and sick. "You're right . . . Mrs. Watson shouldn't . . . ."

"I know." Bradstreet murmured. "I wanted you to know, but . . . if you wanted to go home to your wife . . . ."

Lestrade closed his eyes. "I do," he said brokenly. "But fifteen minutes . . . just fifteen minutes. That's all the difference for a man who once saved my life. And yours . . . ."

INTERLUDE
"Just Inspector Will Do"

After the events of May 4th, 1891: Paddington Station

She was no stranger to the crushing sense of defeat that tragedy inspired. Small and delicate-looking – delicate *within*, too, she knew – Mary Watson was still strong in spirit.

She was not completely aware of this. What she thought of as simple decency required much more courage than the average person was willing to take.

And so she waited for the train that would bring her husband home, standing against the pillar, and knew the ache in her legs would become severe soon enough, but to sit in one of the soot-crusted benches was more than she could take at the moment. *I should have come earlier*, she mourned to herself. *I could have at least bought one of the papers* . . . Then she thought of what the papers might say, and stifled a swallow.

"Mrs. Watson?"

Mary blinked and jumped, shocked at being witnessed in her behavior. She wasn't certain she knew the man. Not through the watery curtain in her eyes. He was soberly dressed and another man stood just behind him – she couldn't make *him* out at all in the cloudy night air. The passing crowd flowed and stumbled against a third man, then a fourth. They were dressed neatly and carefully, but there was a unity to their overall look that set them apart from the rest.

Mary Watson blinked her eyes clear. Her face ran wet and the first man wordlessly produced a clean handkerchief. She wiped her cheeks, then had to do it again. As she watched, plainclothed men were slowly filing themselves through the congested crowd, blocking the worst of the traffic with their bodies until she was left in a breathing spot by the bench.

"We heard the news, Mrs. Watson," her spokesman said. Despite the marks of what must have been a terribly long day on his dustcoat and face, his eyes were warm and kind. "Please accept the condolences of Scotland Yard. Your husband has lost a fine friend."

A hollow box had assembled. Mary realized there really were more constables, strolling with their truncheons and clopping their heavy boots, than needed be. She blinked, and wondered how many people on the train station *weren't* policemen.

186

"He was the best man at my wedding," Mary stammered. His handkerchief was all but useless shreds now.

The man smiled. He was so tired his eyes were bloodshot. "I remember," he said softly.

Mary put two and two together. Her eyes narrowed slightly in thought. "I . . . *you* were at my wedding too." She blushed. "I'm so sorry . . . I didn't recognize . . . ." Behind her, the whistle of a train one mile from the station was shrilling. It swallowed up her attempt to speak and she fell silent, abashed.

"Not at all." He touched the brim of his day-battered hat with his fingers. "I believe we were *all* at your wedding . . . Well, save poor Irons. I think *he* was down with the shingles, or something like that." He paused. His lips twisted. Despite the sadness of the occasion, his face was wry, viewing the world in equal parts sadness and gentle humor. "We weren't going to miss the sight of Mr. Holmes *at a wedding,* Mrs. Watson. It was a bit of an historical occasion. Always swore he'd *never* attend one, even if Wagner was playing."

Mary smiled as the lump swelled her throat. She agreed, but the idea of Wagner at a wedding was enough to make her laugh. "He . . . he even managed to pretend he didn't mind being the best man for a few minutes," One of the men had covered the bench with his coat. He offered it with a silent little bow and she hesitantly took it. Her aching body sighed in relief. "He cared for John that much."

"We can understand that." The man nodded. He glanced about to make certain everyone was in formation. "Mr. Holmes would have never accepted any gesture of friendship, Mrs. Watson . . . Consider this our chance to show our respect."

"Thank you, Mr. – ?" Mary sniffed. "Inspector?"

"Just . . . *Inspector.*" He smiled. "Inspector will do."

Minutes later, John Watson peered out the window, looking anxiously for his wife while hoping against hope that she had *not* taxed herself by coming out. Steam and night air mixed and clambered against his face and in his ears. The lantern light threw pools of watery yellow shadow on the scarred platform.

At first he wondered if there had been some mistake. The pools of yellow spread and shifted, ran into each other as more pools emerged.

Then the lights began to rise.

Watson's mouth dropped open.

His wife sat, safe and protected from the worst of the railroad fumes within a dancing bouquet of fire. Balls of oily flame depended from hoops inside held in each gloved hand, until the platform was full of tired and footsore men, uniformed and plainclothed, waiting patiently for his return.

And Watson thought that while Holmes's clients had been Kings and Cardinals, they had *only* given mere accolades and praises. The next morning, when Holmes's solicitor asked about the funeral eulogy, Watson answered truthfully it had already been given.

Epilogue

"Clea Marie, quit chewing your fingernails," Charles Cheatham said patiently.

Clea yanked her hand out of her mouth. "How did you know?" She demanded. In the large open drawing room, her brothers had collected with her to await the cab.

"When you're oddly quiet and pacing . . . ." The old wrestler shrugged his shoulders.

"We could have met them at the station," she mumbled.

Charles only smiled. "That would have been hard on the boys, dear. You know that."

"I know . . . ," she muttered. "I'm just . . . I'm just glad there's a happy ending." Unlike what had happened elsewhere. Only a few newspapers had picked up the death of the Great Detective. Their words had been short and sere. Clea wondered if they would have done the same to *Geoffrey* had he been the sacrifice.

Charles put his log-like arm around his little daughter. "Shall someone wake the boys?"

"I wouldn't," Myron spoke. "It took them long enough to go to sleep. Let them wake themselves. They shouldn't hold it against us."

"Besides," Andrew added, "they shouldn't have to hear Clea rip the hide off their father."

"I'm not about to do any such thing!" Clea protested a bit too loudly.

"*Whssht*," Bartram grunted. "Someone's coming up the way." He stopped. "It's Geoffrey. He's not alone. There's another man with him." He paused, frowning through the glass. "An old man."

"Now, hold still, Clea." Charles tightened his grip on his daughter. "We don't know who the man is."

Lestrade took in the fact that Bartram Cheatham, his *least*-amicable brother-in-law, was on the other side of the window at the door. "The more things change, the more they stay the same," he said under his breath.

"He's little." Bartram said.

"*That's* no help, Bartram." Andrew sighed. "Next to you, we're *all* little."

"Never were funny, Andrew. It's time someone told you." Bartram leaned forward and opened the door just as Lestrade's hand brushed the knob. "Hurry up," he grunted to his brother-in-law. "It's cold out there."

Lestrade swallowed his astonishment at having been spoken to by Bartram over something that *didn't* have to do with wrestling or eating,

189

and ushered his grandfather inside. The warm was a blessing after the long drive.

And then Clea nearly knocked him flat. He gasped as the impact nearly knocked him into his grandfather. The old smuggler chuckled delightedly.

"Geoffrey Lestrade, don't you ever do that again!"

Andrew sighed superciliously. He looked at Myron. "What did I tell you?"

"What are you complaining about, Andrew?" Myron sniffed. "If she wasn't married to him, it'd be all on us."

Robert sucked his breath in. The brothers followed his gaze. Clea's embrace had pulled the sleeves up her husband's wrists. Bartram grimaced. "And the bastard's still alive." Robert's gentle manners were not much in view at that moment.

"I was worried sick," Clea was crushing his lapels in her fists. "Good God, what happened to you? Did you get hit on the head again? What's wrong with your arm? You're *tanned*! – " She noticed for the first time that a strangely familiar man was smiling at her as if he knew who she was.

"I'm afraid that's because I had to smuggle myself out of the peninsula." Geoffrey was laughing with relief. "Clea, please meet the man who performed that miracle. Triaged Potier, my mother's father." He reversed the greeting. *"Tad-kohz, gwreg."*

"Oh, my Lord!" Clea blurted. She promptly blushed. "Forgive me my manners," she stammered. "At . . . at your service, sir." What did one say to a reconciled lost relative?

The old man beamed, all charm under his weatherbeaten beard. *"Allo, Itron-bihan."* He took her hands inside his own. *"Allo."* And because he wasn't expected to be English, he promptly hugged her and kissed both cheeks. He looked to Geoffrey and rattled off a pepper-pot of words that she couldn't hope to translate.

Geoffrey scowled like a drumhead in July and rattled off something back.

"What do you think they're talking about?" Andrew murmured to Myron.

Myron gave her a droll look. "I daresay something about the possibility of great-grand-daughters."

"I think that's a fine idea." Andrew crossed his arms.

"You don't like children." Bartram grunted.

"That's not the point. Think of Clea with a daughter or two just like her. It's justice incarnate." Andrew raised his voice. "Looks like you know what Geoffrey will look like when he's that old. So sorry, Love."

"Ha!" The old man displayed a grasp of English with a laugh. "You Andrew!" He pointed. "Autrou Beg!"

Geoffrey clapped his hand over his grandfather's mouth and said something in a desperate voice. The old man patently agreed to humor him. At this point Martin and Nicholas came flying through the forest of adult limbs and paid no more respect to their father's bandages than their mother had. Bartram, for one, winced.

"Nicholas," Geoffrey whispered faintly, " . . . watch the ribs . . . ."

"Sorry." Nicholas wasn't. He put his head on his father's shoulders and kept it there, his eyes closed with a beatific smile. Martin stood on the couch so he could take advantage of the height, and grinned at his father. He had a bit more dignity than Nicholas, but his emotions were in his eyes.

"Martin, Nicholas," Clea said softly. "This is your great-grandfather."

Alone at last. It had been a victory in itself. Both men had their job to convince the others they needed nothing in the way of food, but Geoffrey pleaded the need for sleep and left the old men downstairs by the fire with two enamored little boys who were thrilled to have two grandfathers to adore. (Great-grandfather? Grandfather? Small difference to their mind.) Geoffrey said good night to his grandfather in Breton in a way that sounded like he was telling Triaged not to be a bad influence, steal the silverware, or teach the boys anything illegal. Clea waited for the door to click shut in its lock and just stepped inside his waiting arms. For a long time neither moved. Her head fitted against its usual place at his shoulder. Their quiet breathing mixed with the fire's crackle.

"I could start crying now," she said into his necktie.

"I wouldn't blame you," he protested.

"I can't cry. I'm just . . . I'm just too happy to have you back." She sniffed slightly. Finally alone, she was free to stretch up and kiss him. He tensed slightly, an unfamiliar body language but he said nothing. She didn't understand. Her hand touched his shoulder. "At any rate, you need to get that soot off. Let's get you undressed."

"*Ouch!*"

"Sorry!" Clea's hands shot away from the dark bruise on Geoffrey's arm. "Geoffrey, how am I supposed to get you ready for bed if I can't touch you?"

"Just." Geoffrey shook himself. "just *don't* . . . touch . . . *there.*"

"I'll have to if I'm to get that sleeve off." Clea protested. She looked at him. "No, *we're* getting this off. We'll just have to be careful."

"I'm not even going to move," he promised. She smiled.

He waited uneasily for the cufflink to fall away. The material opened up like a book, showing the marks on the wrist bones track up past the elbow.

"Oh, Geoffrey," she whispered.

"It's all right," he said – stupidly, really. *Now* she was crying.

"I know," she sniffed. "And I'll be all right. I think this just has to come out now . . . like my mum used to say. How in the world are we going to get you clean? Hot water's going to burn like the devil."

"It won't be as bad as seawater." Geoffrey said philosophically. "But I think this calls for a sponge, not a scrub brush."

It was over with quickly, and Geoffrey was asleep as soon as his touched the bed linen. Clea didn't blame him one bit – she felt as though she hadn't slept in months – but she did envy him that ability. Tomorrow he would be finishing his report to all his superiors and going back to his thirteen-day working schedule. She didn't know if he would give them the same story he had to her.

"Crime is changing. More organization. We were up against one army with the Professor, Clea. But now that he's dead, there will be more than one army, all of them trying to take his place."

And most policemen didn't even carry a gun. Geoffrey's high levels of work among the undesiribles gave him some concessions there, and he never went without his weapon on his private cases . . . but still.

Clea held him as he slept, as he had so often held her, but her eyes were on the ceiling moulds and she thought before she finally let herself sleep. There was another thing her mother used to say, something she hadn't thought of until now.

"Things get worse before they get better."

It was the witching hour. The fire crackled in the sitting room, casting light across the sleeping faces of Martin and Nicholas, who had tumbled up with Ada and a blanket. The two patriarchs sat, facing each other for the convenience, though Charles had no vision, and spoke quietly.

"Nicholas looks like his mother," Potier said. Alone and with an injection of very good wine, his English improved. "I hoped for this day."

Charles Cheatham smiled all the way across his white beard. "I know Clea did . . . with any hope, she won't be too hard on him. She is every time he returns from a case . . . I think it's just a formality for her."

Potier chuckled. "My wives were all the same way. They never used the frying pan, but there were some nights I would have deserved it."

Cheatham sighed. "Was it worth it?" He wondered. "Many people paid deep prices in this work."

Potier finished drawing fire into his pipe bowl before answering. "Your city will be safer," he said at last. "Or, shall I say, it will be safe for a while. That makes a difference, does it not?"

Cheatham's hand moved as if it were the sighted part of his body. His blind eyes shone white in the firelight. Potier smiled as that large paw reached down and stroked a grandson's small head.

Coastal outskirts of Benodet, Brittany (not far below the city of Kemper, and against the ocean)

Jethro Quimper closed his eyes as the weak morning sunlight filtered through the cloud banks of the ocean to touch his face. That face still felt raw, every thread-fine nerve exposed and tortured by the events of the previous week. His physicians – solicitous bastards, the lot – had protested his getting out of bed so soon. His stitches would open, they scolded. His over-extended sinews and tendons and muscles would suffer and delay his recovery.

But he was still the leader, so they again let him have his way. Not a one of them would ply their medical oath and professional worries against the fear they had of him.

He enjoyed the fact that they could still be afraid. That said something about the way he was when he was hale.

Quimper was sitting at a little traveling desk brought out for his purposes on the stretch of plank that connected his private dock with the actual office of "legitimate" business he kept with the authorities. It resembled a small cove-stop decorated with tiny stores and warehouses, but it was quite the decent crossroads of information inside those brightly painted wood walls and hand-dressed stone trims. A cup of coffee rested at his elbow, cooling to the point where he could drink it with his bruised face. Two stacks of papers rested, one to be read, the other to be written in French, the language of politics. He was trying to address a particularly difficult letter right now – *two*, actually. It wasn't just the soreness of his body that conspired against him.

Before him the ocean was lazily frothing at the docks. This little port was as much *his* as *Corinten-avel* was old Potier's. *Kemper's Port.* Nicknamed after the family, although it went by many other names on the paper maps. It was an extension of both the city and the family by the name.

The city was such a perfect opportunity in itself to gather fortune. "Quimper" or "Kemper" referred to the confluence of rivers. The Odet and the Steir mixed their waters here, while two other rivers, the Jet and the Frout, flowed underneath the city, following deep underground passages.

193

And of course, the ocean rested nearby with its ships . . . flowing all the way to this point, and from here, to everywhere else in the world. For hundreds of years his family had used it for their business, professional and personal. Quimper was the city of the "Founding Fathers" of Brittany, after all, when immigrants from Cornwall, Ireland, Scotland and Wales fled invasion to start anew between the fifth and sixth centuries.

Things were changing. Once the dialects had been so insular that even another Breton had difficulty in understanding a man from the next town, and the shape of his hat spoke of his origins as loudly to the eye. That insular quality had been useful to his family. Slowly at first, and then by degrees, they had worked this inability to communicate to their own advantage. Families like the Glenan and L'estrades had initially started out as equal partners, but always the Quimpers had waited to work their own advantages. Some fruits did not ripen once a year, but once a lifetime.

It was the Potiers who had *truly* threatened his family's interests. Slowly at first, the population of corsairs and pirates and smugglers had gained autonomy, as well as a disturbing egalitarian approach to life. A man's rank and placement was no longer as important as what he did with his own two hands. That had threatened Jethro's great-grandfather. He had seen the beginnings of the end with the slow power the pirates formed in their independence.

Like the Romans before them, the Quimpers had profited with taking over their enemies and making them into allies – or pawns. There was little difference in the long run. But Potier's people had been intractable, gun-shy from any potential trap in alliance with larger powers. They gained their wealth by themselves, notch by notch, until their value rivaled Ivo's empire.

Marriage to Triaged Potier's favourite daughter had been the logical method of undercutting this canker. And when she had found herself unimpressed with the quality of his wooing, the older custom of kidnapping had been employed.

What a disaster that was. The Potiers might have been a mighty family, but they were as wild and stubborn, and unreasonable as any savage out of the wilderness.

Jethro Quimper sighed, wearily turning over the same exhaustive numbers in his mind. He pulled his small cup of coffee to his lips. Defeat rang up, over and over and over, flat as broken bells.

He knew his men were dead. What Potier had *done* with them was a chilling mystery. Quimper now knew that Potier had refrained from war because of his daughter's pact. It had been a mistake to challenge the old man *on his own ground*. Foolish to chase the shark into a sea cave. *Potier had been ready*. How many years had he quietly bided his time, waiting for his moment as patiently as Quimper's people had waited for their own coups?

Quimper slowly drew his arms across his chest and breathed quietly until his thoughts settled. About him was quiet. Guards ensured his privacy in in own personal dock. No one could get in or out without being seen. He took comfort in that. This place was safe from the damned *floders*.

Doue, but he ached. His walking stick would be more a thing of *use* now. The doctors weren't certain if he would walk a straight line ever again. He thought of L'estrade's twisted foot, and his own lip twisted at the acidic irony of it. Less than seven years' difference hung between the two men (though the little detective looked far older). Seven years. But as far as Jethro could remember, his life had been painted with hatred of him.

Still no trace of his men . . . Craddock . . . Griox . . . Hout . . . his best men. All gone. Obviously dead.

Across Brittany, the story had it, the Wild Hunt had swept upon the land like the old days and made prey of some evil men. The fact was, many individuals known for their cruelty or their work with the less savoury sides of the law vanished without a trace when that moon was full last week. An ordinary hunt at night, it was said, gone terribly, terribly wrong. Eventually, King Arthur finds his guilty subjects, and punishes them. No doubt he conjured them into shapes of his black hounds, and they were now hunting to his commands across the night skies.

Griox was gone. Craddock.

Of the entire Wild Hunt that had rode out with him that night, only himself and Judicael were still here to tell the tale. Ironically, that was an alibi in itself to the local peasantry. To their limited thinking, their continued existence was proof they had *not* rode out on that full moon.

All his life, Quimper had used folk myth and legend to his own ends, the way his father had and his father before him. He was now seeing what a two-edged sword it would be, and once it turned on the user, it was quite final. If you let someone believe a fairy tale, then you yourself are forced to admit defeat when the fairy tale turns on you.

Also vanished were most of the old smugglers in Potier's gang. *Most* – but not all. There were a few who had stayed behind, with yards of alibis on their neighbors and families. They were no doubt scattered across the peninsula, remaking their lives with the same easy confidence of their youth . . . Jethro now knew better than to persecute them. They were the bellwethers of the gang. If *anything* happened to them, Potier would return with a vengeance. He knew that now, just as he knew that he had grown weak, and Potier . . . .

Potier had not lost a jot of his old powers. He was as ephemeral, as strong, as crafty as ever, the Seagull who rose above the highest winds and escaped the worst storms. There was no telling what resources the old man had left. And without that knowledge, Quimper would not try against him.

Defeat was as bitter as the salt-pans of the coast. He was not used to this sensation. It left him confused and dazed, as if he had taken many blows to the head and not just to the body itself.

I challenged him. He faced the bilious truth bravely, much as it hurt him. *I challenged him when I sent him to identify his grandson's remains. He took it as a red flag to a bull.* And he had thought he was being clever. One would never be struck by a L'estrade's cleverness . . . but a Potier . . .

Lestrade's family had worked its latest defeat upon his. And it hadn't even been *personal*. It had been the sort of revenge a boulder would get when a person foolishly strikes his fist against its surface.

An Ermine will fight a fox . . . .

They had mocked the boy in their youth, Paul trying to push him into a mud puddle and Geoffrey fighting him with a fury that led to his nickname. *Are you the Ermine, to die before you muddy your coat?* Perhaps not . . . but being disowned had freed L'estrade from having to concede to Quimper's authority. An ermine was nothing if not tenacious. It was small, it was resolute, and when it wished, it challenged animals many times its own size. His father had shot an eagle once, when Quimper was a boy. Buried deep in the bird's breast was the weathered-white skull of a weasel. It had died with its final statement into the bird. It still gave him the chills to remember it. L'estrade was that kind of a fighter. He knew that . . . now.

He didn't know *what* he would tell his father when they were face to face. Plymouth had never seemed so terrible in his mind. Nor could he take revenge against the damned Korrigan's family. They had disowned him after all. Their ties were severed. If they thought of their youngest son at all, it was in terms of the dead.

The *Kelenner* was dead too. Small matter that Sherlock Holmes had died with him. Holmes had been *one* agent, a fluke of physics against the Criminal King. There would be other smaller, paler, duller, and weaker forces than Holmes now. But Moriarty had held London together like fine glue. Already the lines were being drawn as the nobles of Moriarty's crime ring fought over the title. Unfortunately, the two sides were evenly matched. Moriarty's trusted assistant Colonel Moran, and his *just* as formidable brother, the Colonel James Moriarty. Quimper wasn't certain which choice he should make. His living away from London had created a liability with his ignorance.

He should speak to John Clay. The ink pen hovered over his paper. *This* was the subject he'd been struggling with as much as his troubled thoughts. Clay's perspective was cold and reptilian. He would not make *emotional* judgments. He also knew both the Colonels who were fighting for the *Kelenner*'s title.

John Clay had his regard. He also responded to the noble blood in Quimper. Yes . . . it was time to start working, and to start *now*, before any more time was lost. At the very least, he would send for Clay and they would palaver their own solutions against the blood-bath forming.

Both sides were united in their hatred of what Holmes had done, but what would they do after? Colonel Moran wanted the Empire to continue on, to slowly grow and expand the way it had been doing for years. But Colonel Moriarty . . . *that* one had something else in his crafty mind. The *Kelenner* had as much admitted his brother had his own agendas and they came first before his own work. It was the true reason why the deputy had taken his mantle, and not the brother.

Still . . . .

Who are *their* enemies? Quimper realized in a flash that this question would settle the confusion in his mind. A man's enemies would say much of what they did and how they would act. With a sense of relief, he finished up the closing paragraphs as carefully as penmanship and his aching arm would permit, sealed it tight and tapped his stick against the plated dock bell bolted to the pier at his side. It was the work of a few minutes. Judicael, his new valet, was off taking the letter to personal post.

That was that, he thought. An invitation to John Clay. An offer of information, collaboration . . . and perhaps, a weather eye out for their mutual enemies. No matter what happened next, intelligent men had to be prepared for the storm that was coming.

His mind exhilarated by this solution, Quimper rose to his feet and gingerly stretched. The play of the surf crossed his eye and he found himself lingering on a discolouration just below the surface of the waves lapping gently at his feet. The servants had proclaimed the table-fishing excellent of late, far beyond the usual seasonal limits.

Bubbles were rising up to the edge of the sea-water below his private dock. He craned his aching head, a chill running through his body. Something was coming to the surface. No. S*omethings*.

Bound together by their own clothing, made bouyant by the collection of gases of decay, Griox and Craddock burst to the surface, bodies bloated. Crabs crawled out of Craddock's mouth. Their eyes and lips were gone.

It was Jethro Quimper's last sane observation for a very long time.

The story continues in:
A Sword for Defense

MX Publishing

MX Publishing is the world's largest specialist Sherlock Holmes publisher, with over six-hundred titles and over two-hundred authors creating the latest in Sherlock Holmes fiction and non-fiction

The catalogue includes several award winning books, and over four-hundred-and-fifty have been converted into audio.

MX Publishing also has one of the largest communities of Holmes fans on Facebook, with regular contributions from dozens of authors.

www.mxpublishing.com

@mxpublishing on Facebook, Twitter, and Instagram

www.ingramcontent.com/pod-product-compliance
Lightning Source LLC
Chambersburg PA
CBHW071201260626
47162CB00003B/1127